WORLDSOUL

Liz Williams

WORLDSOUL

Liz Williams

PRIME BOOKS

To Trevor and Kari.

⚘Prologue⚘

Fire tore through the library, scattering burning scrolls across the floor, inscribing smooth marble with letters of ash. With a breath of the sea wind through the glassless window, the words were gone. The pale-haired woman turned, a silhouette against the fire, took a dying word in her hand and stared at it. Flames licked the hem of her robe, leaving the linen untouched.

"This is an intriguing tongue," she said. "Runic. From before the ice, perhaps? What do you think?"

"*Beheverah*." The name was accented with exasperation. "We need to *act*. Before They realise what's happening. Before They come."

The woman arched an eyebrow. "You overestimate them. They're savages, nothing more. Mindless . . . Although I grant you that their masters are not. There's no rush."

"Maybe not in the Liminality." His voice was still sharp. "But here—this doesn't work the same way. And we need to take action before it's too late. Think of all the stories here they will devour. You can look at them at leisure, later, if you wish. All those stories," he coaxed.

"Very well." Beheverah sighed. It was so *interesting* in here, with everything changing so quickly, the flames climbing up to swallow marble and paper alike. She brushed a smouldering fragment from her skirts. "If you really think so . . ."

Shouts were coming from outside, cries of panic and dismay trickling up from the harbour.

"The scrolls!" someone cried, an old voice, a heart breaking. "The scrolls!"

Raising her gaze beyond the blazing papyri, the woman could see out past the torchlight on the quay: a green sky, a greener sea, merging into one as the twilight deepened. A good time to steal something away; an edge in time. She reached out and touched her companion's fingertips, stood on tiptoe, called on the horizon and the dying day. His murmuring voice summoned up power, drawing it from the fire and the cracking stone that surrounded them, making the spell concrete, then deconstructing it again. Beneath her bare toes, the library started to shift. She smiled. This was almost easy. She spoke three careful words, spells of *moving*, and the floor rippled as though she was standing on ocean.

More shouts. She knew what they'd see, those horrified observers. They'd see something that couldn't possibly be happening: their beloved library—the greatest repository of knowledge in the world—first in flames and blazing, then starting to shimmer and glow, the gleam of magic blinding out the glow, then the whole magnificent columned structure meteor-shooting out of sight and taking its consuming fire with it.

Gone from Alexandria. Gone from Earth. But not gone forever.

⟶⟩One⟨⟵

At dawn, the distant hoot of the Golden Island steamer split the moist air and told Mercy Fane that it was time to get up. Mercy hauled herself out of bed. For an acknowledged insomniac, it was surprisingly difficult to get out from between the sheets, as though she might trick herself into dropping off after all. But work was beckoning; she'd told Nerren that she'd be in early. Big day today.

She dressed quickly in leather trousers and a crisp white shirt; oiled her hair and bound its springy coils in a club at the nape of her neck. She didn't want any stray strands that something might be able to clutch. Then Mercy drew a line of kohl around each eye and inked the tattooed sigil spirals between her brows and around each shoulder—just in case—waiting a moment for each sigil to glimmer darkly, then fade to matte. After that, she fastened the ward-bracelets around her wrists and ankles, slipped a charm into the hole in her left earlobe, placed her sigilometer on its chain in her pocket, and was ready. A quick glance in the glass reassured her: Mercy Fane: Librarian, a chess-piece study in white and black.

She'd think about weapons later.

She went downstairs into the yellow-painted kitchen. Sunlight poured in through the branches of the apple tree outside the open window, the rosy fruit already ripening. Midsummer was past, the year was growing on. As she stared at the apples, the *ka* leaped in through the window to land on the table below.

"Morning, Perra. Good night?"

The *ka* yawned, stretching small leonine paws. Its grave golden eyes regarded her, from a human face. "Good enough."

"Anything of interest?"

The ancestral spirit blinked. "Rumours. But there are always those. I have visited an astrologer, a friend. She says that there are curious configurations in the heavens."

"There are always *those,* too."

The *ka* nodded and sat back on its haunches. "Portents of change, throughout the city. Planetary alignments, signifying shifts of power."

"Oh dear," Mercy said. "Maybe the Seal is up to something again?"

"I do not know."

"I don't expect you to. I know it's one place you can't go."

"They experiment on my kind," Perra said.

"They experiment on everything," Mercy replied. *Bloody* alchemists. It was different in the Eastern Quarter, where alchemy was a different, and honourable, science. Not so with the Seal, who regarded everything as grist for its sinister mill. She left the *ka* curled up on the couch and headed off to work.

Outside, the morning was already warm. Mercy walked along the canal bank, glancing down occasionally at the shoals of small golden fish whisking, in amoeboid commas, through the clear water. The city had known days when these canals ran red with blood—a long time ago now, but not quite long enough. And now there were these new attacks, the lethal flowers falling from the skies and bursting like bombs, the petals deadly shrapnel.

Mercy had only been a small child, but she still remembered the last days of the Long War, before the Quiet, and then the bloodspill of the Short. She felt a prickle at the back of her neck but the morning seemed peaceful enough.

On the Street of the Hunter, the cafés were already doing a roaring breakfast trade. Mercy stopped under an awning and bought a bun, eating it on her way to the Library. The way to work took her up the hill. As she climbed, she looked through the gaps in the buildings to the blue arc of sea, fringed with mimosa and oleander. Ahead, she could already see the Library and the other buildings of the Citadel, the gold-and-cream domes butter-bright against the morning sky, the gilded spell-vanes of the Court of the Bond glittering in the sunlight. She fancied for a moment that she could almost hear them creaking in the wind, turning on their spires to catch every whisper and breeze of passing magic and siphoning it down into the bubbling crucibles of the Court. But the roofs of the Court itself were darkly tiled: it sat like a jackdaw among doves, upon the hill. Black and bright-eyed, stealing anything shiny . . .

Still, it all looked so *quiet* from down here.

When she reached the steps of the Library, the bun was finished and Mercy's monochrome outfit was covered in crumbs. She took a moment to brush them off. Why could she never stay tidy, unlike the many chic women she saw coming out of the Citadel buildings first thing in the evening, their chignons intact and free of escaping tendrils, their shoes as polished as beetles' wings? Mercy felt as though her clothes and hair were perpetually escaping from her control, in spite of a reassuring glance down at her now crumb-free shirt. Sure that her hair was coming loose, too, she checked it. It seemed smooth enough. For now, anyway.

At the top of the Library's steps she paused again and looked out. From this height, you could see as far as the Eastern and Southern Quarters; although the Northern was blocked by the towers of the Citadel and the looming darkness of the Court, Mercy could still feel the blood-tug, the pull of ancestral tales. A very long way away, she could see the billow of the flags that flew from the Eastern minarets, marshalling winds to the burn of the Great Desert beyond. An azure banner, fringed like a centipede, snapped and sang above the distant dome of the Medina. Below, the faint rumble of the monorail slid up between the buildings, a low thunder. She caught a flash of brass and bronze as the little carriages whisked along it.

A long way, to the south and to the east. Longer than it looked. Mercy thought she could taste rain on the wind. She turned, pushed open the Library's heavy bronze doors, and went inside.

There did not seem, at first, to have been any crises during the night. Good. The Elders had planned an inspection this morning and Mercy, Nerren, and their colleagues wanted everything to go smoothly. Things were quite unstable enough, Mercy thought, without the poor Elders having a conniption— at least, not more of one than they were having already.

However, the huge, echoing foyer of the Library was as austere and tranquil as ever; the smoke-dappled marble columns rising out of a floor so polished that it looked like a pool of grey-green water. Touches of silver—on lecterns, on the spine of the Great Book that stood on its plinth in the centre of the hall, on croziers and the Librarian's Crown—caught the sunlight filtering in through glass that was stained black and white and grey; the windows being one of the few parts of the Library that were really new, untainted by ancient fire. Above, soaring above the motes of light and dust, flew the ghosts of birds.

"You're early," said Nerren, bustling out from behind the reception desk.

"I said I would be. Did anything—?"

"No." Nerren's brow creased. The Senior Librarian wore a man's suit: narrow tapering trousers, cream silk shirt, a frock coat. A black curl of hair had been coaxed to rest on her brow; it looked varnished against her brown skin. Sigils glowed dark-bronze on cheeks and throat, in the manner of the Southern Quarter, but southerner though she was, Nerren had eyes like Mercy's own; the same shape, the same shade. Dark and disapproving. Mercy sometimes wondered whether being a member of the Order of the Library had endowed her with a permanent frown. Now Nerren was frowning, too. Nerren added, in that beautiful musical voice with its accent of the Islands, "At least, not that I'm aware of. But I haven't checked Section C."

"I'll do it."

"Are you sure? Do you want some help before the Elders get here?"

"No, it's all right. I'll do it myself." Mercy had entertained doubts about Section C for some weeks, and had not mentioned the extent of them to Nerren. The Senior Librarian had quite enough on her plate. But now she wondered whether Nerren knew anyway.

"There's more. Bad news." Nerren's fluid voice was not suited to staccato, but it obviously matched her mood. "We're due for a Citadel inspection as well. They'll be coming on Third Day."

"What, *this* Third Day?" Mercy stared at Nerren in dismay.

"Yes. That's the whole point. Not to give us time to cover things up. I suppose we should be grateful they haven't just showed up this morning. At least we've had some warning."

"Two days," Mercy mourned. "Doesn't give anyone much time."

"We haven't been doing anything *wrong*, Mercy." Nerren's voice was sharp.

"No. We haven't done anything wrong," Mercy echoed, as if repeating it would make it true. And in a sense, it *was* true. It was just that they hadn't been entirely . . . forthcoming.

Nerren gave her a beady look. "Section C. Do you want a coffee before you start?"

"Perhaps a stiff brandy." She hadn't meant it to sound quite so sour.

→⟡←

In the weapons room, Mercy stood considering her options.

The bow: taut as a razor's edge, sensitive as the antenna of a moth. The bow, all gleaming silver-black, called to Mercy and she whispered to it, "Wait. Not long. I have to be sure."

There were other bows, but only one that spoke to Mercy and of course, one could take none other.

It must be strange, Mercy reflected, to be someone to whom no weapons spoke. But then again, such people probably didn't become Librarians.

The sword: a thin-whipping rapier, also in black, also in silver, with a curling intricacy of guard fretworked in Kells-coils. Old Irish, from the look of it. Mercy had not seen this blade before, it was newly arrived from the lands of Earth, and its slender length sparkled with stories. It spoke to Mercy of moorland, peat-dark under a new moon, of bogs of sooty water into which horses vanished, of cold high cliffs and seas like thunder. A broch, rising out of the heather, grey as an old bone, haunted by the ghosts of the warrior dead.

"You," Mercy murmured. "Might take you."

A knife: short-bladed, stoical, with little to say. Mercy passed it by, but not because of its relative silence.

She paused before the guns, but guns boasted too much for Mercy's liking. They were not quite a woman's weapon, she always thought, though she knew those who considered differently. They shouted to her of their kills: street kills, Northern Ireland, in Spain, the islands of the Small Realms, Nicaragua, Los Angeles. They had their own legends and she did pause before a musket, speaking of blood and bayou.

"Not in this day and age," Mercy said aloud. She'd probably blow her hand off if she touched the thing. She was almost at the end of the armoury now, by the high windows that looked out over the Citadel as if the presence of the weapons alone was sufficient to protect it. The rows of weaponry and munitions stretched back to infinity-point, the armoury far larger from within than from without, as befitted the nature of the Library. Mercy walked back to the Irish rapier, said, "I'll take you, then." To the bow, she said, "Next time." The bow acquiesced with grace; she would have expected no less from it. But she had a feeling that the sword was right for the day, without knowing why. If she knew why, the story would be over.

The sword had a scabbard—ebony leather, slightly worn but carefully tooled. She strapped it around her waist, slid the sword inside and walked from the armoury, taking care to bolt and bar and spell-ward the door as she did so. Things had been stolen before and not just weapons. The sword tapped lightly against her boots as she walked, a deathwatch clicking.

Section C was located up ten flights of stairs, the winding steps giving a panoramic view of the Library entrance hall below. She could see Nerren's bent head, an ink blot against the marble of her desk. From this height, she was level with the bird-spirits: their shadowy wings beating in ceaseless rotation. They did not appear unduly concerned, but this meant little. Nerren and Mercy had long since given up using the bird-spirits as a barometer of danger, their canaries in the mine.

Finally, she reached the tenth floor landing and paused before the door. Moving with great care, one hand on the hilt of the Irish sword, Mercy leaned an ear to the door.

Inside, something was whispering.

Two

The man stood at the window, staring out over the fragile scattering of roses in Citadel Square. He watched as a golem trudged across the flagstones, the spell parchment protruding from its half-open mouth like the tip of a tongue. It carried a lead box, something from the Court's own vaults, and Jonathan Deed wondered idly who had sent what to whom. As Abbot General of the Court, he preferred to know as much as possible about what was going on in the Court. How else could he fulfil his office as the Court's Abbot? More importantly, how could he attain his own goals?

Thick walls and thick glass cut out the city's murmur, the creak of the spell-vanes on the roofs above. But his office in the Court was not far from the Library, and Deed could almost hear the weight of history, years of hushed whispers in marble corridors, years of policy-making. But now the Skein were gone. Deed smiled, thinking of that. Over there, the Librarians believed they were the ones running the world—and so they had been, but only on the microcosm. The macrocosm, ah, now that was something else entirely.

"Abbot General," the woman said. "What is it? You're making me nervous." She stood, just inside the door, her feet on the outer border of the Persian carpet.

"Perhaps you should be nervous," he said, without turning his head. He tapped the tightly-rolled scroll on the study's windowsill. "It's falling to us, Darya. Did you ever think you'd see that day?"

"No. But maybe—you did?" There was the faintest trace of accusation in her voice, and he grinned, turning to her at last. Amusing, how she tried not to recoil.

"*Darya.*" His voice was a caressing purr. "Mage Nem. You ought to be proud."

"I *am* proud." There was only a little hesitation in her voice and that was good enough. For the moment. Later on, maybe Darya would have to be taken down a peg or two, but there was no rush. Plenty more apprentices waiting in the wings, after all. The Sept had made sure of that in its breeding programme down the long years. Thinking of that, Deed studied her as she sat on the divan, deliberately not looking at him. He knew he frightened her—Abbots General were supposed to be intimidating—but, of course, that wasn't the whole story. He could see the traces of it in her angular face: typically Northern Quarter with the high arched bones of her cheeks, the wide-set blue eyes, and square jaw. She looked so demure in her neat black gown, with the silver charms and wards dangling along the chain of her sigilometer. But there was more than demureness behind her face if you knew where to look, just as there was more than the human behind his own. As the sunlight grew stronger, you could see the silver light at the back of her eyes, a faint mirrorglow. And for a moment, the bones of her face seemed to shift into something not-human, so subtle that he doubted anyone not of the Sept would have noticed it. Naturally, if you looked at her with the sight-beyond-sight, the difference was a great deal more marked: the aura so indigo that it was nearly black, with a sparkle at the edges like distant starlight.

Disir. He doubted whether any humans other than the Court and their Adepts, the Sept, even remembered the word, let alone what it meant. Not even the Librarians: it was too long ago, too far in time and space. Poor Darya. You don't like what you are, do you? But you couldn't run from it, couldn't

change it, and why would you want to? thought Deed. It wasn't
as though you were something banal—a wampyr, for instance.
Something with *penalties*, whereas all the Sept had to deal with
was an unreasonable amount of power. Who could possibly have
a problem with that?

"Abbot General? Has something amused you?" Darya asked,
and for a second there was a feral flash in her sea-coloured eyes.

"A great many things amuse me," Deed told her. "But now, I
need you to do something. A nice little trip to the Library."

She was looking at him now. "The Library? But—"

"No one will *know*, Darya. You don't have *disir* emblazoned
all over your pass card. They don't have magicians working on
the front desk." He smiled again. It wasn't quite true, but she
didn't need to know that, and Deed was all about the need to
know. "Typical Librarians. Always overstretched. No one will
know who you are." *Or what.*

"What do you want me to do?"

"I want you to be charming, Darya, which shouldn't be
too difficult." He smiled, winningly. "I want you to make an
appointment with a gentleman named Jehan True. I've spoken
to him in the guise of one of my other personas, a professor from
the Spellmarkt, and mentioned my delightful young cousin,
Mage Darya Nem, all the way from the Northern Quarter and
keen to make a start on her postgraduate research. A young
lady who is very eager to see certain elements of the Hidden
Collection. I've said nothing about you being of the Court,
don't worry. Anyway, in the highly unlikely event that you were
troubled by a surfeit of conscience, I *am* a professor and you are
in many ways a student."

Darya looked doubtful, but Deed knew this was due to
caution, not inexperience. "You've done this before, Darya. And
so well, too." He pitched his voice lower, verging on the hypnotic,
and though she was of disir blood she failed to notice it.

Darya nodded, once, as mechanically as a golem, and rose. He held the door open for her as she left and watched her recede down the hallway, her heels clicking on the old wooden floor.

Outside, the sun had gone behind a cloud. The city was once more grey and cold. The roses looked out of place, as though they had sprung before their season. Deed felt himself strip down with the day, his face becoming less human, closer to his ravening ancestry. He knew that if he looked in a mirror right now, the bones would be blade-sharp, the eyes behind the expensive rimless spectacles milky or night-dark, the shadow of the unhuman rippling beneath the skin. He preferred it this way: it was sometimes difficult to maintain the façade. But just in case, he took a breath and settled back into the human once more—a man still relatively young, snow-white undershirt, small starched ruff, black tunic, everything perfectly correct. The distinguished contributor to distinguished literary collections. The distinguished Abbot General of the Court. He liked that adjective. What could be more suitable?

It was time to make another attempt. Far away, he could feel the planets moving into alignment, Jupiter a great lamp in the heavens. The familiar aspects of the World Tree were briefly imposed on his vision, with himself surrounded by the sphere of Malkuth at the base of the tree. The Dead Road beckoned beyond the confines of the city of Worldsoul, beyond the Liminality itself. For a moment, the whole universe glittered around him, gloriously outlined. He glimpsed Earth, and Earth's moon; the planets beyond in the realm to which Worldsoul adjoined, a dimly-seen neighbour, visible only in humanity's dreams.

Deed raised a hand. The plain iron band on his index finger flashed. Deed stepped through the hole created in the air, leaving the opulence of his study behind.

Beyond, it was difficult to breathe. The Dead Road seemed even narrower than before, even more restricted. It wasn't the only storyway, by no means the only way into the nevergone, but it was one of the most dangerous. Deed fought for breath, ramped up the entry spell but felt his features once more slip and slide. In the formal suit, his limbs thinned, sharpened, elongated, his clothes shifting with the change. The starched ruff bit into his throat like sharp little teeth. He tried to get a glimpse, at least, of what he sought but—as ever—it eluded him. Frantically, he parted the swirling vapours with his hands, catching snatches of vision—a white city beside an azure sea, a long reach of birch forest—but not a glimpse of the thing he was looking for, the thing he knew was finally within his reach.

Suddenly, amazingly, there it was: an immense pale-columned building, the Grecian roof slightly scorched with fire but still bearing the golden letters on its architrave. The Great Library, in sight at last, but in another time than his own. Deed opened his mouth to speak the first words of the spell—

But then the world woke up. It flung him backwards, the mist swirling up and filling his mouth so that he choked. He was hurled back onto the Persian carpet and it was fortunate, he thought a moment later, that the windows were indeed so thick, for the silence swallowed his roar of fury.

⚬Three⚬

Shadow, stepping into the Medina, glimpsed herself reflected in the shining surface of a copper pot. In the curving metal, she looked like a fragment of sky, no features visible, but Shadow didn't believe in taking chances. She thickened the azure veil a little further. Suleiman had magics learned in the Great Desert, conjurations stolen from the back alleys of Cairo and the cedar groves outside Baalbec, and from worlds other and further than Earth. One of those magics was said to be the charism of discernment of disguises. A charism perhaps, but Shadow doubted that it came from God.

She wasn't in disguise, not really. The veil permitted a greater degree of communion with the divine, shielding her from the invasions of the worlds, unless she chose to invite someone in. To an ordinary person, it would look like just another veil: its secrets were well hidden. Shadow had confided the central mystery to only one other person: Mariam Shenudah. Because if something ever did go wrong with the veil, Mariam would know what to do.

Another twist to the magic of the veil, just in case. Shadow, looking into the surface of the copper pot, saw a glisten on the air, a smear on the shining metal. Only then did she glide away, keeping at first to the old walls on the outer perimeter of the Medina, occasionally running a hand across the cool stone to see if there were any traces.

There were not. She planned to spiral in towards the Has El Zindeh, keeping south-west-north, using left-hand magic. That had its own penalties, but Suleiman deployed it, so why should she hesitate? *Fire with fire, my Shah.*

Shadow passed ovens smouldering with the smell of newly baked flatbread, slipped past golden mounds of turmeric and saffron, past baskets of glittering benzoin and crumbling myrrh, skirted jars of rosewater that sparkled in the lamplight. She would have liked to linger, especially around the conjuration stalls, but it was too risky. But Suleiman had said: *Meet me at noon.*

The Medina, being roofed, was hidden from the sun, although when Shadow looked up she could see the old images of the constellations of Earth inscribed across the ceiling. In the western section of the Medina, the goddess Nuit's body, bent like a bow, arched from floor to floor, carrying the stars within her. She disturbed Shadow, being a representation of a figure, and Shadow turned away, but not before she thought she saw Nuit's painted smile. And here was further representation amid the sea-blue tiles: suns and moons and lions and deer, in endless procession over the Western Quarter's door. Shadow bent her veiled head and passed them by. She circled away from the walls, passing deeper into the maze of the Medina. Here were the weapon makers: the blasting heat of forges, the hiss of metal into water. Shadow's own blade had not come from here, so no whisper could betray her. Her knife, forged out of sunlight and moonlight, came from the Khaureg, the deep desert a long way away. Shadow fingered the gold and black hilt as she walked quickly past the weapon makers, still taking the small modest steps that would proclaim her housewife, not alchemist.

And certainly not: magician.

What did Suleiman *want*? The summons, sent by dove the day before, made Shadow uneasy; it was not like the Shah to have much to do with her profession. He had his own necromancers and thaumaturges, and Shadow doubted she could offer anything they could not. But it was intriguing, all the same, that the Shah would consider hiring a woman. If hiring was what he had in mind.

She would soon find out. Turning the corner of a row of stalls, she saw the Has rising up before her, hidden in the Medina's heart. The market had grown up around it, concealing it in onion layers, but the Has had come first, hewn out of the rock two thousand years before. Its doors were as old-oak so pale and hard that it looked more like carved stone, taken from forests that had long since passed out of existence, and decorated with an intricate repetition of calligraphic patterns in a language older than Arabic. She'd heard that every panel was a spell. Perhaps so. She could not deny that she was eager to see inside the Has, after moving around it for so many years. There were numerous stories . . .

Time to find out. Shadow raised a hand and knocked, once, then diffused the veil to thinness.

"Salaam aleikum," she said, when, after a moment, the doors opened.

"Salaam. You are the alchemist?" A woman, very old, her face unveiled but shaded by a black headscarf, her skin so lined that she might have been the same age as the doors. But she opened them easily, and they looked heavy.

"Yes. I was told to come at noon."

"Good, and here you are, a little early. Well, come in."

Shadow had expected something different from the Has' personnel. Male, she'd thought, and disdainful. Somehow, she'd expected resistance. But this old lady was perfectly courteous and it was hard not to respond to that.

"Rakhmet," Shadow said and passed within.

Inside, a cool, dark hall led into sunlight, surprising in the centre of the Medina. Shadow blinked. She could see a tree, starred with lemons. The plash of a fountain echoed through the hallway like a cascade of arpeggios from a lyre.

"Follow me, please," the old lady said. Shadow did as she was bid, walking down the panelled hall and into the courtyard. Here, like parts of the Medina, all was blue and gold. The courtyard was tiled, and this must be more recent than the Has itself, for passages from the Koran flowed across the walls, the calligraphy bright liquid gold against the blue. Shadow looked up into the midday sky, colours reflecting those of the courtyard so that the two seemed to spill into one another.

"This is—pleasant."

The old woman clapped her hands. A girl appeared, clad head to foot in drifting green. She carried a tray, on which rested two tea glasses, also green with golden filigree, and a pot of tea. The astringent sweetness of mint filled the courtyard. Setting the tray in front of Shadow, the old woman disappeared. A cloud passed across the sun, Shadow blinked again. When she opened her eyes the Shah of Has El Zindeh stood before her, subtly attired in a grey robe.

"The Alchemist Shadow." Suleiman gave a bow, which Shadow returned, more deeply.

"My Shah. Thank you for the tea."

Suleiman smiled. "Ah, you're most welcome. I thought—a noon meeting, where everything can be clearly seen. I hoped you would appreciate the symbolism. But it *is* hot."

In that case, Shadow wondered, why not keep to the cool of indoors? She suspected that despite this earnest avowal of a love of clarity, there were things inside that Suleiman might not want her to see. She took a sip of tea, in response to his waved invitation.

"Enjoy," the Shah said.

One of the many advantages of a veil, under normal circumstances, was that it enabled one to see and not be seen. But Shadow was not confident that Suleiman could not glimpse behind her veil and she did not dare insult him by thickening it further. She studied him anyway, covert and careful. Impossible to tell where he was from, how old he might be. He had an accent, but it shifted, and she could not place it. A placid face; thin, a great many angles, and sad green eyes like old jade. His skin was neither dark nor pale, one of the thousand shades of sand. He carried sorrow with him, a weight of pain, and again, she did not know why. There were stories, but there were always those.

"You will wonder why I've asked you here."

"I do," Shadow acquiesced.

"You are an alchemist."

"That is so."

"You deal with transformation, so I am told?"

"It is the essence of alchemy," Shadow said, polite.

"Can you transform the living?"

She could not resist the temptation. "Into what? The dead?" That was easy enough, as he should know.

Suleiman smiled. "That's a difficult issue, here in our city of Worldsoul. What's dead doesn't always stay that way."

"And equally, when you say 'living,' what exactly do you mean?"

"Ah," Suleiman said. "You see, that's partly the problem. I think I will let you finish your tea."

She did so, wondering. The fountain gave a sudden gurgle and rush, sending water drops pattering out across the tiles. Somewhere, high in the eaves of the Has, a bird began to sing. Shadow looked up.

"A nightingale?"

"They're all around here. Even at noon. Allow me to take your glass. Thank you." The Shah stood in a sweep of grey. "Come with me."

His gentleness was deceptive; she was almost lulled. As she followed him across the courtyard, he raised a hand and plucked a handful of sunlight from the air. It dripped down his wrist, honey-thick. Shadow forbore from asking what he was doing. Keeping close behind, she passed from light into shade, the veil gathering a little strength from sudden gloom.

"It's down here," the Shah said, over his shoulder. The captured sunlight lit their way.

Curious, she let him lead her along a colonnade and through a door. A flight of stairs led up. At least, Shadow reflected, she was not being taken to the dungeons.

But in this, she was wrong.

~Interlude~

In an iron fortress on the shores of a sea of fire, the Duke was waiting for her audience. It was beneath her to seem nervous, especially in front of the servants. Once, she had commanded twenty-six legions: it would not do to show anxiousness before a maid, and so she stood at the window with her back turned and concentrated on the view. This was, she thought, glorious. It was almost worth being summoned up here in order to see it again. The window was open and she could smell hot metal, the dusty ash of the shore, the eternal burn of the tide. Far away, against a sky the colour of geraniums, she thought she could see a crescent moon, as tiny as a human fingernail.

The Duke rested her taloned hands on the windowsill and basked in the heat. Today, she wore armour of sombre dark crimson and for jewellery, only her carnelian sigil ring. It would not do to be perceived as trying to outshine her mistress and the Duke had every intention of playing it safe. Things were going well. She had a number of amusing little projects going on in the Liminality: work on Earth might have dried up in the last four hundred years but other places were still going strong. There were a number of minor flirtations, including one unexpected one. This was good because really, after a couple of thousand years or so, you'd pretty much worked your way through everyone worth knowing. It was so difficult to meet anyone *new*.

"Your Grace?"

She turned. The servant was small and had curling horns, gilded with metal lace; she was dressed in a neat black and white gown. She bobbed a curtsey. "The Prince is ready to see you now."

"Very well," the Duke said. She strode through the iron doors at the end of the entrance hall, and bowed. "Madam."

"Ah. I did hope you'd have the sense to come in *that* aspect."

"I know you prefer it." The Duke looked up. In one of the metal panels that lined the audience chamber, her other aspect was dimly visible, hovering about her like a shroud. She dispelled it. Beside her, one of the astrolabes creaked suddenly into position, the tiny planets shifting about their axis. Astaroth made a note.

"Some people think it's funny to show up in character," Astaroth said, plaintively. "I really don't like enormous toads. Or even deer. I mean, do I still go around riding on a dragon?"

"We won't mention the 'c' word, then."

"Please, dear, no." The Prince uncoiled herself from her couch and stood. She was taller than the Duke by some three feet, nearly nine in height, and her black hair was coiled around her head in a plait. She wore a black trouser suit: with the dark skin and eyes, she looked like a slice of night. "That's why I like you, dear. You're so *understanding*."

Astaroth came close, reached out a hand and stroked the Duke under the chin like a favourite cat. Inwardly, the Duke sighed, but Astaroth did have a point: the Duke did understand. Out of the lords of Hell, Astaroth was one of the handful who still had regular dealings with Earth; that old jurisidictory pattern still held. The Duke knew that Astaroth had petitioned the other team for release, as had her colleagues, but she had been told that some line management was still necessary.

The Duke did not fancy being responsible for America, personally. Although other people had a rather worse deal.

"Madam," she said again.

"I have a problem. I have lost something. Someone has stolen it."

That got the Duke's attention.

"An ambitious thing to do!"

"Do you know, that's exactly what I said. And dangerous, though that goes without saying. Obviously, I want it back."

"May I ask what it is?"

"No."

"It's going to be a bit tricky to find it, then."

"All I know is that the person who took it has fled into the Eastern Quarter of Worldsoul, in the Liminality. So I immediately thought of you. That's one of your stamping grounds, isn't it?"

The Duke bowed. "Yes, indeed."

Astaroth put an arm around her shoulders. "You see, it's like this . . ."

Four

W*hispering.* Yet when Mercy opened the door, Section C was silent, encased in the gloomy panels of the room. The lamps were still lit, suggesting either that Nerren had not got around to turning them off, or that someone had lit them again, but their light did not touch the echoing shadows of the ceiling. Their bronze fittings gleamed. Occasionally there was a clockwork whir from some piece of equipment. Mercy debated whether to go back and check with Nerren, or proceed, but it did not really make a great deal of difference: something was brewing in Section C and she'd find out what it was soon enough. Hopefully she could sort it out before the Elders arrived. She glanced down at the Irish sword, as if to reassure herself that it was still by her side, and began to walk slowly along the row.

In this part of the Library, the books were all necromantic, and all ancient. Some of the editions were no more than fragments, encapsulated in protective wards and filed face out, so that one could see what one might be dealing with. Many were heavily guarded, glittering or shadowy with spellcraft. The texts here were properly the province of the Northern Quarter, but of course the Library was supposed to be neutral ground, containing *Matter* from all manner of places. It wasn't the full body of lore, of course. The Court had its own collection of grimoires and who knew what else besides—Mercy would have given, if not an eye, then certainly an eye tooth to have an hour in the library of the Court. Not that it was ever likely to happen. She lingered over Anglo-Saxon annals, over eddur that were fringed and crackling with ice even in the carefully controlled climate of the Library. She did not touch anything, being careful to walk down the middle of the row. Frequently, she swung around, to see if anything might be following, but there was never anything there. Within a few minutes, she was approaching the end of the row, where the oldest texts of all were held. As she walked, she took note of the unusual silence. In ordinary circumstances, the Library was filled with whispers, scraps and rags and tatters of speech, murmured incantations, soon dampened by the spell filters that constantly flickered, electric-azure, across the high dim ceilings. Mercy glanced up: that was wrong, too. The spell filters were still there, but greatly muted to an occasional dragonfly snap. So something had been through here—perhaps was here now—and diminished the filters' power as well as silencing the other texts. Why would something do that? The answer was obvious, Mercy thought: to increase the power of its own story.

Mentally, she sifted through the kinds of things that could do that. Dark powers, or one of the angelic lords, perhaps, but Mercy thought that would have been more noticeable. Demons, likewise. Demonic incursions were an occasional occurrence in the Library and the filters were usually strong enough to cope: Mercy quite often came in to find a nasty stain on the parquet, still smouldering. In the event of something really unpleasant, the Elders would occasionally counsel taking expert advice from the Court, whose practice was principally with the Goetic powers of Medieval grimoires and whose knowledge of demons was second to none. But that had been in the days before the disappearance of the Skein; now, with them gone for more than a year and distrust ruling all, the two organisations rarely spoke.

And if you asked her, it had been the Court who had sent those demons in the first place.

However, there were any number of things besides demons and angelic powers, things both known and unknown: a person could not read *everything*, after all.

Towards the end of the row Mercy paused and sniffed the air, head up like a hound. Something had definitely been here. She could smell wood smoke and snow, a fresh wild scent in the muted, dusty air of the Library, with an astringency running underneath it—pine, fir? Then a chill brushed the back of her neck, a draught of icy air coming from between the books. Mercy swung round, to find herself facing a sheet of paper—but that was wrong, it wasn't paper at all, but something thicker, the shade of bone and covered with scratched markings. The draught was coming from the text and it was murmuring. Mercy glanced up at the spell filters and saw a blue electric flicker as something shorted out. The sword leaped in her hand. She braced her heels against the parquet floor. *Something's coming through.*

Mercy raised her free hand and spoke into her palm. "Nerren? Section C. Incoming. Sorry."

"On my way," Nerren said, out of the air.

In fact, Mercy was not sure she was right. Sometimes, storyways took a long time to open up. Sometimes, they took years . . . Then, just as she thought she might be mistaken, a word in a harsh and unknown tongue spoke out and the storyway opened.

Mercy stood on an ice shelf, looking out over a landscape filled with blowing snow. A river snaked in a series of startling curves, oxbow lakes in their birthing, out to a frozen horizon where a red sun was going down. From her vantage point, Mercy, teeth chattering, heard the crack and roar of breaking ice from the direction of the river. Wind whipped the pins from her hair and took the strands streaming across her face. A black, attenuated shape was racing over the snow on all fours.

Mercy tried to speak the spell-word—emergency override—

but her mouth was blistering with cold. The shape was swarming up the cliff: long black limbs whirling. It whistled as it came, singing in the wind. A flurry of blizzard spun up around Mercy's feet and she staggered back, but not before she swung the sword. Confusion. Glowing bright eyes in a face as white and sharp as a knife, hair as black as her own swirling over a ridged skull. It had sharp teeth, it snapped at her out of the snow and Mercy brought the singing sword down.

She felt the Irish blade bite and exult as it did so. But the thing knocked her to one side, sending her sprawling on the wooden floor of the Library. The temperate air seemed unnaturally hot after where she had just been. The thing had closed the storyway behind it; there was now no sign of that snaking river, the thin pink line of the sunset horizon, the endless waste of snow. Nor was there any sign of what had come through the gap. Mercy looked at a blank parchment, its words stolen and gone.

"Bollocks," Mercy said aloud.

⋯⊷⊜⊶⋯

"There's no trace of it," Nerren said, peering into the scrolls of readout spilling onto her desk. The old Library monitor whirred, brass cogs churning and turning as it rolled out data.

"Her," Mercy said. She was huddled in a blanket in one of the cosier armchairs of Nerren's study, hands cradling a hot cup of tea. She felt she would never be properly warm again. "Any word from Security yet?"

Nerren frowned. "Not yet. *Her*? Are you sure?"

"She had breasts. Well, teats. I saw them under the cape. And she was either piebald or tattooed. Or both."

"But the basic skin colour was white?"

"Yes, white as snow. Black haired."

"A witch figure," Nerren murmured. "Baba Yaga?"

"Too familiar. Something else. This wasn't human. It was a crone, yes, but something else besides."

"Demon?"

"I just don't know. C's one of the oldest sections. Who knows what's lurking in those pages?"

"There might be a duplicate," Nerren said. "I'm looking now."

Mercy craned her neck to look at the former text, which now sat in a humming lead box with a glass panel on Nerren's desk. "It's cured skin, isn't it? Was it human?"

It was Nerren's turn to look doubtful. "I'm not sure. Might be. But the texture's wrong; it looks too thick."

"Ancient, though. Definitely from the north."

Nerren gave her a curious look. "Don't some of your relatives come from the far north?"

"Yes. But I've never been there myself." *Except just now, with the wind knife-hissing over the snow.*

Nerren sat back. "There's nothing duplicated on the monitors."

"Any record of the filing?"

"Yes." Nerren spun the monitor so that Mercy could see. "There."

Mercy leaned forward, noting serial numbers. "This was one of the first things ever acquired by the Library. It survived the fire."

"I know. It's that ancient."

It wasn't Norse, as Mercy had wondered. Before that, long before, from lands that no longer existed on Earth, although recent experience would indicate that they were still present *somewhere.*

"This dates from the Ice Age."

"One of the oldest things written by humans," Nerren said. "That is to say—there is older material, texts from the Fertile Crescent. But so little from the northern lands . . . "

"A treasure," Mercy said. "A *spell*."

She thought of the thing she had seen; the thing that, mentally, she had started calling "the female." Part of a story from so long ago that any humanity had surely been leached from her, if indeed she had ever possessed any. Something forgotten, that raged, like so many forgotten things. Something that wanted to be known.

And something that, now, would be.

⟣⟶Five⟵⟢

The grove lay a short distance from the Dead Road. The mist gathered around him as Deed moved along it, not bothering to pretend to walk, just letting the Road carry him forward. Behind, in Worldsoul, the Court lay in the late afternoon light. Darya was still at the Library, hopefully far advanced in the process of beguiling its curators.

A crossroads, fog-wrapped, with the gate-stone rising from the white swirl. Deed stepped past its looming bulk and took the small path off the side of the road. He could smell the grove. Not far now. The path was overgrown with the ghosts of bramble and wild clematis, but Deed spoke a word and the spectral plants parted before him, withering back into the undergrowth. Then he glanced up and there was the grove: the bones arching up, the curve of immense jaws snatched from a sperm whale from the northern seas, inscribed with runes. Beyond were ribs, and at the centre of it, a skull mounted on a plinth as black and grainy as the crossroads stone. Deed bowed his head for a moment before stepping into the grove, not an action he cared to take, but one which was wise. Reaching up, he brushed aside the sprig of mistletoe, not the dull green of the Earthly plant, hanging on apple or oak, but white as snow, the berries veined with red.

The old god was waiting. He could smell that, too.

He came as close as he dared to the skull. The basalt in which it was set had partially grown up around it, but still could not quite dim its light. From certain angles—ones that Deed took good care to avoid—the skull shone like the sun. And so it should, given the fairness of its owner in life. Bright Baldur, slain with a mistletoe dart.

"My lord?" the magician said into the waiting gloom.

He came out of the depths of the grove in a clank of chains, true disir and one of the only and oldest males. Deed, accustomed as he was and knowing that the god was chained, still had to concentrate on standing fast, not running. He despised the weakness, but it was an old fear too deeply rooted to be eradicated by force of will. Loki's narrow head turned from side to side, the white eyes gleaming. He wore ancient leather armour, still supple, with splits and rents where the sharp bones pointed through: the armour had been made for a man, ransacked in the long-ago when the gods had gone to war. It was hard to look Loki in the face and Deed centred his gaze instead on the disir's hands, the long fingers and sharp silvery talons.

"You're so like me," the disir said, and chuckled. It didn't sound remotely human and Deed remembered what his old mentor of the Sept had said once: *They are beasts in the guise of men.* The raveners, the scavengers of the battlefields, the initiators of war. Deed had taken care to keep his ancestry from the old man, and had been hard-pressed to school his face into polite interest when these words were spoken, which he supposed proved the old man's point. The words rang cold in Deed's memory and he forced his gaze upwards. Loki was staring at him, the disir's head on one side.

"Well, now, little named one," the disir said. "What have you brought me this time?"

Deed reached into the pocket of his coat and drew it out from its leather box. A scrap of flesh, green as mould and still wet. Scales shifted, opalescent in the bone light as the disir held out a taloned hand. The god never snatched. He took the flesh with a mincing, pinching movement and then it was gone.

"Not bad," Loki breathed. "Rusalka?"

Deed nodded. His pocket still felt river-wet. "From the Northern Quarter, the forests." The hunter had overcharged, too. Deed was not inclined to argue, at least, not just yet.

"So," Loki said again. "You've brought me a little present. How kind."

Deed took a breath, wondering if he'd have to invoke the old law, remind the god that an offering required a reply. But the disir took pity on him.

"What do you want, O my descendent? Answers? Or a question?"

"I've seen the Library," Deed said. He felt he was radiating excitement. "As it first was when they stole it, not as it is now. The predictions didn't lie. It's there, in the past of the Liminality."

"We knew *that*," the god said, reproving.

"But no one has been able to see it. The Skein kept us out. And now—I *saw* it, Lord."

The skull-face of the disir grinned wider. "But what are you going to *do* about it?"

"Get it back. Bring the Library of Alexandria through, replacing the version that now stands in the Citadel. Place it and the knowledge that it contains under the control of the Court." *Under the control of you.* The subtext hung briefly in the air.

"Ah," said the god. He knew damn well, Deed thought. Generations of preparation had gone into this. He just wanted to hear Deed say it. "How do you propose to do that?"

The Abbot General, at last, turned to face him. "I need your help."

⤞⊙⧉⤝

With the god within him, the Abbot General walked to the edge of the ridge and looked down. Loki was an uneasy rider; Deed felt like a horse whose reins were in a cruel grip. He did not trust the old god not to jerk them at a whim, tearing at the mouth. But for now, Loki's presence was bearable. Just.

The encampment sprawled along the edges of a lake. It was ice-bound along its shore, but further out Deed could see the gleam of sullen water, greasy with cold. A low range of hills, furred white, ran along the furthest shore. Deed did not know where this corresponded to in Earth's past: probably Lapland, or northern Russia. It didn't really matter, this far back along the storyways: the tribes had held much in common.

It would be going too far to call them "tents." They were stretched hides, tied to poles. The disir did not suffer from the cold, as humans did. There were no fires—they were afraid of fire, an atavistic dread that Deed felt superior in having conquered. The disir ate their food raw, and preferably bloody. At the far side of the encampment, a range of poles each boasted a severed head: some human, some not. One was a wolf's and Deed could not help wondering if this had belonged to an animal, or one of the clan members.

"See her?" Loki whispered, inside his mind. There was the sound of smacking lips, a lecherous sigh. "Fancy a tumble in the snow, Deed?"

Deed did not. The disir was tall, well over six foot in height, and as gaunt as a goat. Her long face was tattooed in the tribe sigils and she had a long crest of hair, bound with an iron band, on the top of her head. She wore armour of skins, and her person clanked with hoops of silver, lead, and carved coal encrusted with protection runes. At her waist, she wore a small skull with a long snout and sharp teeth.

"Not my type," Deed said.

The old god laughed. "I can see a little thing inside your mind: half-human, eh? So refined, with those tip-tapping heels."

"Her name's Darya. Don't go imagining any great romance." He'd have to take better care to school his thoughts.

Loki laughed again. "Does she change when you fuck her?"

"No more than most women."

The god within nodded towards the tall disir. "She's the shaman. Or one of them. You can see—she whispers with magic. She's stolen power from animal totems, mainly bear, wolverine, raven. Anything that likes a fight."

"Why are you telling me this?"

"Well, you see," the god said, "this is nearly forgotten, this story. People have progressed too far." He made Deed's head turn, and spit into the snow. "They've forgotten these old tales of the old north lands. They remember me—quite well, actually—and the others, but the Vanir—not so much. Frey was fading even in my day. Anything further back from that, forget it. Literally. So you have a storyway on a siding, a tale that no longer grows, changes, moves. All these creatures are just hanging around here with nothing to do. Do you think that's *right*, Deed? Do you think that's fair?"

Deed shrugged. "*I* remember them."

"Yes, but you're not exactly some tribal chieftain, are you? You're a descendant, partly human, mainly changed. I know you can show the teeth if you want to, and sometimes when you don't, but there you sit, in your fancy clothes, in your smart office of the Court—not exactly roaming the tundra, are you? Not exactly hunting and gathering?"

"So what are you suggesting?"

"Deed, Deed." The god's chastisement was like having a slap to the brain. Deed reeled, and only regained his balance on the ridge with difficulty. "Look at the opportunities. There are thousands of the disir, all with raging aggression and nothing on which to vent it except bunnies. What does that suggest to you?"

"An opportunity."

"Quite so. I've conducted a little experiment. Some days ago, one of those dear ladies strayed a little too close. So I sent her on a little holiday down a storyway, into your city. I wonder where she's ended up?"

"Into Worldsoul?" Deed asked, in alarm.

"Quite so. I lost her after that. Can do the first push, but not much more."

Deed was silent, and into his silence, Loki poured a plan. Then he sealed it, like someone putting a lead lid on a jar and welding it shut.

"You see," he told Deed, just before the magician blacked out, "I don't want you remembering everything. Some, but not all. That might lead you to tell other people, especially under duress. So you just go back to that city, and do my bidding, and everything will become clear. Eventually."

⋯⊃ ⊂⋯

Returning to the Court, Deed felt as if he'd been gone for years. The Dead Road was like that: it was one of the most dangerous storyways of all. He doubted that anyone outside the Court even knew of its existence, although perhaps some of the Eastern mages trod their own version. Had Deed been truly human, it could have snatched him away, showing him its beautiful, flower-filled face, leading him lost and uncaring until the moment when it revealed itself for what it was and spat him out.

Good thing he wasn't truly human. He thought back to the meeting with Loki. He remembered that the god had told him about a disir, sent into the city. That had to be a priority: he made a note on official parchment, and sent it to the Sept. But for the rest—try as he might, he couldn't uncork the jar of memory. The old god had programmed him, as neatly as if he were a computing machine. Deed was disir enough to resent this, but man enough to recognise the sense behind it: any conscious information can be extracted under enough torture. The trouble was, how can you trust a trickster god?

The answer was: you can't.

He sat back in the deep leather chair of his chamber, nursing the whisky. It tasted of peat, of age, of blood. He savoured it with disir senses humans did not possess. Even the disir needed downtime. Deed adjusted the cuffs of his jacket, meticulously picked a speck of lint from the black velvet. He was slightly disappointed when Darya walked in, her clicking heel-taps muffled by the thick carpet. She was smiling, and for a moment, Deed felt something that might almost be described as affection.

"I spoke to True. A dear old man," she said. Her smile grew sharper.

"You've got the permit?"

"Oh, yes, Abbot General. He was so helpful," Darya said. She sat down opposite, sinking into the seat and taking the glass of whisky that Deed proffered. "We had a most interesting chat and he's given me a letter. Also he talked to the Librarian in charge of the collection and she'll make sure that everything goes smoothly tomorrow."

"Very good," Deed said. He turned the glass in his fingers, admiring the glow of the whisky in the subdued light. "This Librarian. Do we know anything about her?"

"I've done a search of known . . . personnel," Darya said. "I can't find a reference to her. Her name is Nerren Bone."

"Ah, Darya, Darya. If she's in charge of a collection like the papers under discussion, then she's almost certainly one of the opposition. But she won't be able to say the same about us. People are interested in that sort of thing for all manner of reasons."

"And you, Abbot General?" Darya asked politely, after a short pause. "How was your afternoon?"

He shrugged, thinking of the bone grove, the red-veined mistletoe, the blade-presence of one of the oldest and most dangerous gods of all. "Oh, you know. Quiet."

⊸Six⊸

S hadow stood before the cage, looking in.
"Meteorite iron," the Shah explained, giving the bars a light
tap with an ivory wand. "It's the only thing that will hold it."

The cage shook as he tapped it, causing the floor to shudder.
They stood in an upstairs chamber, fretworked windows looking
out onto the roofs of the Quarter and across to its wall. Sunlight
patterned the floor, chequered into diamonds and triangles by
the carved wood of the shutters. The room smelled of spice, and
smoke, and fire. The room was a prison.

"Let me guess," Shadow said. "You found out the hard
way?"

Suleiman gave his saddened smile. "You might say that. We
lost . . . some personnel."

"Oh, dear." She looked at the thing in the cage. Impossible
to see it directly: this was a thing to be glimpsed from the corner
of the eye, and even then it was unclear, an amorphous shifting
mass, boiling cloud, a localised storm. It had eyes.

"A djinn," Shadow said.

"An ifrit, to give it the precise taxonomy. Not a common
one, either. This is a rare species."

"Then why isn't it in the zoo?"

"People bring me things," Suleiman said. "Things that they
can't . . . look after . . . elsewhere."

"Ah," Shadow said. "Now I'm with you."

She was not inclined to elaborate. The Shah being a fence,
a nexus point between worlds, people must bring all manner

of stuff. Girls, guns, drugs, jewels. Stolen heirs. Missing spells. Ifrits.

"Does it have a human aspect? An animal one?"

"Almost certainly, but it hasn't manifested it yet, despite efforts to force it to do so. A pity. It's so much easier to engage with something that looks like a man. This is its natural shape— if they can be said to *have* a natural shape. You might have gathered that this isn't my normal area of operations," Suleiman said. "I'm not a naturalist."

"They're known to have sentience," Shadow murmured. "That makes it doubly illegal. Did it come from Earth?"

"I don't know. There are very few ifrits on Earth any more. The oil business, you know, and less . . . *superstitious* forms of Islam. Somewhere else, perhaps."

"I am not a naturalist, either," Shadow said, although she had a nasty feeling where the conversation might be heading.

"No. You are an alchemist. You change things, as we have mentioned, in the universe's refining fire."

"I change *things*," Shadow replied, more sharply than she had intended. "Not living beings."

"And yet," Suleiman mused, "it is well known that the alchemy of the East is concerned primarily with the transformation of the human soul."

"Something that the alchemist willingly undertakes," Shadow said. "Not something that is done *to* someone. Besides—" She should not ask, she *would* not ask, and yet curiosity drove her to it, backed her into the corner of the question, "What do you want it changed into?"

⊷⊙⊜⊶

"No," Shadow said, an hour later, for perhaps the dozenth time. "I cannot do it."

"Cannot? Or will not?"

"The latter. It's against my vows." She hoped he couldn't hear the weakness in her voice, for she could not help wondering *what if, what if*? That was the problem with science; it was so rarely pure. But surely that was the essence of the battle, that one must struggle with the baser instincts of one's own nature, transform them into the gold of mercy and compassion? In that, at least, Suleiman had been correct in his views on alchemy. If she had wanted to go down the left-hand route, she'd have joined the Court. Rumour had it that they had no such scruples and Shadow knew that rumour was right. She picked up her glass of tea, newly refreshed by the silent green-clad serving maid, and stared into it as if it might furnish answers. In the corner of the room, a plangent note came from the cage as the ifrit struck the bars.

"Against your vows? Or are you simply afraid?"

O Allah, thank you for not making me a man, Shadow silently prayed. She could afford not to sink under a weight of pride. "Of course I am afraid. What do you think, my Shah?"

Suleiman smiled. "I think anyone in your position would be afraid. Anyone who was either intelligent or sane."

Shadow could not, however, say that what really scared her was the knowledge that he would force her to do it. The only question was how. She had isolated herself over the years: parents dead, family estranged, lovers nonexistent. Mariam Shenudah was her only real friend and Mariam, thank God, was well protected: as the Vice Chancellor of the quarter's principal university, she was in too prominent a position for frivolous attacks. Shadow couldn't afford to risk other people and that was an old sorrow. But that she had been brought this far, that the Shah had showed her what was within the cage of meteorite iron—that meant that Suleiman would not take *no* for an answer and *no* was the only answer she could give.

"You'd be rewarded, of course," the Shah nudged gently.

Of course. And he'd have a hold over her forever. This was illegal, and more than illegal, it was wrong. She had some ideas as to why Suleiman wanted the ifrit to be transformed, and none of them were good.

"Your generosity is well known," Shadow responded, automatically.

"Oh, come now," the Shah said. "You don't need to take refuge in platitudes. Will you do this for me, Alchemist Shadow? You can quite literally name your price."

"May I ask a stupid question?"

The Shah's courteous silence told her that there was no such thing.

"Have you considered bringing in the Court? I'm assuming that politics precludes it, which is why this is a stupid question."

"It is not, but you are right. Even if relations were cordial, which they are not, I could not trust them, and I do not want them here within my walls—there is too much that they might glean. Besides, I believe in keeping things in the family, as it were, and there is bad blood between myself and the Abbot General."

"That doesn't surprise me."

A struggle, that was what she had told herself. It did not take long. "I can't," Shadow said. "You do understand? I took certain vows and I cannot transform a living thing—I could easily kill it. You have told me that you wish to make it into a man. I do not think I have the skill."

"They say you are the best," Suleiman said.

"Then they don't know what they are talking about, whoever they are. With gold, yes. With jewels, yes. Give me a lump of lead and ask me for a sapphire, you have it, my Shah. But this—no."

Suleiman inclined his head. "Very well. I understand your reservations, even if I do not agree with them. I need not caution you to say nothing of this, to anyone. Now, we both have work to do."

"I promise you my silence," Shadow echoed, although she knew, as did he, that this was only a preliminary skirmish. The war was yet to come. As a servant girl ushered her through the door, a shaft of fragmented light fell on the girl's face, illuminating it briefly through her veil. Milky eyes stared straight ahead, seeing nothing. Shadow nodded once, as she walked through the doors of the Has.

Outside, the humming throb of the Medina seemed oddly peaceful and Shadow's sense of oppression lifted. She walked quickly down the narrow streets, leaving the veil in thinness but resisting the pleas and blandishments to buy saffron or linen or beans. Her head was spinning; she needed to get home, to the garret laboratory and silence. Suleiman would take action of some sort. It might be a long time coming or mere hours. This was the trouble. He knew he had her now, and even if it was months before he acted, he knew that the knowledge that he *would* act was enough to stop Shadow from doing anything unwise. A little alchemical puppet, dancing back through the Medina . . .

Through the Medina and out. Here, the streets of the Quarter were wider, but not by much. A boy on a brass scooter zipped past Shadow's feet, nearly knocking her flat. She thought of shouting after him, thought better of it. His eyes, glimpsed in the fleeting rush, had been a deep and fiery gold. She walked slowly back through the afternoon heat and it was quieter now, the Quarter settling down before the evening cool, shutters bolted and doors locked to keep out the sun. She thought of the Has, its deceptive tranquillity, of the ifrit in its cage. She was glad to reach the crumbling tower that contained her own laboratory, to climb the baked earth steps to its summit.

Not many people were prepared to live in the city wall. It added to her cachet, the spice of risks taken, and moreover, because of the danger, it was cheap. Shadow ascended the stairs into darkness and spoke the words that opened the old oak door.

Once inside, she stepped past the table that held alembics and retorts. The morning's experiment still bubbled, without the aid of flame. Shadow, putting aside the veil, sniffed it, recoiled, and went to the window to throw the shutters open. The wall curved off to her right, with a second tower some distance along its length. Shadow studied this for a moment and then her gaze flew outward, as if drawn by the magnet of the desert. The great dunes stretched to the horizon, endless colours and shadows, rolling up and down in patterns that were different every morning, and yet essentially the same. Shadow drew strength from her proximity to the desert; if she had to live within the city, it might as well be here, perched like a dove in the wall. She stared at the desert for a long time, trying to empty her mind of memories of Suleiman, of the caged ifrit. But it was not until the muezzin sang out across the Quarter, comforting in its regulation of the day, that she was able to gain a little peace, kneeling with her forehead touching the bare scrubbed boards, distantly noting little acid burns where an alembic had splashed, finding within the thread that led to God. And praying for delivery from the attention of Suleiman the Shah.

Seven

Mercy and Nerren went down to the security office later that morning, after the Elders had gone, and had spent an hour searching through the records. Their efforts had produced little and the Elders had been predictably querulous. What *was* it with senior Librarians? They'd presumably had the same adrenaline-filled life as any other staff member, but as soon as they passed retirement age and went on the council they became trembling and sheep-like and nervous. Perhaps it was some kind of reaction? She hoped it wouldn't happen to her.

If she lived that long. Nerren and herself, by mutual accord, had not mentioned the episode in Section C to the Elders in case someone had a weak heart. Actually, there was a lot of other things they hadn't told the Elders either, also by mutual accord.

Mercy was trying not to snap, a measure of her frustration. This was not Nerren's fault, after all. Better to blame the Skein, whose vanishing had led the Library to its current state of instability. But she hated to think that they were failing; they had held the Library together for a year and now it was starting to crack . . .

This was paranoia, she told herself. There had been a few incursions, all dealt with. Library security knew what they were doing. The Citadel inspectors continued to oversee the longer term administration and, as Mercy's earlier dismay had proved, they made regular checks.

Sulis was there in the office now, an Enforcer with twenty-three years behind her; a big, calm woman in grey. Massive ward bracelets enclosed her thick wrists; her hands were stiff with spellrings.

"It's unlikely to be connected with the flower raids," she was saying. Mercy, perched on the edge of Sulis' desk, nodded.

"That's what I thought. It feels totally different. This is something else, something from a much earlier time." *Mind you, we've all been wrong before.*

"But we don't know who this female entity is?"

"No," Mercy admitted. "Who or what. I wounded her, I'm sure of that."

"Jonah's still looking at the blood. Wasn't able to give me any quick conclusions. Whatever she is, she disappeared as soon as she left the Library. The spell filters couldn't hold her."

Mercy swore under her breath. As soon as she'd heard the female had left the building, the gnawing worry had grown.

"That doesn't surprise me," Sulis said. She touched a bronze knob and the machine once more whirred into life, hissing with electric azure. "Actually, you can see from this that they're functioning perfectly well. It's just that with very old things, the magic's correspondingly ancient. The filters can't cope with it, because they don't know how: the equipment's too modern."

"This is what pisses me off," Mercy said. "We've got all these old texts—all these old *stories*—hoarded like a . . . a dragon's gold, and no one seems to have *done* anything about them."

Sulis did not reply, nor did she need to. It wasn't as though the origins of the Library had been in any way scientific. The Skein had brought it through when the building had been set on fire—by enemies about whom the Skein had been remarkably closemouthed—the flames lighting the Egyptian night. Even though that was long ago now, they had just kept accumulating material. People all had their areas of expertise, but there was simply too much to analyse and it hadn't been until relatively recently, Mercy reflected, that a proper cataloguing system had been brought in.

A different agenda for humans, was the charitable view. Charitable, but possibly not accurate.

"A collection, nothing more. But the Skein were able to handle it. And we—"

"Well," Sulis said, mildly. "We're doing our best."

"But what if that's not good enough?"

—◦▬◦ ◦▬◦—

It was not until mid-afternoon that a positive sighting came in. Someone had seen an odd thing on Orchis Hill, crouching in a back alley. Mercy and Nerren got there as soon as they heard, taking the monorail from the stop at the back of the Citadel. It was the fastest means of transport they had, which wasn't saying a lot. Mercy stared out of the window as the monorail creaked along, fingering the Irish sword, wondering how long it would be before the monorail fell into disuse. Its brass wheels clanked; the red velvet seats were faded and threadbare. Fireweed and oleander grew along the rusting tracks. Mercy saw a fox slink into the weeds, not hurrying, evidently undisturbed by the nearness of the rattling vehicle. What would it be like, to live in a city you could really change, that did not alter itself around you? Ask one of the Earthbound. Ask one of the Skein.

The monorail cranked on and Mercy grew more irritable with every passing mile. Through Sweetside, across the Lesser Channel, under the long-browed hill of Ferria Gracia with its white balconied buildings. Graffiti was inscribed everywhere along the sidings: curling, glowing words of power. Mercy winced. The Skein had ruthlessly eradicated this in their day, just as they had maintained the monorail, and made Worldsoul run efficiently. Had they really been kidnapped, as popular wisdom claimed? Or had they removed themselves, impatient parents casting their children into independence? It seemed impossible that she might never know.

Her meditations were interrupted by a gasp from Nerren. Towards the front of the monorail, the sky had turned to rose. Mercy had a moment to think, *But it isn't sunset yet*—before she saw the molten core of a falling flower and the front of the monorail erupted into a tangle of twisted, screaming metal.

⊷═◉═⊶

She was under something. It pinned her to a mass of soil and torn foliage. A hibiscus blossom was nodding like a sage's wise head, inches from her ear—a white bloom, dappled with crimson. It took her a long moment to realise that the crimson was supplied by her own splashed blood.

"Nerren!" She tried to rise, but the beam, or rail, or whatever it was, held her fast to the earth. She ached all over and she could feel something wet running down the side of her face, but it did not seem as though anything had been broken. She could move both her head and her feet, and this boded well.

But Nerren did not reply. Mercy struggled to look up and found herself staring at the underside of the monorail, contorted into the air, a rearing caterpillar shape. The blast had bent it back on itself, so that the first of its three carriages was vertical. She twisted her head to the side and saw an outflung hand, very pale and still.

"Nerren!" Someone groaned and the hand twitched. Mercy exhaled in relief. Fragments of burning petal were still drifting down out of the smoky sky: the flower must have fallen only a little while before, and Mercy knocked unconscious for seconds. That was reassuring, at least; it explained why no assistance had appeared. Then she heard shouts. Turning to the other side, she saw a man running down the bank, taking great leaps and bounds down the steep siding of the monorail.

"Over here!" Mercy cried. The weeds were on fire, smouldering into dampness. He was a young man, wearing a workman's tunic and boots. He tried, and failed, to lift the girder, grunting as he did so.

"Hey, careful!" Mercy said in alarm. She wanted to be free, but there was no point in her would-be rescuer undergoing a hernia for it. But more people were arriving now, at a slightly less precipitate pace, and she heard the clanging of an emergency bell. Then someone called her name.

"I'm here," Mercy said. "I'm all right." Not quite true, perhaps, but she did not want to frighten Nerren, whom she could see scrambling to her knees a short distance away. The girder was lifted up by a dozen hands and Mercy, disregarding offers of help, got to her feet and stood swaying.

"Hey," Nerren said, and started to laugh. "Look at us. Black and white and red. We're all fairytale now."

Mercy, to her infinite disgust, felt the laughter and the light recede to a small pinprick point as she slid once more to the ground.

⤖Interlude⤖

He often walked to the edge of the world in the evening, heading out from the beehive hut into the nevergone. The garden was quiet, then, and there seemed to be something about dusk that dimmed the story-streams to calmer tides. He liked the peace, although there had been a time when he had not. Loneliness is something you can outgrow, given enough time.

He wondered, sometimes, whether it was possible to outgrow every emotion. Messengers were not supposed to feel hate or rage, but sometimes, in his younger days, he had been aware of a spark deep within like a burning coal, especially when he looked upon the Legions. Those had been the days of the great conflicts, the sweep of the wars, when the Legions had amassed on the edges of their fiery shores and a roar of defiance had been raised from thousands of throats. He had, so secretly that it was barely recognisable, exulted at the sight: the clashing spears and flashing banners against the cloudscape, the behemoths bellowing as they lumbered into position, bearing the castles of their dukes and princes upon their backs. The devil-beasts: great white gibbons with yellow eyes, unicorns with iron spikes jutting out of their bony skulls, the crab-men with their pincered arms and scuttling gait.

He had tried, as he had been instructed, not to look at the women, and had not always been successful. Manytongued the Beautiful, riding on her loping hydra. The War Dukes, clad in their shining armour, kissing their weapons. He had been taught to know that beneath the glamourous guises lay putrefaction and decay, but seeing them strut against the cloudscape it was hard to remember that . . .

Harder still, several thousand years later, in the depths of the quiet desert night.

When such memories rose to the surface of his dreaming mind, he tried to recall instead the memory of the Hosts: the ranks striding through the Gates and down the sunlit air. The warriors, fiery haired, bearing golden swords and silver bows, their calm faces shining with the rightness of their war. The heralds, sounding the charge. The Archmessengers, clad in sapphire and emerald, clear garnet and diamond fire, speaking courage to the troops.

But now the war was over and the Hosts had won.

He should not, then, still wake from dreaming of a red-clad War Duke with brass talons. Maybe it was evidence of senility, but he didn't feel that old.

He stood at the edge of the world and looked down. The Pass was silent now, a guard patrolling along the farthest slope. He could see its fiery silhouette flickering against the shadows. Silent. But recently there had been a shift, a change. He could feel it in the green evening air, sense its presence, but he did not know what it heralded. He turned, walking back past the glimmering storyways to the peace of the beehive hut and his dreams.

⚡Eight⚡

Life was full of irony, Deed thought in frustration. He studied the message that lay before him on the desk, marked with a top-secret sigil. It had come in that morning, from one of the Library moles.

The Library. Trust Loki to manage to send something in through the *Library*. The disir had been disruptive, apparently, which came as no surprise. Mind you, Deed thought sourly, to the old codgers who ran the place, "disruptive" probably meant putting a book back in the wrong place or abusing your lending rights. The disir had not remained long in the place, anyway. She had fled, somewhere in the city. But where? They were likely, Deed thought, to find out reasonably soon. Wild disir were not unobtrusive.

He turned again to the report. The Librarian who had made the discovery had a name: Mercy Fane. Well, Deed thought, let's see what we can find out about Miss Fane, shall we?"

⚡

The curse hung from the lower branches of a pine tree, about head height. It was made of feathers and bone, tied together with sinew. A shrew's skull, the jaws curved in an elegant arc and ending in small razor teeth, surmounted it and it carried the rune for winter.

The shaman of the wolf clan studied it for some time in silence. He took a rattle from his pouch and shook it, making a dry sound of falling seeds in the still air. His grey pelt was starred with snow, as stray flakes drifted down from the pines. Then he turned to Mercy, dreaming, and said, "Of course, it's an enemy's work. The question is, which one?"

"No shortage of *those*," Mercy heard herself reply. As with all dreams, she did not question how she knew this. "The White Owl Tribe, or the Shinbone People."

"Not quite their style," the shaman said. His lips drew back over his long teeth. "Look at the back of it."

Mercy did so. The back was a small flayed skin, stretched out. She could see the remnants of black fur. "What does that mean?"

"It's hunters' work."

"We're all hunters, aren't we?"

"Who hunts everything? Including the wolf clans?"

Mercy thought. "Death?"

"Nightmares. Everything is hunted by nightmares."

"I don't understand," Mercy said.

"You don't have to understand. All you have to do is remember," the shaman said. Mercy once again surged down into sleep.

⊸Nine⊷

Shadow spent the evening in the laboratory, working on a summoning spell for a client. So much of this work required personal concentration—the will bound into sulphur and dragon's blood and myrrh—that she lost track of the time. She was dimly aware of the sun slipping over the edge of the world, the blue fall of twilight, but when at last she looked up from the end of the preparation, night had fallen and the stars prickled out across the ridges of the desert. She was, she realised, hungry. And there was nothing in the place. Not even an alchemist can eat incense.

Shadow, frowning, investigated the ice-box. Bottled water, nothing else. She sighed. It meant a trip back to the Medina, to one of the all-night chaikhanas, and she was tired. She really ought to have got some stuff in the market. She'd learned long ago that you need to keep your strength up when you do this kind of work, need to keep grounded and earthed. Especially after the use of magic, which would take your light-headedness and spin you away, cause you to follow phantoms and chase illusion. Food would put a stop to that.

Shadow thickened her veil and stepped out into the warm night. The street was still busy: people strolling, bicycles, scooters. Shadow wove her way through the throng and back into the Medina. In a small chaikhana set into the Medina wall, she took tea and *ful mesdames* with pita. Thus sustained, she started back to the laboratory.

The attack came when she was almost back at the Eastern Quarter Wall. Shadow was not expecting it, but her instincts held sway. She was turning almost before the thing was upon her: a swirling form out of the blackness beneath the wall. The air around her was suddenly icy cold, a wind howling out of nowhere. She had a moment to reflect that it felt like the *harmattan* wind that blows from the desert, bringing madness in its wake, but where the *harmattan* was hot, this wind was nerve-chilling. It knocked her backwards, flung her against the wall, snatching her breath for a moment. Paradoxically, this probably saved her life—the wind pushed her out of the path of her attacker. The twisting form—darker than the night—took a mincing step forwards. Shadow's blade was up. The entity spoke in a language Shadow did not understand but which she recognised to be a spell.

The air about her grew black as ink, but Shadow had magic of her own and this was her territory, her strength. She spoke a word, a name, and a lance of light shot through the gathering dark and stabbed at the eyes of her attacker. The thing gave a wordless cry, fell back, and Shadow drew back her sun-and-moon blade, twisted it in her hand and struck. There was a foul billow of cold smoke, making Shadow choke, and then the thing was gone. She had a glimpse of it scrambling up the city wall like a monkey, shrieking as it went. And when the normal lamplight was once more shining down upon the street, Shadow saw that it had left something behind.

A hand.

--==◌ ◌==--

Some time later, she stood at the acid-stained laboratory table, staring down. The hand her attacker had left behind was a mottled black and white, withering as she watched, but it had not had the fleshy consistency of a human hand in the first place: more like a wizened claw. It had the normal complement of fingers, but an extra joint on each and long, black nails as hard as iron. Shadow pursed her lips and tapped a finger against the surface of the table.

"What," she said aloud, "Are you?"

She had consulted grimoires, sought answers in encyclopedias, and done a series of magical tests, but there had been nothing in the tomes to suggest what her assailant might be, and the spells had only shown her glimpses: a wild, bleak land, swirling snow, endless cold. Not the sort of country in which she felt at home. Had that been why it had attacked her? she wondered whimsically. Sensing an opposite: a person of warmth, fire, sun? Surely this was due to more than geography. Shadow, over years as an alchemist, had learned not to discount apparent synchronicities. Her visit to the Shah at noon; the attack, at close to midnight. Was the Shah trying an unusual means of persuasion? If so, it had failed. Shadow did not respond graciously to threats.

She walked across to the open window and took a breath of desert air, hot and clean, to wipe away the sense of foulness. Odd, how something so cold could yet be putrid. When she turned back to the table, the hand had moved.

"Aha," Shadow said, tilting her head to one side.

She walked across to the door and drew it shut, then watched through a crack. Sure enough, the hand—she did not think that it possessed intelligence, animate though it might be—scuttled along the surface of the table, leaving a greasy trail of ichor in its wake. Once at the table's edge, it seemed to be uncertain as to how to get down. It faltered, hesitated, tapped a finger much as Shadow herself had just done. Then, disappointingly, all the life seemed to ebb out of it and it slumped down in a tangle of fingers, unmoving. Shadow was reminded of chickens whose heads had been cut off. Tutting, she went back into the lab and found a small lead box. She picked up the stiffening hand with a pair of tongs and dropped it into the box, then sealed it with a soldering iron and put a binding of spells around it. Magic sizzled and hissed as she did so, flickering indigo-blue about the box, and when she had finished, the box was barely visible, contained in a cloud of magic. That, Shadow thought before she went to bed, would have to do.

⸺Ten⸺

When Mercy woke up, the *ka* was crouched on her chest, breathing out. She felt filled with sudden life, a glittering sense of well-being.

"Perra?"

"I breathe for you," the *ka* said.

"Well, thank you." Perra jumped down, but Mercy barely noticed: the *ka* was as light as air, weighing far less than a cat. It sat, a small sphinx, on the carpet by the bed and gazed up at her with lambent eyes. "Where am I?" Mercy asked. She blinked. The room was panelled in a faint willow-green. A lamp stood by her bed.

"You're in hospital, dear." A nurse appeared, with a white starched cap. "You had an accident."

"Yes, I remember." Her head hurt. "My colleague—Nerren?"

"She's in the next ward. She's fine. So are you. We're discharging you both as soon as I get the all-clear from the doctors."

"All right," Mercy said, relieved. It struck her as particularly ironic that she should have survived the morning's encounter in Section C with the thing from the ice, only to be nearly flattened by a falling flower. "Was anyone else hurt?"

"Yes, and one death." The nurse checked her blood pressure.

"Damn it. Who *are* these people? Who's *sending* these things?"

"If we knew that, dear," the nurse remarked, "We could do something about it."

And yet no one seemed to know, despite all the resources of Worldsoul. The Library had set a team on it, the Court had done so as well, and so had a myriad other organisations. The flower attacks had begun not long after the Skein had left: was this some natural phenomenon that the Skein had kept at bay, or was it part of the same thing that had led to the disappearance of the Skein themselves? No one knew. But they were devastating. Mercy felt lucky to be alive.

"I have given you a life," the *ka* said, in its reedy, whispering voice.

"Thank you!" Mercy raised herself up on an elbow and peered down at it. "You didn't have to do that."

"It's a spare. I have seven left."

They had been granted nine originally, Mercy knew. Like cats. She did not like to ask the ancestral spirit how the eighth had been lost. Not given to either of her mothers, evidently: the heritage was wrong. The *ka* must have come from her father's line, and who he had been, Greya—her mother—had never told.

"I'll see you shortly," the nurse said, giving the *ka* a disapproving glance, and bustled out before Mercy could ask her why they had given her a private room. Perhaps Nerren had pulled strings? The Library was still rich. But Nerren had no private room. She was in a ward.

Mercy lay back and after a moment saw the *ka* jump onto the windowsill. Perra gave a twist, and was gone out into the twilight. Mercy thought she might have dozed after that, because when she woke again, it was dark outside and a man was standing over her.

"Miss Fane?" He passed a hand across her eyes and there was a moment where her vision blurred. Then it cleared again. "How are you feeling?"

"A bit dizzy, actually."

"You had a nasty bang on the head."

He was dark-haired, pale-faced, ascetic. He wore a ruffed black suit, of expensive cut, a crisp white shirt, round spectacles. This must be the doctor, she thought, and wondered why there was such a sense of familiarity about him. Perhaps he was a frequenter of the Library: it had an extensive medical section.

"I've come to give you a final check-up," the man said. "I am Doctor Roke."

"Thanks," Mercy said. "I don't feel too bad."

"A few last checks," Roke said, soothingly. She found that she was lulled by his voice: *Everything,* it suggested, *will be all right.* "After all, we still don't really understand what effects these flower attacks can produce. We need to be sure. I just need to take a quick blood test—" and before Mercy could open her mouth, she felt a needle at her arm and the doctor was holding up a phial of crimson fluid. "There we are. All done. We'll let you know if there are any significant results."

Then he was gone, leaving Mercy feeling safe. Ten minutes after that, the door opened again and the nurse reappeared with a small, stout man. "This is Dr Marlain. He's going to give you a final check-up before we discharge you."

"You're very thorough," Mercy said. "I've already had one of those. Dr Roke did a blood test?"

The nurse and Marlain exchanged startled glances. "Who?"

"A Dr Roke? Tall, dark? Nice manner. Very urbane."

"There's no one called Roke on the register," Marlain said, blankly.

"Ah." She digested this. So someone now unknown had come into her room and, entirely trusting, Mercy had let him take her blood. For what? And from the looks on their faces, they thought she had made it up. "Maybe I was dreaming," Mercy said, dismayed.

⊷═◉═⊷

They let her out anyway. Nerren was waiting in the lobby, bandaged and bruised.

"We've been told to take tomorrow off," Nerren said, rising stiffly from her seat. "You didn't have any appointments anyway."

"I'm going to need it," Mercy replied. "Did you? Appointments, I mean."

"Some northern grad student, but I can put her off." They began to walk slowly towards the doors.

Then Mercy remembered. "Oh, hell. The Citadel inspection."

"You know what?" Nerren said. "Benjaya Vrone can handle it. He's always bitching that I don't give him enough responsibility, but I prefer to ask McLaren—he's just good at dealing with crises. Let Ben handle the inspection and if there is a problem, we'll just have to deal with it later. Having narrowly escaped being blown up, a bunch of civil servants suddenly seems less intimidating." She pushed open the heavy doors and they stepped out into the warm embrace of the night.

"Agreed," Mercy said.

They exchanged weary goodbyes.

Mercy walked stiffly through the darkness to a rickshaw row, and took an uncomfortably jolting ride home.

⋆→◉ ◉←⋆

The blizzard had died out over the pass, but in her dream, Mercy knew that winter was coming. She took the clantrack south, heading down through the silent, snow-weighted pines and into the valley. It stretched, both shallow and wide, for three miles until the estuary, which in summer was a place of leaping salmon and flickering eels, white with water-fowl, but which now creaked and groaned with the cascade of ice floes from the further sea. Mercy was heading for the river and for the traps. She ran quickly, running on back-jointed feet across the hard ground, her pack bouncing against her shoulder blades. High above, a pair of ravens bobbed and wheeled, game playing in the first of the snows.

There was a build-up of cloud on the horizon, golden-grey turrets towering into the sky. More snow before nightfall. She reached the river, and stepped carefully down the icy tumble of soil that had become its bank. The ice was not yet thick and she could see the slow seep of water underneath it. The ice was glassy: it was like a dim mirror and she could see the faint outline of her head—the long muzzle, the golden eyes. In her dream, this did not seem at all strange to her; she had always been like this. She looked like the rest of the clan, although darker of fur than most.

The first trap was close to the bank. A small stick protruded above the ice, marking its location. Mercy took the axe and broke the ice, shattering it star-shaped around the marker. Beneath, under the frigid water, something writhed in the snare. She reached down, took hold of the string, and pulled it up, expecting a fish.

It wasn't a fish. It was a small, man-like figure, dark, with twig-like limbs. It should have been drowned but it hissed and spat in the snare, twisting round to snap at her hand. Its face was like her own: her human face, not the wolf-face she now wore. Mercy dropped it in the snow in a spatter of blood and, to her great relief, woke up.

⊷ ⚬⊶

Daylight was flooding through the window, along with the scent of jasmine. Mercy took a deep breath and sat up. The headache had receded to a dull afterburn and her first thought was that she had overslept and was late for work. Then she remembered: day off, because of the accident. But a day off was the one thing she could not afford to take right now.

Objectively, she knew the house was warm, but Mercy felt cold. She wrapped the robe more closely, flung a wrap around herself and went downstairs. She could not stop thinking about the woman-thing at the Library. It had made more of an impact on her than being caught in the flower blast. For a moment, whirling around, thinking the thing was actually in the room. But it was only the steam from the kettle, rising up. She was starting to become annoyed with herself. *Let's think about what's real.* She heaped green tea into a frog-shaped pot and stood staring at the familiar walls of the kitchen while she waited for it to brew. The walls, painted yellow. The polished boards of the floor, with a speckle of white by the stove where, long ago, her mother Sho had spilled hot oil while trying to make pancakes. Sho, always taking risks, always getting things wrong, but somehow it had never seemed to matter. So different from her other mother, Greya: the cautious, sensible suffocating one, the mother who had wanted Mercy, the single chick, to do something sensible in turn, something safe.

Mercy had never been able to blame her for this. Greya was from the Northern Quarter, after all, and something had frozen inside her, causing icicles in the heart. Greya's mother had been from one of the wolfclans, or so Sho had whispered to Mercy as a child; Mercy had never known whether or not this was really true, although Greya's eyes, in certain lights, gleamed gold. And there had just been that dream . . . But Greya herself—no wolfcub. Whatever fire and spit she'd owned had been burned out of her on the journey south, made her dry as a winter leaf, careful as a cat on ice.

Yet Greya had been the one to go, when the first word of the *Barquess* had come, asking for volunteers. Mercy had resented that, after all the slammed doors and hisses over her dangerous choice of career at the end of her teens. Greya had not stayed to see her try to survive in the now-Skeinless Library, as though she'd just hung around long enough to really piss Mercy off by doing something completely unpredictable.

Sho had gone after her, of course. No change there. She'd bequeathed the house to Mercy, which had been both reassuring and not: Mercy wouldn't lose the family home, but it didn't say much for the chances of either Sho or Greya returning. She'd asked the *ka* about the fate of the *Barquess*, but the *ka* had been unable to tell her, said that no oracle could, said it was "fuzzy." Oh, well. Mercy was used to that.

She sipped her tea, now brewed and sour. It suited Mercy's mood. Something was loose in the city, something for which Mercy felt responsible. If the Library had seen fit to give her a day off, it therefore made sense to Mercy to see if she could find it.

"Perra!"

The *ka* leaped lightly onto the kitchen table. Its feet made shadowy golden traces, like pollen.

"I think," Mercy said, "that I'm going to need your help."

⊷━◯═━⊷

The docks were a hubbub. The Golden Island steamer could not get into harbour, having to wait at anchor in the waters beyond. Mercy could see the passengers milling on the deck, gesturing, but they were too far away for her to hear what they were saying. She doubted it was polite. The harbour itself was thronged with fishing boats, private yachts, a junk from the far side of the Eastern Quarter, and the air smelled of salt and smoke and fish. Mercy and Perra walked to the far end of the harbour, where a thistle-head of bridges indicated the start of the West-East Canal. Here, the gates were being opened. She could hear the creak and tear of the winch and knew that a ferry was waiting, riding up in the womb of the lock, and Mercy's spirits rose with it. Soon, the boathouse came into view and then the ferry itself.

A small crowd was already present, bags and children clutched in eager arms, to take passage to the Eastern Quarter. The *ka* plucked at her boot with a claw.

"I am not sure, mind," the *ka* whispered.

"I know. But you said you heard *something*."

"Rumours are like dandelion clocks. They spread on the wind. There is no substance to them."

"But sometimes seeds take root, and there are dandelions all over the city, Perra."

The *ka's* small solar face turned up to hers. "As I told you, a demon says that there was something by the Eastern Wall last night. It attacked a woman and lost a hand."

"Who was this demon?"

"Only one of the small, the lesser, not a duke or an earl. Those would not talk to me, I am too lowly. But the little spirits like to gossip. It had no reason to lie."

"They can be malicious." Yet this tale sounded too specific, somehow. She thought of Roke, the blood snatcher, and felt herself grow still. Who had he been? She was still sure that she'd seen him somewhere before, but an odd dizzy moment blanked him out. Now that she thought back, he was becoming difficult to recall.

"It spoke of cold," the *ka* said, then fell silent. "The woman is an alchemist. The demon could not remember her name." It looked briefly disapproving. "They have minds like mayflies."

"We'll take the ferry anyway," Mercy replied. "It will be a nice day out."

With the rest of the passengers—mainly Easterners, in all manner of dress—Mercy and Perra queued briefly, then climbed the walkway to the ferry. Standing in the prow, Mercy could see the canal snaking across the city, all the way through the Western Quarter to the banners and flags of the East. And then, with a creak, the ferry cast off.

❡Eleven❡

In his laboratory, back at the Court, Deed held the phial to the light and smiled. Alchemical science tells us that there are demons in the blood, and all manner of spirits flock to its red light, drawn like moths to fire. He was looking forward to seeing what might be attracted to the blood of Mercy Fane, what manner of thing might be conjured out of it.

Mercy Fane. Until now, she'd been just another Librarian and not particularly worthy of attention. But that was before she met the disir. Deed wanted to know whether there was a connection: was she a recruit of Loki? Was it just chance that she'd been in a flower attack? If Mercy decided to investigate the disir's presence, Deed wanted her under observation.

He took a dropper and extracted a small quantity of fluid from the phial, then set it into a glass dish. Around it, he drew a triangle in chalk, then stepped back. Another circle, and then he spoke a word and set the chalk alight, a fire that flickered across the floor in eternal containment. Deed, in shirtsleeves, raised his hands and uttered the name of Mercy Fane, three times. The blood hissed and writhed.

"Come on," Deed said, enticing. A shadow fell across the blood and stepped forth, coming up abruptly against the triangle's invisible wall. "Oh," said Deed, intrigued. "Now what might *you* be?"

But in fact, he knew all too well. The thing was tall, grave, golden-eyed. It had a long muzzle and graceful hands. A wolf-headed man.

"Now," Deed said. "You're from the north. One of the wolfclans. What were you? Her grandfather?"

"I shall not speak," the wolfhead said, glaring.

"Oh, but you will. Don't be difficult. It's boring. You know what I am."

"Loki's blood," the wolfhead said, and growled.

"Of course. I am disir, but not only disir: I have many ancestors, just as your bloodchild Mercy does. They don't concern you. But you concern me. I need information. Who was your daughter, your son?" He spoke another word, forcing names from the wolfhead's mouth.

"Ativana. Soreth. Greya."

"Greya Fane," Deed said. A piece of puzzle had fallen into place. "Aha. Yes, that would make sense. She went out on the *Barquess,* I recall. Nearly a year ago. So noble, heading out into the unknown on the ship that searches for the Skein. I'm sure we'll all be interested to see if they make it back alive. So Greya Fane is Mercy's . . . what? Mother? Aunt? I will have to check."

"Not . . . touch . . . " the wolfhead slurred and Deed looked up in surprise. "Still here? Well, can't have you running off to little Mercy, can we?" He snapped fingers, intoned an incantation and the wolfhead was snared in silvery bonds, threads of fiery shadow that snaked around the spirit's form until it was wrapped as neatly as a fly in a web. "Gone!"

And it was. The chalk triangle flared up and out. Deed sank to his haunches and crouched in the circle. Time to do some thinking.

⊷▷○◁⊶

Later, he went in search of Darya. He found her in the long, lead-windowed gallery at the top of the Court, looking out over the city. The four o'clock rain had swept over Worldsoul, drenching the roses and oleander and leaving a humid warmth in its wake. He could smell it through the open window and wondered what Darya might be thinking, but only for a moment. Nothing very deep, that was certain. She had cast off her jacket in the afternoon heat and her spine was bare in the cowled blouse that she wore today. He could see the little knobs of her vertebrae protruding through the flesh. Seamed stockings ran down to her high heels, but Deed knew that those heels were her own bones, the spikes of her heels arching her feet and making her teeter. It was appealing, but he knew how fast her kind could run if it came to the chase. Perhaps that would be entertaining, if Darya ever over-stepped the mark. As seemed likely.

"Darya?"

He had the satisfaction of seeing her jump.

"Abbot General?"

"Greya Fane. What does the name mean to you?"

"She was a volunteer, wasn't she? On the *Barquess*. From this quarter, although I seem to recall that she was originally from the Northern Quarter. I saw her name on the list, and I memorised the list. And she is related to Mercy Fane, maybe, whom Nerren at the Library told me about."

"Quite right," Deed approved. "If the crew of the *Barquess* had found the Skein, they would be heroes, but as far as we know, they have not, and thus they are not. They are in limbo, like Odin on the World Tree, waiting to snatch knowledge from the abyss. A nice simile, don't you think?"

Darya's face betrayed unease. "No one knows what has become of the *Barquess*," she reminded him.

"Of course they don't. It has sailed over the rim of the Western Ocean to try and catch the sun, and if they don't make it back, which they probably won't, they will pass into legend themselves, like the Flying Dutchman. On the other hand, if they do come back, everyone will take an interest. But the reason I'm interested in Greya Fane—"

"Is this Mercy Fane?"

"Just so. Well done, Darya. I want you to do some genealogical digging. I want to find out what other relatives Miss Fane might have."

⟢Twelve⟢

Had she not been in pursuit of the creature from the Library, Mercy would have enjoyed the journey along the West-East Canal. She had done it before, and it never failed to be charming. The turrets and towers of the Western Fort were visible above its parkland, as the ferry drifted serenely onward, through rich areas and poor, past city streets and stretches of flower-filled wasteland. From this perspective, the city seemed strangely distant and calm, as if the disappearance of the Skein, the flower attacks, and all the other difficulties that were besetting it had been sealed away behind a glass wall. For the first time in weeks, Mercy felt herself beginning to relax, a completely irrational thing to do under the circumstances. She fingered the hilt of the Irish sword at her hip and pondered. Perra sat beside her on the bench as the ferry wallowed along the canal, occasionally rising up to gaze at some aspect of the changing view that had attracted its interest. Another *ka* accompanied a passenger, a woman in a blue headscarf with a tattooed face, but the two ancestral spirits ignored each other and now that Mercy thought of it, she had never seen *kas* in conversation. Perhaps it was considered impolite. She would ask Perra, when the occasion allowed it.

They were coming to the centre of the city now: the wide circular plaza known as the Heart of the World. Here stood the empty palace of the Skein, built aeons ago of red and black marble, mottled like flesh, its towers arching up into the heavens. A light still burned in the topmost tower, a sacred flame kept alight by servants in vigil for the day when their masters and mistresses returned. Before the palace stood a much more recent statue, a representation of the ship called the *Barquess*. Mercy thought of Greya, and sighed. The statue had emerged out of Worldsoul itself; it had not been commissioned or carved by human hand. One morning, a few months back, it had simply appeared. She watched the statue until it fell out of sight: the bronze sides of the ship gleaming in the morning sunlight, its vanes and sails shifting in the breeze.

They were now in the Eastern Quarter and already the architecture was different: domes and minarets, pagodas and turrets. Some of these buildings had been taken from Earth, others were more recent, but built on ancient lines. Originally, the different peoples of Worldsoul had lived in separate areas in their separate quarters, but without the tensions of Earth, ghettos had not proved viable and now everyone was more muddled up. A good thing, in Mercy's view. She looked down on a street market as the ferry sailed along an aqueduct, the white roofs of the market stalls bright in the sunlight and allowing occasional glimpses of piles of eggplant, oranges, coriander, ginger . . . all the produce that had been brought in from the fields that week. Beyond the Eastern Quarter lay the Great Desert, the Khaureg, but to the south, the land was fertile. Mercy began thinking about supper: she had eaten out these last few days. It would be nice to have the time to sit down and eat properly at home . . .

Now the huge blue dome of the Medina was visible, rising above the rooftops, and Mercy became aware of a growing impatience. She had a mission, after all, unrelated to what was for dinner. The *ka*, seeming to pick up on her mood, sat up straight and stern.

"We are nearly there," Perra said.

Mercy nodded. The terminal wharf of the Eastern Quarter ferry was now visible, a mass of cranes and scaffolding. The ferry sailed into dock with a brief flurry of activity as it was secured and then Mercy and Perra were heading down the gangplank.

"Do you know where this woman lives?" Mercy asked the *ka*.

"No, but it should not be hard to find her. She is an alchemist. She has . . . a certain reputation."

"What kind of reputation?" Mercy asked, intrigued.

"A dangerous one."

⊷⚬⊶

One did not simply enter the Eastern Quarter and start asking questions. First, there was tea. Despite her impatience, Mercy let Perra take the lead. The *ka* found a chaikhana, set into the wall of the Medina where it was safe for a Westerner to go. The heart of the Medina was, so Perra said, best avoided. Mercy was disinclined to argue. She took a seat at the back of the chaikhana, where she could see the door.

"What do we do now?" she asked, in an undertone.

"We wait," Perra said.

Shortly afterwards, once tea had been brought, a man approached the table. He wore an elegant suit, black, with brilliant white cuffs. Sad eyes gazed at Mercy, from a patrician face. The countenance of the mysterious Dr Roke flashed briefly across Mercy's mind, but this man did not, on second glance, bear all that significant a resemblance: it was the suit.

"Madam, forgive me. You are from the Western Quarter?"

"Yes. We're looking for someone."

"May I ask who?"

"We do not have a name for her. She is an alchemist."

"Ah." The man smiled. "Then there is only one person whom you can be looking for. She calls herself Shadow. Would you like me to introduce you to her?"

Mercy smiled. "Forgive me for my incredible rudeness, but what is in this for you?"

"I am a facilitator, you see. A number of individuals have me on commission. I effect introductions, engineer chance meetings, arrange coincidences and synchronicities. My name is Georgiou Sephardi."

"So if you introduce us to the woman who calls herself Shadow, she will pay you?"

"If she considers you are worth meeting, yes."

"Well," Mercy said, after a pause. "Let's hope that she will. Tell her that we know about the attack last night."

Sephardi vanished into the maze of the Medina, while Mercy and Perra sipped tea. "This is going too smoothly," Mercy said. "I don't trust that."

The *ka* managed a fluid shrug. "Such things happen with grace here."

"So you say." And then, because that sounded rude, she added, "I am sure you know this better than I, Perra." The headache was coming back, like an oncoming warning of storms. Mercy frowned. Yesterday—and then, all of a sudden, she knew what was happening.

"Perra, quickly—outside!"

The *ka* did not question her. They ran for the door, startling the other customers of the teahouse, but it was too late. Mercy smelled an acrid, fizzy burning, heard a firework hiss, and felt an indefinable sense of wrongness that grew and grew until the explosion itself came almost as a relief. *Not again . . .* Mercy and Perra dropped under a table just outside the door and covered their heads. The world was swallowed in a billow of scarlet and for a second, Mercy thought that she had actually been blown up. But it was only the red awning of the chaikhana, torn free by the flower-blast and floating down to cover the wrecked frontage. There was a minute of intense silence, then screams.

Mercy started disentangling herself from the collapsed awning, Unseen hands helped, until she was able to free herself from the weight of the material.

"Are you all right?" Sephardi did not have a hair out of place.

"Yes. Perra?" But she knew that the *ka*, being a spirit, would be all right.

"I am here," Perra said.

"I lament," Sephardi remarked, "my timing."

"Maybe it's not *your* timing. This happened to me yesterday. Are they following me around?"

Sephardi spread his hands. He was accompanied, Mercy saw now, by a woman. She was veiled: dressed in a grey tunic and silvery trousers that billowed like a bell. The veil itself covered her entire face, a gauzy blue mist, and nothing at all could be glimpsed behind it.

"This is Shadow," Sephardi said.

"I'm Mercy Fane. This is Perra. We've come—" But there was a flash. Mercy, turning, squinted past the collapsed awning. A lamp hanging above the street illuminated the now-roofless interior of the chaikhana. A pool of light shone on overturned tables and utter chaos. A blossom drifted down, glowing like hot blood, and just as it reached the level of the lamp it burst silently apart, the crimson petals flaring out and setting fire to everything they touched. The awning ignited like dry tinder.

"Oh, shit," Mercy said, retreating further into the street with the others. Bits of blazing fabric fluttered down.

The veil turned in Sephardi's direction. "Do we not," the woman said, "have emergency services?"

"I'm assuming that's rhetorical," he replied.

Shadow sighed, stretched out a hand, uttered a long liquid word and the flames subsided into ash.

The core of the blossom had embedded itself in the pavement with a soft, corrosive hiss. The glowing stamen was quivering.

"*Don't* look," Mercy said. She flung up an arm, shielding her eyes, and the thought rushed through her mind, *This is too close, we're going to get—*

Her skin was suddenly flushed, her mouth filled with a dry desert heat. She could feel the ends of her hair sizzling. The afterimage of the flash, the white-hot flare of the core, still glared against her shuttered eyelids. But something was between the stamen and herself, a soft rustling wind. Shocked, her eyes snapped open to see she was enveloped in the azure gauze of the woman's veil. Dark eyes, golden-black, heavily kohled, were staring into her own.

"Good to meet you, too, Mercy," Shadow said, and to Mercy's surprise, she was smiling.

--→=●=→--

They had been lucky, Mercy thought. Shadow stooped to pick up a charred curl. Perfect, the raised lines of the petal still clearly delineated, but as Shadow's fingers closed a little, the petal disintegrated, showering into a stream of ash.

"Be careful," Mercy warned, "Handling those things can hurt you."

Shadow nodded. "I've done it once before. I'm—good with fire."

"So I saw." The expression in those troubled eyes was still with her, burned onto her retina like the implosion of the core. "Your veil—"

Saved my life was one of those things better left unsaid. People could expect the honouring of obligations; you had to watch your spirit, living here.

Shadow made a negligent gesture. "It was for the benefit of both of us."

"I think," Sephardi said diffidently, "that perhaps we should find another teahouse."

They followed a disconsolate crowd of those who had been in the teahouse at the time of the attack, those who had been walking by. Mercy looked at two blue faces, serenely displeased, then at a tall person in black, with a ridged and tattooed skull.

"Too many nightlighters living here," Shadow said. She nodded in the direction of the skull. "But you can't prevent people from going about their business."

"I suppose not," Mercy said. "And speaking of which . . . "

"You'll understand," Shadow said, "that I'm reluctant to take you to my place. Besides, it's a mess. May I suggest another chaikhana?"

"We shall be guided by you," Sephardi told her.

Mercy was relieved that their short trip through the now-crowded streets was without further incident. People were beginning to congregate, knot, then disperse like a kind of tidal flow. Even without the aid of technology, news of the flower attack was spreading throughout the quarter. Shadow ignored covert stares and strode ahead, her veil billowing behind her.

The new teahouse was set into the wall of the Eastern Quarter. Mercy stepped inside to sudden coolness and peace. The chaikhana was spacious, with oak tables and low benches set far apart, and at the end it opened onto a balcony.

"Let's sit," Shadow said. Mercy followed her out onto the balcony and found herself gazing out across the expanse of the Great Desert. Dunes hummed and shifted in the tides of the desert, moving imperceptibly, but Mercy knew that if she was to look again an hour later, the landscape would have changed. A kite, in search of carrion, wheeled high above the sands. But the balcony of the chaikhana was shaded and cool.

"Here," Shadow said to Mercy, "one is able to breathe."

Mercy knew what she meant.

"Sit," Shadow said, "Please. You are my guests here."

"Thank you. By the way, they don't have an objection to my being armed?"

"They'd consider you foolish if you were not." Shadow ordered more tea and was still for a moment, gazing out across the sands. Then she said, "Rumour moves faster than anything. A pity they can't harness it to drive engines."

Mercy laughed. "They don't refer to it as a 'mill' for nothing."

"Sephardi tells me that you're seeking information."

"I'll get straight to the point," Mercy said. "Perra, my *ka*, heard that you were attacked last night."

"Yes, I was. I defeated it. I don't know what it was. It left a hand behind—I have it in a box, at my laboratory."

"Left a hand?"

"I sliced it off." Shadow drew a blade from beneath her veil and placed it on the table, turning it over quickly so that it flickered light and dark. "This is one of my weapons."

"Impressive. What's it made from?" She knew better than to reach out and touch, but Mercy could hear the voice of the blade, a whispering, and it spoke of darkness and light, noon and shade. The Irish sword murmured at her side.

"Meteorite iron. It was forged with moonlight and sunlight. It can cut through almost anything. I have many enemies. But I would not," Shadow said, turning the weapon from side to side, "have wanted to go up against the thing I saw last night with any less a weapon. What's your interest in this?"

"I'm with the Library," Mercy said. "I let . . . the thing . . . loose." She could see Shadow's eyes on her, from behind the veil. It occurred to her that the other woman might easily think Mercy had sent the thing, and was now checking up on its success.

However, Shadow said, "But not deliberately, I think."

"No. Not at all." Briefly, she recounted to Shadow what had happened. When she had finished, there was a short silence.

"You don't know what it is?"

"No, I've no idea. Except that it's from the north. It wasn't a Wolfhead. I know what those look like."

"They are a civilised people."

"Yes, they are." Mercy was pleasantly surprised by this; there was a great deal of prejudice about the northern clans, a lot of misunderstanding. "But no, I didn't recognise this thing and we can't translate the text that it came from."

"Then," Shadow said, "I suggest we use other methods."

⋅─≡ ⊂≡─⋅

From Shadow's laboratory, hewn out of pale golden stone and with graceful arches, the view across the desert was angled but, by now, familiar. Mercy, Sephardi, and the *ka* stood across the room, as Shadow opened the leaden box. Shadow had been deceptive: the place was not a mess, and she had obviously made the decision to trust Mercy enough to let her into her home, at least for now.

Mercy was under no illusions. The alchemist did not know her, could not trust her beyond a certain point. Mercy had no doubt that Shadow did not leave her most interesting experiments in public view. She had caught a glimpse of other rooms in the walled-in apartment, doors that whisked silently shut. But the weight of the Library was a compelling authority: Mercy, as its representative, had garnered Shadow's attention, if not yet her respect.

She watched as Shadow knelt and swiftly scratched a triangle on the wooden boards of the laboratory with the sun-moon blade. A moment later, and the edges of the triangle flared up into light. The alchemist was taking no chances.

Mercy and Sephardi were contained within a separate circle. The *ka*, not as subject to magical pressures, elected to remain outside, perching on the windowsill. Its small face was creased in a frown, or perhaps simply concentration. Shadow fetched the leaden box and placed it inside the triangle, then retreated to the containment circle and spoke a quick incantation. The lid of the box sprang open.

"What I am intending to do," Shadow said, "is as much science as magic. I want to take a close look at this thing. That means building up an image from its DNA."

Mercy nodded. "All right."

She was unfamiliar with Persian magic, with the long streams of syllables, but this was ancient craft. It was linked to mathematics, to gematria, and to the stars, but the magic of the old lands from which this spellwork had come went further, all the way back to the Fertile Crescent, the dawn of Earth's history. It harked back to the oldest goddesses, women who were half-bird, women who later became demons. Astarte into Astaroth, Prince of Hell. Lilith, and her storm brood of the deep desert. Cybele, Lady of Lions. Mercy did not know whether it was on these that Shadow was calling: in the teahouse earlier, Sephardi had described Shadow as a devotee of Allah, and devout. But she was also a magician, and magicians are pragmatic.

Gradually, drawn forth by words, spirals of DNA began to wind upwards in hologrammatic formation. Mercy knew that this was an illusion, but it was compelling. The DNA twisted, turned, and began to fill out into bone and sinew and flesh. As they watched, the figure that Mercy had seen in the Library began to take shape before them. Its bones were long and sharp, the dappled hide too tightly stretched over them so that the thing appeared lightly fleshed, mainly sinew. Its face was human, of sorts. The black eyes, whiteless, glinted with intelligence. Its long hair, also black and matted into ropy locks, fell down its back, Mercy was now able to get a closer look at the tattooed symbols covering its visible flesh. Runes and symbols, ancient in configuration. She said urgently to Sephardi, "Do you have a pen?"

When he complied, Mercy took a notebook from her pocket and began to note the symbols down as accurately as she could. Shadow made the image turn, and it did so, revealing glyphs and spiked sigils down the length of its spine.

"It's definitely the thing I saw," Mercy said.

"Good. It's definitely the thing that attacked me. The question is: What is it?"

"I cannot help you," Sephardi said. "I am not an expert on the north."

"I know someone who is, though," Shadow said. She turned to Mercy. "Have you finished?"

"Yes. Can it speak, Shadow? Can you make it talk?"

"No, this is just an image." She sounded apologetic. "I've tried making them talk before."

Mercy could not help having the disconcerting feeling that the thing was watching them, linked, somehow, to this conjured representation. But there was no awareness of them in its eyes. "This person you mentioned, who is an expert on the north. Where might they be found?"

Shadow laughed. "You'll like this. She's employed by the Library. As a consultant. She's also Vice Chancellor of the University."

⊷Interlude⊷

She had lived in this apartment for over twenty years, ever since Ibrahim's death. It would have felt wrong to leave it, as though she were leaving him behind, and she was not ready to do that. Some women married again, but she knew that she would not: the inclination was not there. Besides, his spirit returned to her, on the great days, and although she knew he was at peace with God, she was always happy to see him.

If she had gone to live somewhere else, he would not have known his way around.

With care, because her joints were not good today, she re-arranged the roses in their bowl. Her daughter brought her these, grown in her courtyard garden. They reminded her of sunsets and she loved to look at them.

On this particular evening, she had left the windows open. A ward glistened across the open space, so she was surprised to turn and find someone there.

"Oh!" she said, relieved. "It's you." She put a hand to her heart. "For a moment, I thought it was Ibrahim. Or, Allah forbid, an intruder."

"I am sorry," her visitor said. "I should have knocked."

She smiled. "On the air itself? Sit. Have some tea. Or at least, the pretence of tea."

It was his turn to smile. "I like the smell. I'll have some, if I may."

She brought it on a silver tray and they sipped, inhaled, in silence for some minutes. Then her visitor said, "You're wondering why I've come. I'm afraid it's not good news."

Her heart sank. "I thought as much. There have been signs, the usual portents. Someone saw a bloodstained lion in the Medina last week. People have had visions. There's been a great deal of astrological mayhem going on: peculiar conjunctions of the heavens."

"I can't tell you what it heralds, because I don't know. But there's been a change at the end of the world."

"That's not good," she said. "The end of the world—well, if you walk far enough away from there, you'll end up here."

"Something's happening, Mariam," the Messenger said. Against the brocaded cushions of the couch, she could see his faint illuminated transparency, visible only in certain lights. This was a projection, if a good one. Messengers can do that, dissolve and reform at will. "Something's changing," he continued. "The question is, what?"

⇒Thirteen⇐

Darya had done well in the limited time he had given her, but Jonathan Deed had no intention of telling her this. Instead, he frowned down at the collection of parchment that she now placed before him and said, "Is this all?"

She hid her feelings well, but he saw her mouth tighten a fraction and her fingers clench. "It was all I could find, Abbot General," she said, with a deference which clearly did not come naturally. Darya was learning. Good.

"Very well," Deed said, with a sigh. "I suppose it will have to do."

He waited until her bone heels clicked away, then turned back to the parchments. These were fragmentary: Mercy Fane's genealogy was likely to be held in full by the Library, as the Skein had liked to keep tabs on their personnel, but locating her personal details would be troublesome given the level of security. For the moment, he would work with what he had.

They knew that Mercy was descended from the Wolfhead clans, via Greya Fane. That didn't mean very much: half or quarterbreeds didn't usually exhibit the Wolf Clans' particular brand of magic. As Deed knew well, that magic was heavily dependent on place, on the ice fields and pine forests of the north: wild magic, drawing on earth and sky and all the winds that blew.

So. Greya Fane. But what about the other mother, the woman called Sho? She would, Deed knew, have contributed to Mercy's heritage—a magical binding, a connection, was usual in such partnerships, even though Mercy would have had a biological father as well and he would need to be taken into consideration. If they could ever find out who he had been . . . Sho herself was, apparently, missing. Looking at the partial family tree, Deed worked out that she had come from the Eastern Quarter, and that gave Mercy links with Eastern magic, too. An interesting combination and one that could prove powerful. Mercy would have skills in a number of areas, otherwise the Library would not be employing her.

"So," Deed said, aloud. He looked up from the parchments, into a sudden shaft of sunlight. "Time to ask some questions."

⊷═◐═⊷

He did not enter the Northern Quarter by the usual route, the North Road that led up from the Heart of the World. Instead, he chose to slip into the Quarter at night, through the Ancestral Gate itself. He was entitled, and its magic would not snare him, but even so, Deed felt a faint prickle of what in a human might have been called fright as he stepped beneath its huge stone-and-iron portal. The ground beneath the Gate was red. This was not, Deed knew, symbolic.

In this district, the buildings of the Northern Quarter were massive, resembling forts, and the castellated pinnacles of the castles of the old Northern lords fragmented the skyline. It was cold, too: snow crunched beneath Deed's boots as he made his way through the quiet, dark street. He was heading for Bleikrgard, the Pale Castle: not a trip he cared to make, because the northern lords were fractious and twitchy, disliking his kind. Insularity, Deed thought, had long been a problem, and would doubtless continue to be so long after he was gone. But when they had heard what he had to tell them . . . Loki's plan still itched inside his subconscious, like a burr inside a shirt.

A silvery thread of sound broke the silence: sleigh bells. Deed stepped back into the shadows and waited. The sleigh came around the corner of the street, travelling swiftly. It was drawn by two white deer, with bells woven into their ruffed manes. A woman sat inside it, wielding a whip. Deed, in sudden alarm, took care to wrap invisibility about himself, drawing it up from the snow and the cold air, freezing the world around him, but the sleigh came to a halt nonetheless.

"It's no use doing that," the woman called. "You're perfectly visible."

Deed sighed. "My apologies." He spread his hands in deprecation. "I'm used to the West."

"The West," the woman said, in contempt.

"I am not a Westerner myself." Deed, caught off guard, was annoyed to find himself sounding defensive.

"I can tell," the woman said. "You are disir."

Deed froze, and not because of the cold. "How did you—?"

"Ah." The woman laughed. She looked over the side of the sleigh and Deed saw her face for the first time. She was beautiful, but not young. White hair was piled high in a chignon, secured with silver icicles. Her eyes glittered silver in the lamplight.

"What are you?" Deed whispered.

"My name is Mareritt."

It meant "nightmare." That placed her as something out of story, and not quite of the world. Silently, Deed cursed. Trust his luck to be badgered by some stray tale.

"You see," Mareritt said, smiling thinly, "Your kind and I have had a long and profitable history." He felt her reach out through his own defences, take his name out of his head like someone plucking fruit from a tree. "Where are you going, Jonathan Deed?"

He did not want to tell her, but again, she stole it easily from his mind and laughed at his discomfort. "You can't have too many secrets from me, Mr Deed. I am inside everyone's head sooner or later."

Deed swallowed. Used to being the one in control, he was finding it hard to know how to proceed. He gave silent, fleeting thanks to Loki then, for burying the plan so deep that no one could find it. Then the woman said, "I can give you a lift, if you like?"

Deed opened his mouth to say that he would prefer to walk, but instead he found himself stepping onto the lip of the sleigh and sitting uncomfortably beside her. She was dressed in rags and tatters beneath her cloak, which he could now see was made of feathers, white and black. Swans and crows . . . but he could not quite place her. She seemed to embody elements of different tales, a ragbag of stories. He glanced behind him into the body of the sleigh, behind the driving seat, and froze.

The sleigh was filled with severed heads, perhaps a dozen. All of them were male, and their necks and brows were bound with metal bands, bronze and silver and lead, brass and the soft gleam of gold. Each band was covered with runic signs and Deed felt the tug and pull of magic. Their eyes were closed but they mumbled and muttered to themselves in sleep. The pallid lips of the closest head, bound in tin, smacked with a wet sucking noise. Deed, accustomed to gruesome sights, found himself unable to tear his gaze away.

"These are my kings," Mareritt said, and laughed. "Do you like them?"

"I—" With difficulty, he wrenched his eyes back to her face. She smiled at him and he saw she had teeth as sharp as his own.

Mareritt cracked her whip and the deer sprang forward in a flurry of snow. Bleikrgard rose up ahead.

⊶Fourteen⊷

Shadow should have been suspicious of the woman from the Library, and indeed, retained a certain level of paranoia out of habit. However, when she consulted her intuition, it told her that Mercy was sound, and the presence of the *ka*, Perra, was further testament to this. *Ka* spirits did not take well to evil, sent from the gods as they were. As ancestral guides, they were evidence of a degree of divine faith. Besides, she thought that Mercy would have concocted a less bald narrative, had she been lying.

She checked anyway, leaving Mercy alone in the lab. The Librarian on duty said placidly that Mercy Fane was currently on sick leave, but would be back soon.

Therefore, Shadow had little reservation about taking Mercy to meet Mariam Shenudah. The latter would, she felt, have her own opinions on what had transpired, and if she did not trust Mercy, she would have little hesitation in saying so. And doing something about it.

They had sealed the severed hand in its box. Shadow had no intention of letting it out of the laboratory, but she had taken pictures. Interesting to see what Shenudah would make of it.

They reached Mariam's apartment close to twilight. Mercy would not, she had told Shadow, be obliged to return to work immediately: she could call in sick, and muttered something about preferring her to do so—something about an inspection. Shadow had not offered to put her up overnight, but had asked Sephardi to find her a room in a nearby guest house. The Librarian had not seemed to take affront at this.

Shenudah lived at the summit of an apartment block, one of the many that had gone up around the Medina in recent years. It was rickety, covered in bamboo scaffolding and tangles of plants where enterprising dwellers had made the most of their balconies, given the lack of a garden. Mercy followed her up flights of winding stairs.

"She says it keeps her fit," Shadow said over her shoulder.

"I'm not surprised."

The building creaked and groaned like a ship in a high wind. Shadow was almost relieved when they reached the final flight and an ancient door, incongruous in the modern setting of the apartment block. Shadow knocked, once. "Mariam? It's me."

A pause, then the door opened and a small face looked out. Shenudah, like her door, was elderly, but as usual she was dressed with the utmost smartness: a neat black suit with a rose and lily corsage, sheer stockings, high-heeled shoes.

"Good evening!" The voice was brisk and educated.

"Mariam, I've brought a visitor. From the Library."

Shadow was conscious of a piercing stare over her shoulder, then the old woman said, "You look like someone I used to know, once."

"Who was that, Mrs—er,"

"It's Dr Shenudah. But you may call me Mariam. Come in."

On her first visit here, Shadow had expected a motley, shambolic apartment filled with books, but Mariam Shenudah's home was tidy and controlled. All four walls were covered in bookcases, but these were neatly filed and the books were in alphabetical order, in a range of languages from Arabic to Mandarin. A polished wooden table stood in the centre of the room, bearing a vase filled with roses and the curving statue of an ibis. Shadow looked with pleasure at the familiar deep, rich colours: gold and dun and deep red, rose pink and ivory, the colours of a desert at twilight.

"Sit, please," Mariam Shenudah said. "I will bring tea."

"I hadn't forgotten that the Eastern Quarter runs on tea," Mercy said, with a smile.

"The West, too," Shadow murmured.

"Or booze. But I don't suppose you drink alcohol, do you?"

"No. I am observant. But I don't object to others doing as they see fit. We all have different paths, after all."

Once Mariam had brought the round silver tray of tea glasses, she once more looked at Mercy. "Allow me to guess. Your mother is called Greya Fane. She had a partner called Sho."

"You knew them?"

"Yes, well. Perhaps forty years ago, now. A long time. How old are you, Mercy?"

"I'm twenty-eight."

"I knew Greya in the north, when she lived in Aachven. She was a child of the Wolf Clans, as doubtless you know."

"Yes. They're my family, but I've never met them. Sho and Greya . . . kept themselves to themselves. I've never been sure what had gone wrong." She paused. "I'll be honest with you. I don't know who my father was. Greya chose him because she and Sho wanted to have a child, but I don't know anything about him."

How odd Westerners could be, Shadow thought. But that wasn't quite fair: Sho had come from this quarter, evidently.

Mariam said, "Greya was always—reckless. She took risks—magical ones. She associated with people whom a wiser, older woman would not have gone near, but Greya was young, and I'm afraid she was easily beguiled by glamour. I'm sure you are more sensible, Mercy."

"I always thought of her as cautious," Mercy said. "Annoyingly so, actually. But then she bolted into the blue on the *Barquess*, so . . ."

"Maybe she'd learned from experience, at least until the Skein departed. But when I knew her, she courted risks like another woman might court lovers. There was a forest lodge, a cult dating back to ancient times. Blood magic and sigil magic. Greya became involved. I am telling you this not because of any interest in your family history, but because it relates to your current situation. Sephardi has spoken to me, about the thing you have both seen. I know what that thing is."

"What is it?" Mercy and Shadow both spoke at the same time.

"Disir."

Shadow saw that Mercy was frowning. "I know that word. I've heard it before, but I don't know what it means. Is that thing a 'disir,' then? What are they?"

"They are the children of Loki, the lord of misrule and more than misrule. Their story says that they were born out of the drops of poison and blood that the god shed when he was chained, springing from the earth and the ice. Their name means 'the ladies' and they are essentially ancestral spirits, but some stories are not meant to last. They have curdled and turned foul, like sour milk."

"And now one of them has escaped from an ancient text."

"They have bred with men although the Wolf Clans would not touch them, and there are rumours that their descendents are active in Worldsoul. They reap chaos, they are dukes of blood."

"We need a magic to stop it," Shadow said. "We can't have it running around attacking people. There are practical considerations here, regardless of its history."

"I understand," Mariam said placidly. She took a sip of tea. "There is a spell to bind them, but it is not easy. It's blood magic, as I have said, and requires a commitment."

Involuntarily, Shadow and Mercy glanced at one another. "Whose blood?" Mercy said.

"That would be yours. You released it, Shadow injured it. You both have a connection to it and thus, it is your blood which must be given, but given freely."

"As long as it's only a drop," Mercy said, after a long pause. She did not seem keen; Shadow could not blame her. There was something in her expression which Shadow could not interpret.

"The same for me," Shadow said.

"Then I will show you the spell," Mariam told them.

⤖ ⬅⤖

Mercy and Shadow stood side by side that midnight, in the middle of Shadow's laboratory. Shadow had put the veil aside. Out of respect, Mercy had glanced at her face only once, even though she had seen it before. The alchemist had the fierce profile of a falcon, a curving nose, high-angled cheeks.

She had asked the *ka*, privately, if the alchemist could be trusted. Perra had said that in its opinion, the answer was yes, but Mercy was still unhappy about the blood ritual. Maybe it wasn't just Greya who was a risk-taker . . . the thought that she might be treading in her mother's footsteps was a dismaying one.

The *ka* stood watch as Shadow once again inscribed a circle in fire and placed a silver bowl filled with water and roses before them. They spoke the spell together, Mercy trying not to stumble over the unfamiliar words, and then Shadow took the sun-and-moon blade and nicked first her own palm, then Mercy's. The drops of blood fell, mingled, into the bowl and the roses went up in a hiss of flame.

" . . . and I abjure you now, in the name of Solomon the King and the Book of Solomon which holds all the names of God . . . "

Shadow's voice, quiet and firm, spoke through the sudden roar of fire. This was the old magic of Asia Minor, winding its way through Europe in the Renaissance and perhaps before, a magic of fire and bare rock and burning sky. Here, on the rim of the Great Desert, it seemed appropriate, Shadow's voice whispering out of the ages and conjuring ancient names. Mercy looked down into the bowl and saw that the roses were gone; the bowl was bubbling with blood. Her sigilometer was ticking like a metronome, registering magic. Across the room, in the triangle, the writhing mottled form was once again appearing, but this time it was solid.

"Hold!" Shadow's voice rang out across the room. Mercy could see the disir clearly now, the rows of teats down her abdomen between the cracked leather harness, the razor-toothed mouth.

"Hold!" The blood, far more than the few drops that Mercy and Shadow had shed, boiled over the lip of the bowl and surged towards the edge of the circle, then beyond, a thin line of red reaching out to the triangle and extinguishing the fire. The disir sprang out, crouching for a moment, then rushing forward. Shadow's blade was already out and Mercy freed the sword, stepped back, and came up against a wall of air. The circle was still holding her in; if she tried to strike, she was likely to hit Shadow. The alchemist cried out and struck down with the blade. But the disir had learned from the loss of her hand. Mercy could see the stump, wrinkled and seamed, looking like an old injury. The disir moved with unnatural speed, up the wall and across the ceiling like a spider. Shadow uttered an imprecation and cast a Name upwards: it missed the disir by inches and scorched itself into the ceiling to flare for a moment before flaking out into ash.

"Take the circle down!" Mercy yelled. Shadow did so, and she was free to move. She vaulted across the work table, sending an alembic crashing to the floor in a shower of glass and landing in a defensive sprawl as the disir dropped from the ceiling. As Mercy had already briefly grappled with it, she was almost prepared for the blast of cold that the disir brought in its wake. The disir raked out with long claws, but the lost hand was hampering it. Mercy, on her feet again, dodged back, slashing out with the Irish blade and severing the disir's harness. A streak of welling black blood appeared in the sword's wake and the disir hissed in pain. The blood spattered across the floor. The disir rushed at Mercy, who ran backwards and slipped on the pool of the mingled blood that had seeped from the bowl. She fell and the disir was on her, but there was a sudden blast of light and heat and the intense cold was blown back by warmth. The smell of roses was all around, sandalwood, myrrh, filling the laboratory in an intoxicating wave of perfume. Mercy gasped, scrambling to her feet. The disir was backing away. She heard Shadow say something, urgently, and turned to look at her, but the light was too bright, too blinding. Mercy threw an arm across her eyes but as she did so, she glimpsed the diminished spidery shape of the disir clambering up the wall to the high arched window. There was a shatter of breaking glass and the disir was gone, scrambling down the city wall.

Light, and a presence that filled the laboratory. Shadow was speaking, but Mercy did not understand the language. Something laughed and it was not human. Then it, too, was gone, leaving heat and the scent of roses in its wake.

"Shadow?" Mercy's vision was still blurred.

The alchemist was huddled on the floor. "Are you hurt?"

"No." Shadow looked up and Mercy realised the alchemist was consumed with fury. "That was—well. Someone who has no business in *my* business."

"Who are you talking about?"

"Suleiman the Shah. That was one of his spirits, his djinn. He saved my life—and yours. That means he's bound me to him, when that has been the very thing that I've been trying to avoid."

Fifteen

Deed reached Bleikrgard in a skating flurry of snow. It had begun to fall from the skies again, as Mareritt's sleigh raced through the streets, the deers' feet unnaturally sure on the icy stone. When they reached the looming grey stone palace, Mareritt brought the sleigh to a skidding halt and said to Deed, "Here we are."

"I can offer payment—" Deed began. Resolutely, he did not look behind him again, to where the heads muttered and twitched.

"Oh, yes, you certainly can. And you will, but not now. I shall take my payment when I see fit."

Deed did not wish to show how unnerved he was by this remark, nor could he—for he found he was already out of the sleigh and standing on the stone flags of the palace. Mareritt veered the deer about without another word and was gone into whirling white.

Deed was relieved to see her depart. He went quickly across the courtyard without looking back, but it seemed to him that he could still feel Mareritt's gaze on his back and the sensation was an unfamiliar one, therefore unsettling. His pride was affronted and that made him angry, made him feel the disir bones start to thrust at his cheeks and rib cage. If anyone had been watching, which perhaps they were, they would have seen his eyes darken and his teeth grow sharper. Deed took hold of himself with an effort and forced the human semblance back.

The steps up to the palace were icy and needed care to negotiate. Reaching the massive doors, Deed knocked once, hammering the iron ring back against cold oak. The sound resonated throughout the courtyard like a rifle shot, though the snow muffled all else. Deed waited for a moment and then the door swung open.

He had been here many times before, but the hallway always looked different. Deed could not say why this was, although he suspected that it had to do with the magical overlay that Bleikrgard would have continuously deployed: the warding/guarding/binding spellcasting that kept the fortress secure. The exterior of the fortress was ancient, castellated, but the hallway was modern: a marble floor with the patina of ice, mirrored walls, a gleaming blue ceiling the colour of an arctic sky, and a soft illuminating glow which was diffused throughout the hall. No one was in sight. Deed walked along the hallway, catching glimpses of himself in endless mirrored permutations. He did not care to look directly at his reflection, in fear of what it might reveal. He had forced the disir-self back, but it might not last: Bleikrgard had a way of revealing weakness, not the disir-nature itself, but the loss of control.

He reached the end of the hallway. Here stood a wall that seemed made of ice. Deed placed a hand upon it and, as always, felt its cold beating into his bones. He did not fight it off, but tried to welcome it, let it enter into himself. The cold was so intense that he felt as if it was transforming him, taking him somewhere that was very far from Worldsoul, perhaps all the way down the storyway of the Dead Road to the wild old lands of Earth's far past.

Then, it was gone. A dim blackness took its place. Deed smiled for the first time since Mareritt's intervention. He took strength from the cold and the dark, drawing a breath of pine-scented, smoky air. He stepped forwards into the dimness and spoke.

"I am here."

"Abbot General. Again, welcome."

Light flared and it took a moment for his eyes to adjust. The Lords of Bleikrgard, the lords of the north, were seated around the chamber. Nine of them wore business suits, of conservative and old-fashioned cut, with greater or lesser ruffs. The tenth wore rust-red armour, and carried a sword. The helm was down and Deed had never seen it raised, but he knew what it was supposed to contain. A skull, some claimed, but Deed thought this clichéd, and therefore tedious. The tenth lord was not human, Deed knew—at least, not any more. What he was, however, was open to some question.

The third lord spoke. "Abbot General." The voice was weary, long since burned of any fire. "What did you have to tell us?"

"I have a proposition for you. Of all the Quarters of this city, the Court has greatest allegiance to the Northern. To yourselves. How would you like that power to spread?"

"Of course we would."

"The past is stirring and the Ladies are coming to town," the fourth lord, who was prone to oracular announcements, said. He smiled a sudden and terrible smile. The others ignored him, which was just as well, Deed thought.

Deed pursed his lips. "How would you like to possess the Library? And all the magic that it contains?"

The Lords drew forwards. "The Library, you say?" the second lord said.

"Yes. I can give it to you."

Loki's plan was bubbling beneath the surface of his brain. He could not reveal it yet, but they would trust him enough to believe that he could make good on his promise. He was Abbot General, after all.

" . . . we need to take power, and that time is now."

"Yours is a savage ancestry, Abbot General," the third lord said. He meant it as a compliment, without reference to the disir: Deed had taken pains to keep that quiet, but he winced anyway.

"It's a matter of family pride," Deed said, modestly.

"We depend upon you, Abbot General." That was the armoured lord, in a voice that sounded as though there were no larynx behind it.

"Whilst regional feeling may account for something," Deed began.

"You will be paid, naturally. What currency do you wish?"

Deed showed teeth. "Blood."

"From whom?"

"None of you. There are debts that I would like settled. I shall give you a list of names. If you have objections to any of them, then we can negotiate." But he knew they would comply. He was their link to the oldest lord of all, he who lived in the wood, he who spoke chaos to the world. Deed was their link to Loki, whether they realised it or not, and thus they would do exactly what he told them.

Mareritt was a bad dream, nothing more. Deed walked out on a cloud of power; he had got what he wanted.

~Sixteen~

S he must have slept, Mercy told herself later; must have done so, because she dreamed. She was standing in the entrance hall of the Library, one hand resting on cool marble. The other hand held a small book; it seemed she had been reading. Those who had interrupted her were walking down the middle of the hall and Mercy's heart leaped to see them: they had come back, at long, long last. Their year's absence was ended and they had come home. Smiling, Mercy swept down into a bow.

The Skein acknowledged her with their customary remote smiles. There were two of them, one male, one female. They were twice Mercy's human height and their long robes fell to the floor as smoothly as water, a pale, fluid grey. The male Skein's skin was night-black, underlain with gold, and black hair reached his waist, tied with a gilded thong. The woman was white: snow haired, paper pale. Her eyes were jade; his were azure. They were talking and laughing in their own unknowable tongue, a language in which every word held weight, and their long hands glided in graceful, sweeping motions, adding emphasis to their words.

"You've come back," Mercy breathed, and bowed lower. But when she straightened up again, the hall was empty. The Skein had gone and the marble paving was blowing with dust and cracked with age. It frightened her so much that she woke into the unfamiliar confines of the guest house, and she did not sleep again.

Interlude

The Duke knocked, once. She had never been to this place before, but it seemed to her that there was something familiar about it, as though someone lived here whom she had once known. But she was used to palaces, mage-houses, fortresses, not ordinary apartment blocks.

The door opened. She looked through twisted coils of magic.

"You are a demon," the old lady said.

"That is correct." The Duke bowed.

"I'm afraid I have no intention of letting you in."

The Duke had expected this.

"Not a problem. I have no intention of hurting you, however."

"Then why have you come?"

"I am told that you know a great deal about this quarter, about its magic. I'm looking for someone. A djinn."

The old lady laughed. "There are many djinns and ifrits in the desert. Have you tried there?"

"I'm reliably informed that this one is in the city itself."

"I think your informant must be mistaken," Mariam Shenudah said. "An ifrit in the city would cause a small sensation. They're quite large, you know."

"Nevertheless."

"I can't help you. I'm very sorry." Then, guileless, she added, "Have you tried asking Suleiman the Shah? He's *very* well connected."

The demon grinned. "Perhaps a small social call is in the cards."

Later, she crouched on the roof of the Has, tapping a brass fingernail against the tiles. It would not be wise even for a duke to try to break into the Shah's palace, but there was more than one way to go about things. From a pocket of her armour, the Duke took a small golden fishing hook and a long line of thread, also gold. Then she cast about for the nearest storyway.

These were evidently rigidly controlled around the domain of the Has. She finally found one, the slightest whisper of an unfinished tale, so gossamer thin that it had crept unnoticed through a crack in the wards. The Duke raised the fishing hook, attached to its line, and dropped it down the storyway. She felt it slide into the Has, and be gripped by a strong rushing tide. The psyche of the Shah, a lodestone within the palace walls. Gremory let the hook be drawn along until it snagged.

The Shah was sleeping. She supposed he had to do that sometimes. His dreams were bloody, and the Duke smiled. A man after her own heart . . . maybe she'd come back later, pay a genuine social call. Some men were wary of demons, but her grandmother had been a succubus and she could still turn on the charm when she needed to. She sent her own mind down the line, slipping gently into the Shah's dreaming psyche. She included a few erotic thoughts, just to distract him. But the Shah's mind was well-guarded. It was like peering at a sealed leaden egg. The Duke cast about for cracks and at last found one in a dream: the Shah, possibly stimulated by her erotic thoughts, was dreaming about a woman. In the dream, she was behaving in a most wanton manner: Gremory wondered idly if this was actually true to life. She could tell that this was a real person, not a dream artefact. She watched with interest as the Shah demonstrated a variety of perversions, culminating as he cried the woman's name and it snared on the demon's golden hook.

Her name was Shadow.

⇒Seventeen⇐

Mercy had returned to her own quarter, with a promise to return. Shadow, left alone, spent the morning in a quiet, boiling rage that she tried to channel into restoring the damaged laboratory. It was mid-afternoon when some semblance of order had been attained, and her fury had abated a little. She was not surprised when the soft knock on the door came. She had been expecting it.

Before she opened the door, she reset the wards with a gesture of her hand and they burned a dull red around the frame. Someone was standing on the step: a woman in green.

"Yes?" Shadow said.

The woman bowed her head. She handed over a parchment scroll, tied with a black ribbon.

"Who has this come from? Is it the Shah?" Shadow demanded. The woman looked up and Shadow recognised the blind eyes: it was the mute serving maid from the Has el Zindeh. She bowed her head again and melted into the dimness of the stairwell, leaving Shadow clutching the scroll.

Some time later, she perched on the windowsill of the laboratory, looking out across the desert. The scroll sat beside her and she was tempted to fling it into the sands, let it be swallowed by nothingness and shift. But Shadow knew this was childish. It would accomplish nothing; the obligation set by the Shah would still remain. Had she not taken the vows that she had, Shadow would have simply ignored it, but by the initiatory terms of her training, she could not. She even wondered whether the Shah had summoned the disir himself. The timing did not add up, but the Shah had diviners, and more than that, understood people, damn him. Coercion and threats would have made Shadow dig her heels in: this, however, was a far greater compulsion.

She picked up the scroll again and studied the contents. She was required, most politely, to present herself at the Has on the following morning, with a range of tools. The Shah would, he said, leave those to her discretion. There was no attempt to bluster, or to suggest that Shadow herself might call his bluff by not appearing. That still left the issue of the disir. Shadow and Mercy had talked long into the night, but had been unable to come up with an explanation as to why Shadow, in particular, had been attacked. Was it connected with the Shah, or not? Had it been purely random? Whatever the case, two things seemed clear: the Shah had been keeping an eye on her, and the disir was now engaged. Shadow had wounded it, and it was somewhere in the Eastern Quarter. Shadow had no doubts that it would be back.

⁙

On the following morning, after a troubled night, Shadow walked to the Has. She kept the veil as thick as possible, feeling secure behind its magic, but she knew that this was illusory only, no real solution. The ones who wanted her would find her, and Shadow disliked feeling exposed.

The door was opened by the same old woman as before. She gave Shadow a knowing glance. "Nice to see you back."

"Thank you," Shadow said sourly. "Where am I to go, please?"

She was led up a narrow staircase. The Shah stood in a room high in the Has, a turret with fretworked windows that were shuttered against the sun, looking out over the courtyard garden and letting in diamonds and squares of dappled, pleated light. The Shah stood in mingled bright and shade, reminding her uneasily of her own sun-and-moon knife. The floor was tiled in white and blue.

"Good morning," the Shah said, placidly. "I'm pleased that you could come."

"I do not see the need to fence," Shadow said. "We both know what I feel."

"Yes. And although you will not believe this, you have my apologies. I dislike extreme measures. I take them only when they are necessary."

"You are right. I do not believe."

"Nonetheless." The Shah's voice remained mild. "I imagine that, under the circumstances, you are eager to start work."

Shadow did not trust herself to speak. She walked past him to a window, hearing the heavy cream robes that he wore rustle against the tiles as he turned.

"I will have the ifrit brought up," the Shah said. "Here in the heights, overlooking all, it is closer to the air and fire which is its element, and it will prove more compliant."

"I would have thought that miring it in water and earth would have been a more sensible solution."

"No. A curious paradox. Using its own elements against it has proved more helpful. Please don't think that we have not tried."

"I do not want to reinvent the wheel."

"Of course not."

She looked out over the quarter as the Shah clapped his hands and spoke into the air. The turret was higher than it had appeared: she could see the curving dome of the Medina and then the jumbled buildings of the Quarter beyond. There was the wall, her own windows mercifully not visible from this angle. There was the apartment in which Mariam Shenudah lived. Shadow blinked into the morning sun as the sounds of something heavy being carried up the stairs drew louder.

⇥Interlude⇤

The young man was walking quickly, his footsteps unsteady on first the steps and then the cobbled street as he made his way up from the cellar bar. She had not hunted here before, and she was enjoying the change of scene. Had this been the Northern Quarter, she would never have taken this sort of risk, but it was not. She was enjoying that, too.

In her mother's house, she would be expected to bring back any kills. The cub was told to do that; any transgressions would earn a beating. But then, it was exactly the same in the Court. It did not occur to her to miss her mother's house, that blackstone fort near Bleikrgard, but she did want to make her family proud. And jealous. She planned to accomplish that on her next visit home with a casual remark.

I've become very—close—to the Abbot General.

If they didn't believe her, she'd show them the bite marks.

She watched, now, as the young man wove his way along the street. It had recently rained, one of those sea-stained downpours for which the Western Quarter was famous, not good cold northern snow. It occurred to her that had the Skein still been in dominion, she might not have taken such a risk then either, but they were gone and she stretched, luxuriating in unaccustomed freedom.

She wasn't supposed to be out but, well, windows could be opened. It was a relief to be naked and free of all those formal gowns. She knew Deed liked them: that was the human half. His little disir doll. But he liked the row of multiple teats and the spiky spine, too. She watched the young man with eyes grown luminous until he reached the end of the street, and then she stepped, clicking, from the shadows.

She didn't drink his blood. She wasn't *wampyr*. But she did take a little memento.

⚬Eighteen⚬

Nerren was due in later that morning after a doctor's appointment. The Library inspection had apparently gone as well as possible and Benjaya informed her that it had been thankfully brief.

"They said they'd do a more extensive one later."

"Oh, good," Mercy said. "Something to look forward to."

Predictably, she found herself with a mountain of paperwork, and some explaining to do. She spent most of the morning of her return with the Elders of the Library, trying to work out where the disir had come from. Nerren had told them about the events in Section C, eventually. Mercy called on Librarian McLaren for moral support: he could be relied upon to talk sense, and he looked more like a warrior than a Librarian. She felt she needed that.

"It must be a priority," Elder Tope said, her elderly face creased in concern. "We simply cannot have leakage."

"This never happened when the Skein were here," Elder Jonah lamented.

"But now the Skein are gone," McLaren remarked. "We have to shift for ourselves."

She looked at the Elders and suddenly felt very sad. Despite their age, they were like children whose parents had suddenly disappeared, leaving them alone and defenceless. She had thought this before and, of course, it was no more than the truth: the Skein had always taken care of everything. They might not have been gods, but they were god-like—powerful, benevolent, remote. Not for the first time, however, Mercy started to wonder whether this was really an accurate perception. How much had they really known about their masters and mistresses, after all?—although the Skein had changed gender seemingly at will, adopting new bodies as one might put on another set of clothes. They had always seemed kind, but when Mercy thought about it, she had the impression that the Skein treated humans as a sort of amusing pet, that their agenda lay entirely elsewhere. These thoughts did not make her comfortable, but this was not a comfortable world. And looking at the faces of the Elders, creased with worry and bewilderment, Mercy was conscious of a growing anger. *Did you go away on purpose,* she mentally asked the Skein, *so that we would grow up? But in that case, why didn't you prepare us better?*

"Don't worry," she heard herself say. "I'll take care of it. I promise you that I will."

Outside the doors, McLaren gave her a quizzical look. "We've known each other a long time, Mercy. Are you sure you can handle this?"

"No," she said. "I'm not. I'm not sure at all."

⁘

The *ka*, Perra, slipped on velvet feet through the labyrinthine passages of the Library. These were the secret ways, that even most of the Librarians did not know. Only the Librarians were allowed entry here, but Perra and *ka*-kind, along with others, used the secret routes: the little-known pathways of forgotten stories, the backdoors of tales, the null-spaces between lines of text and subtext. The route that Perra now took had brought the *ka* through an ancient tale of a winged bull and the sun, a fragment of poetry from an Elizabethan noblewoman's writing desk, and a folktale about fox witches from nineteenth-century

China. Nimbly, Perra skirted hooves crashing into sunwarmed dust, tasted old rose petals and disappointment, glimpsed a galleon on a far and silver sea, and pattered through snow under pine trees, before coming out into the liminal space between Sections C and D of the secured section of the Library.

Perra was curious, like all spirits. Perra wanted to *know*.

This section of the Library was very quiet, even compared to the usual silence of all libraries anywhere. Perra, being a spirit, was noiseless, and yet felt a distinct tinge of the ominous in the air, glimpsing shadows from the corners of the eye that had no relationship to the storyways.

This ka, thought Perra, *is being watched.*

The spirit spoke a name into the air, experimentally. Nothing answered, but Perra was not really expecting it to. The name hung for a moment, glimmering, then shattered like glass, the shards falling to the floor and disappearing.

This ka sees.

The name had been a revelatory one, calling the invisible into being, and it was a powerful and ancient word. It took a considerable resistance to protect oneself against it and the non-appearance of anything significant gave Perra two theories: either there was nothing there, or there was something *big*. Perra, from both experience and a natural caution, was inclined to favour the latter.

Mercy had mentioned the problematic section and so Perra approached it with a considerable degree of caution. As soon as the relevant stack was reached, the *ka* became aware of a tingling in the air, a jangling resonance which a human would have been unlikely to pick up. To the *ka*, however, it was as though someone had stretched a wire far too tightly and made it sing, sending ripples out into the surrounding air. It ruffled the goldensand fur of Perra's spine and set the *ka*'s small sharp teeth on edge. Reflexive claws slid out from Perra's toes to make small indentations on the parquet floor, which lingered briefly and then vanished: spirits leave little trace.

Cold/drivensnow/blackice/wrongness.

All of these things were familiar to the *ka* by now, in direct opposition to its own ancestral magic, which was of the desert, the warm breath of the sand-laden winds, the heat of stone and the cooler shadows of moonlight. Golden magic, and old. But the *ka* had seen what had come through this ripped gate in the world and what now haunted the Eastern Quarter: the disir. The *ka* had some other ideas about that.

Pausing before the stacks, Perra could see where the disir had come through. The rent would be invisible to Mercy and her colleagues, but to Perra, it looked like a black shining rip in the air, the edges hanging loosely and occasionally billowing outward as the between-worlds wind caught them and sent them flying like a ragged banner. Perra made a small, clucking sound of disapproval. Not Mercy's fault, of course. How can you mend something if you don't know that it's there? But the *ka* could see it and with sight, came knowledge, and with knowledge, came responsibility.

Perra knew that the sensible thing to do would be to close the rift at once. But *kas* are old, and although they are wise, they know that wisdom sometimes has to be earned and won. Thus Perra did not close the gap immediately. It thought it would take a little look.

⊷═◉═⊷

Together, Mercy and Nerren studied the map. Its edges bristled with thistledown sigils: the spells that were keeping the map's representation three-dimensional, and mid-air. Occasionally, Nerren cranked the bronze and silver sigilometer up a notch, bringing the map into sharper focus.

"It's too far," Mercy said. "It's off the map." But they had known that. They were looking for loose threads and there were plenty of those.

This part of the map showed the northern storyways. At the top were the more modern folktales, threads of narrative which led down into more ancient groups of legend. Most of them were quests, showing the distinctive golden-brown colour of quest stories and featuring brave children, elf-folk and svart-folk, mythical swords, magical objects. Earlier on, the children had been heroes, usually male, and then gods.

"Here's something," Nerren said, peering. The readout showed a partial tale, of a wonderful necklace desired by a goddess: this one was multilayered and emergent into Earth's present day, but at the bottom a thread disappeared into nowhere. Nerren sighed. "It's slid past the Holdstockian layer into the nevergone. Looks more like a love story, though."

"I'm not really interested in those," Mercy said.

"What *happened* to what's-his-name, by the way?"

"I'd rather not talk about it." Mercy winced. *That* story, which had reached a conclusion shortly before the Skein had disappeared, had taken the pattern of all her other romances: Library coming first, everything else coming second.

Nerren seemed to understand this. She said, "Well, never mind that now, then. How about this?"

It was the story of a woman who tried to fly to the moon, in a chariot drawn by deer, or sometimes swans. It was very old, and petered out some three thousand years down.

"I like it but I can't see how it's relevant. What we're looking for are legends of warrior women, ancient nightmares . . . "

"Those all seem to be from around the Black Sea," Nerren said. "We'd have to bring up another map."

The oldest maps of the storyways were from the Middle East, with some from China. The Australasia department on the ninth floor was doing sterling work transcribing songlines, which were much older, but those responded to pictures, not text, and Mercy did not think they would be relevant to mainland Continental Ice Age myths. Eventually, she and Nerren gave up.

"We're just going to have to go in there and have a look," Mercy said. She watched as the sigilometer powered down and the map faded back into its parchment. "And keep our fingers crossed."

⌐◉═⌐

Mercy took the Irish sword with her when she went back into Section C. She also took Benjaya, one of the more active of her colleagues. Benjaya was young, male, and keen, which were not necessarily good qualities, but Mercy felt that enthusiasm would make up the lack. She gave him a lecture anyway, as they climbed the stairs, about appropriate behaviour and lack of experience. Benjaya listened earnestly, but she had a nasty feeling that he might not have taken it all in. With Nerren recently injured, however, she needed someone who could provide backup and Benjaya, despite inexperience, had muscles. He was also on the Library's fencing team and Mercy thought this was likely to be useful. He brought a sword of his own with him, a long whipping rapier which sang softly to itself, in a language that Mercy did not know.

⌐◉═⌐

The *ka* stood on a ledge of ice, small wings folded against the wind. Golden eyes were slitted, trying to see. To the left lay a long line of forest, shadow-dark. To the right stretched a broken landscape of ice, a wide tumbling torrent, and the glimmer of oxbow lakes. The sky was heavy with storms. As Perra watched, a vivid bolt of rose-coloured lightning broke the cloud and struck down into the forest. Perra heard something cry out, a long forlorn wail which did not sound human. The trees went up like torches, burning a strange, unnatural blue.

Perra had the feeling that this had happened before, many times. The *ka*, eyes closed, sent senses out into the overlight, the place which lies between the layers of the nevergone, and saw, very far away, a huge construction like a sundial. This confirmed the *ka's* suspicions that this scene, unfolding now, was no more than a bubble in time, a trapped loop on endless replay.

Nonetheless, it was interesting. And something was running from the forest, a tall thing that loped swiftly over the tundra. Perra braced clawed feet against the ice, but this thing did not look like the disir. A narrow muzzle swung from side to side, scenting the air. It was dressed in strips of leather that hung down like moss; a clawed hand gripped a staff. It sang as it came, a plaintive wail that was nonetheless rhythmic and compelling. Perra felt a thread of old magic spiral through the air, conjured from ice and water and wind, and speaking to the far stars. The figure raised its staff and behind the *ka*, the rent in the air grew wide. Perra was lifted from the ledge and carried through. The rift snapped shut.

⊷≡◌ ◌≡⊶

Mercy, stepping cautiously through the double doors of Section C, had to duck to avoid the flying *ka*. Benjaya cried out, lashing up with the rapier.

"No!" Mercy cried. "It's Perra!"

She felt the *ka's* passage merely as soft feathers brushing her face, and when she straightened up, she saw Perra sitting on the ledge above the door. The spirit looked slightly ruffled.

"Perra, what are you doing here?"

"This *ka* wanted to see what was here," the *ka* said. "Now, it has seen."

Mercy stared at her. "What did you see?"

"An age of ice."

"Why was the rent still open?" Benjaya asked.

"A very good question."

"You would not have been able to see it," the *ka* said. "It was visible to me, but only in the overlight, not the everyday."

Mercy sighed. "So all the time we've been thinking of the rent as closed, it's been gaping wide open letting through who knows what?"

⠤⠂Nineteen⠂⠤

Deed had been more relieved than he cared to admit on his
return from Bleikrgard. The meeting had gone well, better
than he'd hoped, and despite the encounter with Mareritt, which
still unsettled him, he thought he had the upper hand. That was
the way Deed liked it.

This flying blind was making him nervous, however. He
did not know exactly what Loki's intentions were, although he
thought they were now becoming reasonably clear.

The lid taken off the cauldron of the city by the disappearance
of the Skein and a power vacuum in Worldsoul, with the Court
facing powerful former allies turned enemies.

The chance to retrieve an earlier version of the Library and
bring it under Court control.

The disir, trapped in their ancient storytime and awaiting
the possibility of release.

You didn't have to be a genius to put those things together.

Deed stood now in one of the Watchrooms, on the long
gallery that went around the perimeter of the circular chamber.
The walnut panelled gallery was lit by sconces, dim gaslight
which flickered and hissed, but which proved as far as the spirits
who inhabited the Watchroom were willing to go in terms of
technology. Demons, so Deed had discovered, were conservative
and slow to change. There was a moral there, but he was damned
if he knew what it was. Well, probably damned anyway.

The triangle for the conjuration floated in the middle of the
shadowy cloud that filled the inner part of the chamber. This

was classical magic, very formal, tried and tested. The magician stood in a circle, bound about with the Key of Solomon. A triangle, inscribed with ward words, formed the holding pen for whatever was summoned through the overlight from the infernal regions of the nevergone.

Deed had done this on many occasions, and the process was one he considered routine. That did not mean that it was perfunctory: he took care to make certain that the chamber was as secure as possible. But there were two parts to this particular ritual and he wanted to make sure he got it right.

Demons do not come for blood, or death, or even pain. They do not need to. They come for one reason only, and that reason is curiosity. Deed made sure the spell he was reciting would pique the interest of any demon listening to it, but he had a particular target in mind.

As he spoke the words of the spell, he could feel the twitch and twinge in the overlight, which meant that he'd attracted attention. Whether it was the right attention remained to be seen, but he continued to speak and gradually, a shape began to form in the triangle. Its head was bowed. It wore a veil and a long mantle, both of crimson. There was a shape behind it, something not human, but as he watched, it dissipated like smoke. One hand, ringed with a great carnelian seal, gripped the veil at its throat.

Deed spoke a name. "Am I addressing Gremory, Duke of Hell?"

The demon looked up. He saw eyes like rubies, over the folds of the veil.

"Who asks?"

"My name is Jonathan Deed." Names had power, even children knew that, but there was nothing to be gained from hiding his own. The demon would have been able to pluck that out of the communications directory, if she so chose. Mareritt— well. Best not go there.

"Deed." The demon spoke wonderingly, savouring it on her tongue. "I have heard of you. Abbot General of the Court."

Deed bowed. "Madam. The honour is mine."

The demon looked idly around her. "What does a mage of the Court want with me?"

"Ah," Deed said. "I need some advice."

The spirit put her head to one side and slipped the veil from her face, which was, predictably, cold and beautiful. The more human demons always had something of the same look, as if there was some form of genetic stamp, but since their manifest appearance was illusory, Deed could only assume that they simply lacked imagination. Or perhaps it wasn't that important. "Advice, indeed?"

Deed aimed for an expression of humility, but did not feel he was entirely successful in achieving it. "Yes. I have a question concerning the Eastern Quarter of this city, regarding a woman named Shadow. An alchemist."

Gremory grew still, the garnet eyes filmed like the bloom on a plum. "An alchemist named Shadow? Yes, I know her."

"What can you tell me of her?"

"I hear that she has courage and intelligence. She has integrity, and cannot be easily bought." The demon grinned. "And she is under the protection, if you can call it that, of the Shah of Has El Zindeh. I would suggest that even the Court treads carefully."

"I see," said Deed. This confirmed what he already knew. "Do you know anything more about this protection? Is she working for him?"

"Oh," Gremory said, with a laugh. "She will be working for him. The Shah does not give something for nothing."

"Do you know," Deed asked carefully, "of an ancient race known as the disir?"

"The Ladies?" the demon said, with scorn. "Of course." She put her head to one side again and touched a finger to her lips.

Deed could not help but focus on the long, curling claw, of polished brass. "Now let me see. They are from the north, an ancient people, as you say, bred from clans that roamed the snowlands long before the ice. They bred into the northern tribes, mingling the bloodlines—one of which you come from."

She pointed her brassy claw at him and, to his horror, Deed felt himself start to change: flesh drawing back from the bones of his face, his fingers elongating, back hunching, vision altering— "Enough!" Gremory said and Deed, human once more, again stood straight in his formal ruffed suit, feeling as though he had been wrenched out of his skin. As indeed, he had. It was Mareritt all over again and within, Deed cursed all female kind. A boil of hate rose up inside him. Never mind that now; he could take it out on Darya later.

"You are one of Loki's children," the demon said and an expression of extreme distaste crossed her beautiful face. "Be careful, Abbot General. I know much more than you think. There is a disir in the Eastern Quarter; she has been hurt and she is angry. Even for you, I don't think she will come back."

"Oh," Deed said, more sharply than he meant to. "She'll come. I sent her, after all. Now—" for he felt the need to move from these dangerous waters into others, which might prove equally treacherous, "—I need to speak about another matter. The *Barquess*."

The head-tilt was to the other side this time, but just as irritating. "Ah. The ship of souls."

"Yes. What can you tell me about the *Barquess*? She and her crew were sent in search of the Skein, but since then nothing has been heard, and nothing can be found. Can you tell me? Is the ship lost?"

"The *Barquess* sails on," the demon said. "But not as you know it."

"They *are* dead, then?"

"No." Gremory smiled a curious, secretive smile. "They are far beyond the Liminality, and that is why you cannot find them. But they do live. Would you like to see them?"

Deed felt blood pounding in his head. "Yes. Yes, I would. But why haven't we been told of this before, from your kindred?"

"You didn't ask," the demon answered, mildly surprised. Deed knew that this was not true, at least, not by human standards of truth. Demons did not see things in the same way, however.

"Please show me now," he said, as politely as he could. Obligingly, the demon spread a clawed hand. Lightning played about her fingers and an abyss at her feet began to whirl and bubble. A pale dot appeared, at the centre of the whirlpool, then cast upward, sailing around the rim of a maelstrom. It grew in size and soon it was large enough for Deed to see the familiar configurations of the *Barquess*: its icebreaker prow, the huge engines at the stern, the masts and funnels and, along its sides, the immense folded vanes which would enable the ship to fly, should there be a need. Part battleship, part airship, part behemoth, the *Barquess* had been engineered for many possibilities. It was not beautiful, although the golden traceries along its flanks—indicating the passage of the dimension-breaking magic with which it had been endowed—looked like the veins of leaves. Deed had seen the sails unfurled only once and they, too, were of gold. When he looked more closely, he could see small figures scurrying across its decks.

"Is this as the ship is now? Or a simulacrum?"

"A day or so ago. We are looking into the past, but not far." The demon shrugged. "It is likely that they still live but who can truly say? The *Barquess* sails dangerous waters, if one can call them such."

"Where is it? Tell me the truth," Deed commanded, "in the name of Solomon the King, I abjure you." He made a sign in the air.

A blank cast came over the demon's face, but Deed knew the Name would not hold her for long, and could be used only sparingly, like a rare spice. "They sail among the Western Stars. They chase their quarry, hound to hunter. Their journey takes them further and yet closer—do not try that again," Gremory warned, eyes flashing ruby sparks. "I am not easily controlled."

"Madam," Deed said easily, for now he had got what he wanted. "I would not dream of it."

⚯Twenty⚯

Shadow sat on her heels by the cage containing the ifrit. The thing was vast, far bigger than the cage, its energies contorted within it in a way that could not be comfortable. But who knew how the ifrit saw matters? Shadow did not, however, think the ifrit was happy.

That made two of them.

"You have an entirely free rein," the Shah had said that morning, when Shadow had sourly reported for work. "I trust your judgement." This had not improved Shadow's mood. The Shah was affable, but that meant he'd got whatever it was he wanted and that didn't suit Shadow at all. And her concentration wasn't up to much, either: memories of the disir, of the wrecked laboratory, and of Mercy Fane kept intruding. She wished Mercy was still here and that made her very nervous. Apart from Shenudah, Shadow was not accustomed to friends, and really, her friendship would not be doing the other woman any favours. Yet she'd felt that she could discuss things with Mercy, that the woman understood, and she certainly wasn't used to having a sounding board. The fact the Shah was funding full repairs to the lab hadn't helped, either. More unwanted obligations, more requirements for gratitude. Shadow had insisted on hiring the workmen herself, but she knew it gave the Shah the possibility to get someone inside the lab, perhaps sabotage the equipment for who knew what purpose further down the line. She could see a future in which she remained permanently tied to the Shah and she did not like it at all.

Now for the ifrit.

She could see nothing resembling features, or an eye. The ifrit could take semi-human form, but Shadow knew from experience that this was a loose term only: they were beings of fire, silhouettes of flickering eldritch light that freeze-burned the touch. Humans did not always survive long in their presence and this was why the Shah had confined this ifrit here, in a very expensive cage made of meteorite iron, and therefore holy. Shadow could see the many names of God as they wove and coiled around the bars, and resisted the urge to bow her head. She did not want to take her eyes off the ifrit for too long, wary of what it might do.

She had already tried speaking to it, in the old language of Persia, a tongue now lost or kept secret by the Fire Worshippers, the Zoroastrians. But the ifrit had remained within a vast and distant silence, like the quiet of the desert itself, at the breaking of the day. Shadow had not really expected anything else and repressed a sigh. They were not like angels, who might deign to talk to you, or demons, who were eager to do so in exchange for something else. They had an agenda which Shadow did not understand, and even the great mystics had failed to delineate their thoughts.

"If you will not talk to me," Shadow said aloud, "Then I cannot give you what you want." Yet she knew this was meretricious. She thought she did know, indeed, what the ifrit wanted: it wanted to be free, to roam the high places of the air beneath the stars, to step lightly with feet of flame upon the sands of the desert, to burn to a blaze that lights the night. She could not give it that, because the Shah had imprisoned it. So that meant forcing it into action.

Shadow swallowed, and went over to the latticed window. Below, the fountain played its music in the centre of the courtyard and a flock of golden doves wheeled above the Has, before settling onto the opposing roof where they cooed and quarrelled. That gave Shadow an idea. She walked back to the captive roil of the ifrit.

"You want to go back to your kind, don't you?" she said. She pitched her voice low, almost seductive. "Back to your flock? I can help you."

She lied, but she did not think the ifrit would know that. At least, not yet. The mass of energy slowed a little, she thought, although it could have been her own imagination. Wishful thinking . . . well, that was what magic was all about, after all.

"If you give me what I want," Shadow said, "I will make the Shah help you. And then I will help you get your revenge."

If the room were bugged, if she were challenged, she would say only that it had been a ploy to force the ifrit's cooperation. Perhaps this was even true, in part.

The ifrit said, in a voice that was not a voice, within her mind, *What do you want?*

"The Shah wants knowledge," Shadow said. "Not to live forever—he is too wise for that. But when he does die, he wants to know how he can force the hand of paradise. He wants the name of a particular spirit, and you can get that for me." She lied, of course, and did not like the lie. Once the ifrit had agreed to do her bidding, then she could act: transform the ifrit into other parameters. *That it should be changed into human form,* the Shah had commanded, and Shadow would have to do her best to comply.

"It is a long time," the ifrit said, "since I set foot at the gates of heaven."

"Your kind are not allowed into paradise, are they?" Shadow said, hesitant.

Soft, vast laughter. "We do not wish to go. The sunset airs are enough for us."

"But can you get me the name?"

"Which is the spirit?"

"He is a prince of the air," Shadow said. The Shah had coached her carefully in what she had to say. "His number is nine and his stone is the moss agate. His hour of the day is six o'clock in the morning. That's the only information the Shah has, and do not ask me where he got it from."

"I shall look within memory," the ifrit said. "In return, when will I be free? And what assurance do I have that this will be so?"

"I will go away while you are looking," Shadow answered. "When I come back, I will bring the Shah's own Court with me, as a guarantee. Its use in my magic will set you free."

"Then I agree," the ifrit said, surprising her. (It was only much later, Shadow realised, that she had omitted a crucial factor from her considerations. Set on the notion that the ifrit would want its freedom above all else, it had not occurred to her that the ifrit might have other ideas.)

She left the room, seeking the Shah. She found him in the long room that adjoined the courtyard verandah.

"How are you getting on?" She might have been a new secretary, typing a report.

"I'm not sure." Shadow was determined to treat the Shah with as much neutrality as she could muster. She told him what the ifrit had said.

"Interesting. You may borrow the ring."

Shadow had been expecting more protest, which either meant that the Shah wanted this very badly, or that he was playing a different game altogether. She was inclined to suspect the latter.

"The ifrit will know . . . " she began. The Shah blinked at her mildly.

"If it is a fake? Yes, I am aware of that. I shall just have to trust you with the genuine article, then."

"All right," Shadow said, warily. "I'd best get back."

The Shah removed the heavy signet from his finger and put it into her hand, curling cool fingers around her own for a disconcerting second. "Do try to look after it."

"I'll do my best."

On the way up the stairs, she looked down at the ring. It was a heavy thing of pale gold, with a carved obsidian stone. The letters were in Arabic and glided across the surface of the ring. Shadow blinked, as the Shah had done, and the letters changed. All at once, she was conscious of being watched. It was as though she held an eye in the palm of her hand. No wonder the Shah had not suggested accompanying her back to the room in which the ifrit was held; he had not needed to. He could watch, and perhaps listen, through the very mechanism that she had requested of him.

Holding the ring tightly in her fist, Shadow stepped back into the room to meet the ifrit.

⇒Twenty-one⇐

Mercy and Benjaya sat on one side of the table in a downstairs office, the *ka* on the other. Perra sat with its paws on the ebony wood, a small severe judge.

"You have a choice, as I see it," the *ka* said. "Stay on this side of the world and try to close the gap, or pass through and find out why."

"I told the Elders that I would do my best to sort this out," Mercy said. She felt the obligation like an uncomfortable lump in her throat. The *ka* looked at her. "And how do you intend to do that?"

"I don't know," Mercy admitted. The journey to the Eastern Quarter had clarified the danger, but had accomplished little in terms of resolution. The idea of going through the gap held a dark appeal: Mercy had to ask herself whether this was simply escapism, staving off the problem in the guise of taking action. She looked at Benjaya's hopeful face and thought: *Oh dear. Librarians. We don't get out much.*

When she turned to the *ka,* she saw to her irritation that Perra had already divined what she was thinking. The *ka* was not, so Mercy believed, reliably psychic—although it might just have been that Perra kept its own counsel.

"Should you go," the *ka* said, "I shall accompany you."

"Thank you," Mercy said.

They set out that evening, when twilight was already falling in a soft veil across the city. Mercy once more carried the Irish sword; Benjaya bore his rapier. They had brought suitable clothes. Mercy was wearing one of the thick woollen sweaters that Greya had brought from the north and rarely wore in the temperate climes of the West, and toting a padded coat with a fur hood. The sweater—cream wool, with a design of small black snowflakes—made her conscious of a link with her mother, now who knows where on the *Barquess* . . . Even in the temperate climes of the Library, she was already feeling far too hot. The thought of that Arctic air was almost welcome.

Benjaya wore a leather coat, as dark as his skin, and sensible stout boots.

Perra padded alongside on small lion's feet, saying little.

As they approached the stacks of Section C, Mercy thought she felt a cold wind already blowing through, but she was not sure if this was only her imagination. She looked down at Perra, but the *ka's* face was as unruffled as ever.

"Do you feel a draft?" she asked Benjaya. He twitched as though she had poked him.

"Maybe. I'm not sure."

"What happens if it doesn't open?" Mercy said to Perra. "You said you can see a rift, but I can't. What happens if we can't get through?"

"Then we go home," Perra said, sounding slightly surprised.

Perhaps, Mercy thought, it was that obvious.

But when they were standing in front of the stacks, there was no mistake. The blast of freezing air, seemingly blowing out from the pages of the books themselves, was very marked. Mercy donned her coat.

"Take a book down from the shelf," Perra instructed. Mercy did so, an old fairy story book from Denmark, full of trolls and elves and dark old gods. As soon as she opened the pages, the edges of each page became rimed with frost and she breathed in a fresh clean cold, which soon became stifling, freezing her lungs and throat. Beside her, Benjaya made a small sound of fright.

"It is opening," Perra said, and the *ka*'s calm voice steadied her. Mercy flicked swiftly through the pages of the book, aware of a gradual roaring in her ears. The cold intensified, making her gasp, and when she looked up again the rift was there, gaping up before her and letting through a glimpse of starlit snows.

"All right," Mercy said, her grip tightening on the hilt of the Irish sword. "We're going through."

She stepped forwards. There were words in the air ahead, between her and the rift. Mercy found herself whispering aloud, telling the story, summoning the road that was the storyway that would take them into the world beyond:

" . . . and there was a troll who lived under the bridge, and his name was . . . "

She stopped, but the words were scrolling up from the pages of the Danish fairy tale book, coiling into the air like silver and black threads and pulling them in through the weave . . .

. . . there was a vast tugging sensation, as though the air had been sucked out of the room. Mercy was gasping for breath, the oxygen knocked out of her. She was lifted off her feet and whisked upwards and *through* . . .

Stone hit under her heels. She heard Benjaya shout out. The *ka*, predictably, was silent. Mercy blinked into sudden light.

"Sunshine?"

It was a winter sun, low and red, hanging over a jagged black line of forest. She breathed in yet more cold air. They were high up, standing on stone flags which formed the arch of a bridge. Perra balanced on the low parapet and Mercy noticed that the *ka*'s coat had become thicker. A ruff of gold and cream obscured the sleek lines of its neck.

"I didn't think spirits felt the cold," Mercy said.

"This is a chill of the spirit," the *ka* said, reprovingly.

"If this is the bridge," Benjaya remarked, with unease, "then where's the troll?"

Twenty-two

D eed waited for Darya in the winter garden at the top of the Court, behind the gallery. Here, those of his colleagues who possessed green fingers chose to grow various plants: poisonous verdure, delicate orchids, various aphrodisiacs. Deed was not among them. Plants withered when he came too near. If he planted a seed, it went black in the ground and rotted as if the frost had touched it, which essentially it had. But he admired plants, with a kind of wary reluctance. They grew and lived with no help from him, and he could kill them, yet they always rose up again somewhere else. He sometimes felt the same about people.

Now, he sat, not too close, to a wall of orchids. They were the colour of roses, of bruises, of flesh. Some were like stormclouds, a livid white with indigo hearts, and some were a sooty midnight black. Deed liked those the best, and despised himself for predictability, but only a little. They had very little scent; it had been bred out of them.

He heard Darya's bone heels clicking against the treads of the staircase like some monstrous insect and grew very still, waiting. He had intended to remain human, but that—well, that wasn't happening. Instead, his own bones began to sharpen and change, his jaw elongating and the teeth within growing sharp. His vision changed, the flowers growing darker, a spectrum that humans do not see becoming resonant, a glimmering aura emerging around each bloom. By the time Darya's footsteps reached the door, paused, hesitated, faltered—Deed was a long way from mankind, a skeletal nightmare in a ruff.

He grabbed her from behind, long clawed fingers snaking around her throat and squeezing tight. He lifted her off the floor so that she kicked out, squealing, but Deed evaded the sharp, flailing heels. Then he dropped her so she fell in a heap on the parquet floor, gasping for breath. The marks of his talons showed on her neck, small bloodied new moons.

"Abbot General. What have I done?" Darya whispered. She kept her head lowered, but Deed could see a rebellious silver spark in her eyes and even at the back of the disir emotions, which were not human ones, he took careful note.

"Not a good enough job," Deed said, a man once more. He brushed off his hands against his coat, as if they had become contaminated. "The Watch has found a body. A young man, down by the canal, in a considerable state of disarray. They asked me if I knew anything about it; I have just spent an hour fobbing them off. They believed me, but I'm not pleased."

"I am sorry, Abbot General" Darya said, meekly.

"You should always *share,* Darya. Didn't your mother teach you any manners?"

He waited for her to ask forgiveness, apologise further for her offence, but she remained silent and that made Deed coldly angry, until he realised, with a glow of pleasure, that she was simply too afraid.

Afraid, in spite of that rebellious silver spark. He could taste it against his teeth. It tasted good.

⭜Twenty-three⭜

Shadow stepped back from the cage containing the ifrit. The Shah's ring was changing temperature, first cold, like a heavy lump of ice, then hot as a coal. Shadow gritted her teeth and held onto the ring as the ifrit became a cloud of boiling dark within the confines of the cage, and the room grew oppressively hot. Ifrits were storm spirits in their original form, she knew, denizens of the deep desert where men would never go, unless they were mad. Burning at noon and freezing at midnight, places of extremes. She could sense the ifrit's mood now, plucking at the edges of her senses as if it sought to unravel her, like someone pulling the loose threads of a tapestry.

"I have what you asked for," Shadow said.

"So I perceive." The ifrit spoke softly and its voice filled the world. Shadow was finding it difficult to breathe.

Now. She held out the ring. "Tell me!" There was a silent moment, a waiting, then the ifrit whispered the Name it had been sent to find. In that moment of compliance, Shadow felt a connection between them: a thin, threadlike bridge, made of cooperation and agreement. It was enough. She sent her own spell down it, a spell of changing and transformation, a human blueprint contained within a sigil and translated into a word. She felt the ifrit absorb it. The world stopped.

Shadow looked out of the window and saw the roofs and domes of the Eastern Quarter lined with darkness like the negative of a photograph, flashing on and off. Then her vision cleared. She saw everything in sudden sharp relief: the outlines of the latticed shutters in stark black and pale, the dust motes sparkling in the shafts of sun. Then she looked up.

Entirely unexpected, there was a ship. It hung above her, as tiny as an illustration in a Persian miniature. It was a dreadnaught, but it had sails furled along its sides. It was a monstrous thing, unnatural, made for no worldly sea and Shadow knew it immediately: the *Barquess*. She heard the ifrit hiss. Then the ship was abruptly gone. A bolt of golden light flooded outwards from the ifrit's cage as the ifrit exploded, flying silently apart into a thousand shards. Shadow felt an icy touch against her arm, penetrating her sleeve and then flying inwards through her left eye. She cried out. She felt a sharp pain as if her eye had been stabbed with a pin and then wetness welling up inside it. She clawed at her face, panicking, and felt the wet spreading out from her eye. She looked down, out of the good eye, and saw that it was not blood. A blackness stained her sleeve and her hand, gleaming like ink. She felt it pouring from the socket of her eye and spilling down her face, as though the socket were a bowl which someone had overfilled. Shadow stumbled back against the wall, reeling with shock. *O Allah, help me, help me*—and He must have heard her, for there was a coolness in the air, a soft singing note like a nightingale after rain. Shadow managed a ragged breath. The pain in her eye diminished; she felt the wetness cease to flow. Clasping her arms about herself, she slumped down the wall, crouching on the floor. A single black drop splashed down from her eye and onto the tiled floor, where it remained for a moment before seeping into the tile, swallowed by the blue. The nightingale note sang on and it brought freshness, cutting through the dusty mustiness of the chamber, which now felt scorched as if a fire had raged through it. As indeed, a fire had, and its black knife had cut through Shadow. With great care, wincing, she tried to open her left eye. She raised a hand, gently probing it with a forefinger.

To her surprise, the eye was still there. She could feel it, soft in its socket. She had expected to find the socket reamed and empty, its seed gone. She shut her right eye and looked. Everything was filmed with blackness, as though she looked through a veil, but it was different. Everything was in shadow, but as she looked, the lines at the edges of things became light. Her vision cleared: everything was sharp and vivid. She was seeing more clearly with the damaged eye than she had ever seen: right into the heart of things. She could see their names—a faint script which described everything, God's language underwriting the world. The name of the ifrit was still clear, in the centre of the tangled mass of iron that had been its cage. Shadow spoke the name.

"I am here," said a small, clear voice inside her mind.

Twenty-four

The bridge was high and arched: from the base, Mercy could not see the other side. It did not look like the kind of thing that could exist in the real world, a feat of magical engineering, and she did not like it.

"Where do you think we are?" Benjaya asked. "Are we still in the Liminality?"

She looked in the direction of the *ka*, which shrugged. Mercy sighed. "I doubt it very much—this is almost certainly somewhere in the nevergone. I'd like to see what's at the end of the bridge, though." Without waiting for Benjaya, she started walking upwards. It was a steep trudge and she only realised that she'd reached its summit when she looked up and saw she was standing on the arch. Ahead, the bridge sloped down to a snaking path through the mountains. To its left, stood something that, for a moment, she thought might be a sculpture of some kind. It was not: it was a waterfall, but made of mist. It cascaded silently, falling thousands of feet to the invisible valley below. Mercy stood above cloud. Yet the sun, though thin, was warm on her skin and the air smelled of pine.

"I've heard of this place, this mistfall," Benjaya said. "It's from the Norse myths. I think it's a kind of Hell. Niflheim? I think that means 'land of the mist.'"

"Seems too pleasant to be Hell," Mercy answered, but she thought he was right, all the same. There was something archetypal about this landscape: the towering mountains, the clouds, the waterfall of mist. This was, she felt in her gut, part of the land from which the disir had come, and therefore not to be trusted. "If it's Hell," she went on, "then we need to find a way out."

The trouble was, she had no idea how to go about it. Things like this happened to Librarians. They had occurred before, although infrequently. The last time had been some hundred years previously, when a cache of hidden scrolls had come to the Library from the east. A Librarian had gone missing, whisked into some desert kingdom, but he had been retrieved by the Skein who, like concerned parents with a lost toddler, had searched until they'd found him. But now the Skein had gone. *If we had been trusted with significant magic of our own—safe words, key words . . .* But they had not, and now they would have to make do for themselves. Perhaps it would not be a bad thing if the Skein never came back . . .

"All right," Mercy said, aloud. "If it's a Hell, there will be passage points. Entrances. Exits." In much of the world's literature, these had been situated near water: in wells, over rivers, through cracks in the earth. The mistfall was the closest possibility, and Mercy headed for it.

As she grew closer, she saw that the mist sparkled. A myriad diamond drops glittered within it and it made a soft rushing sound.

"Mercy?" Benjaya said. "I don't know if you've noticed, but the sun's going down."

She nodded. "I know." Looking out from the high span of the bridge, the low red sun had sunk even further, until it was now starting to touch the dark line of the horizon. The sky was deepening to a cold winter green.

"We've got a choice," she said. "We can stay here, or try and press on. I think it's easier to defend a bridge than a mountain path."

"Perra, do you think we should look at the mist, while there's still light?"

The *ka* agreed. Mercy went down to the edge of the bridge, and saw that steps led from it to a narrow platform that ran behind the mistfall. Nothing ventured, nothing gained. With the sword drawn, she followed the steps, Benjaya and Perra close behind.

At close hand, the mist fell across the skin in a moist coolness. Fearing unknown northern magic, Mercy did not care to get too close, but she had to step through the mist to get to the platform. As she did so, there was a long cry from the direction of the forest: something lost and angry. They looked at each other, not needing to ask *what was that?* It could be nothing good.

Mercy slid behind the fall of mist, feeling it speckle her face. She had expected this place to be dark, uneasy, dangerous, but instead it spoke to her. It was comforting. It enticed her inside, a return to somewhere cosy and loved. This alarmed her.

"Can you feel that?" she asked Benjaya.

"Yeah. Reminds me of my mum's kitchen."

"That's not a good thing. I mean, no reflections on your mum or her kitchen, but you know what I mean."

Benjaya nodded dumbly. The *ka* said, "Take great care. It is a glamour."

Mercy held the Irish sword up in front of her face. "What can you cut?"

The sword sang, rejoicing, and there was a spark of light as it cut through the wall of mist and the shadows. As though a curtain had fallen from in front of her sight, Mercy *saw*.

She was standing on a lip of rock, looking into the mountain, and the mountain was hollow. There was a world within it: the world of ice she had glimpsed through the pages of the book, through which the disir had come. She saw, again, the forest, and the snaking river, and across the line of trees she saw the rise of mountains and, again, the high arch of a bridge. She had the feeling that if she had been able to see more clearly,

through a telescope, there would be two uncertain people and a
ka standing on a ledge behind a wall of mist . . .

"The world's an onion," she murmured.

"But we knew that," Benjaya said, reasonably enough. "It's
in a lot of books."

He was right. Stories don't always reflect the world; they
make it, too. A book is a world inside the world, and sometimes
there are worlds within that. A galaxy in a speck of sand; suns
in a water drop.

"Well," Mercy asked. "Are we going in?"

Benjaya nodded. The *ka* blinked. Mercy took a step forward,
into sudden searing cold. She had thought the world of the
bridge was chilly, but the sunlight had meant that she had been
too warm in the heavy greatcoat. This place was really arctic. She
took a shuddering breath and heard Benjaya gasp and snuffle
behind her. She looked back and saw the world of the bridge in
miniature, the fall of mist cascading softly downwards, and then
it was winked out. Night lay ahead. Mercy started walking.

The path wound down a rocky incline. When she looked
back again, she saw a sparsely forested mountain summit, heavy
with snow, looming behind them. The sky was thick with stars
and a great creamy swirl, the galactic arm, lay overhead. She
recognised a few of the constellations: they were ancient, and
were those of Earth, not of the Liminality. No one had ever
been able to explain to her why the stars were different, since
the Liminality was so strongly linked to Earth itself, yet this was
so. A mystery, another to which, presumably, the Skein held the
key. But it was further evidence that this was the nevergone,
some distant storytime. Mercy's mouth tightened and she strode
on, dodging loose pebbles. Was this even a path at all? An animal
track, maybe. She kept the sword drawn and a moment later,
was glad that she had done so when Benjaya cried out.

But it wasn't an animal. Benjaya pointed. "Look!"

The airship came fast over the brow of the mountain. Its sides were rounded and black; it made a rushing sound as it came. A pennant flapped from a spike at its prow and Mercy could see lamplight gleaming inside its carapace, through a round brass porthole. Just as she noted this, a bolt shot out of the darkness and buried itself in a puff of dust, a few feet from where she stood. Mercy and Benjaya threw themselves behind a rock.

The airship shot on, flying across the long river valley. They watched, unspeaking, until it disappeared into the distance. Mercy was afraid it would turn, but it did not. It vanished over the rim of the world, into night.

"Not very friendly," Benjaya said.

"I wonder who they are? I've never seen anything like it before. Well, apart from the *Barquess*. That reminded me of the *Barquess*, somehow."

"There are stories of flying galleons," Benjaya said, standing up cautiously. "One of them sent an anchor down into a churchyard. In England. I read it in a book."

"That wasn't a galleon, but it's the same principle, I suppose. This world is too old for those, though. They must be travelling through."

"Question is, are there more of them?"

"I'm hoping that's a no," Mercy said.

They trudged on, descending the long slope by degrees and eventually finding themselves standing on the flat valley floor. It was tundra, spongy underfoot, and starred with lichen. Here, the snow lay in patches, exposing the permafrost. Mercy pulled her coat closer. The *ka* padded across the lichen, delicate as a cat. As they drew nearer to the river, Mercy could hear the creak and crack of the ice. The river was flowing swiftly, bearing its cargo of ice with it, and an icy breeze came off it that chilled her still further. There was a weird smell, too: something musty and organic. A moment later, she realised she'd smelled it before. It was the odour of the disir.

⊷Twenty-five⊷

Shadow listened to the voice. In a way, it was reassuring to have this rider in her head, and that alarmed her more than anything. It was smooth, decisive, clear. It knew what it wanted and what it wanted was to be free of the Shah. In that, both Shadow and the rider were in accord.

"What *are* you?" But it had to be the ifrit, that inchoate thing of fire and flame.

"I am a word made flesh."

"Yes, in me," Shadow thought, tartly.

"Until I choose otherwise." Smoothly, to conquer her rising anger, it added, "I understand. No one cares to be possessed. Who should know this better than I? I am the essence. You asked that I should be transformed into a human. This is so, is it not? You are human, and I am in you."

And then she understood how the spell had gone so wrong. *Be careful what you wish for.* She was an alchemist, an agent of change—and now change had caught her in its web.

"What sort of spirit are you?" Shadow asked, through mentally gritted teeth. "Are you male or female?" Shadow was dreading this answer. The cool voice could have belonged to either gender.

"We are not like you. But you would see me as a man, were I to choose to appear to you in a form other than the one you have seen."

Shadow, appalled, said nothing. The idea of having this male spirit within her was defiling, abhorrent. But at the moment, there was little she could do.

In the end, it told her what to do. She must go to the Shah, and tell him a tale. The ifrit would dictate it to her, it said kindly, as one conferring a favour. Ten minutes and already Shadow was sick of the thing, quite apart from any other considerations. She did not think that the spirit was the one doing the favour. But she did not have a choice. Shadow had essentially failed, and the Shah would not be pleased unless the situation was finessed.

And so she went.

"The spell was unsuccessful," she said. "I have failed. I am deeply sorry."

The Shah looked at her. "What has become of it, then?" he asked, deceptively mild.

"Rather than becoming human, it has passed into your ring," Shadow said, prompted by the ifrit. "You will, of course, wish to check."

The Shah gave a sad smile. "I wouldn't want to doubt your word. Perhaps we can find a use for it." He steepled his fingers, looking past her. "A truly captive spirit, within the ring. Such things have been known. Maybe this will be more useful than if it had become a man."

You wouldn't doubt my word? Hell. "Of course." The Shah took the ring from her and held it over a flame. Shadow inclined her head, staring at her hands clasped in her lap as he inspected it. Shadow sneaked a look upwards and saw that the blue smoke from the flame was forming words, inscribed in azure light upon the air. A name, and also a spell. She tried to remember the name, but it drained out of her mind like water through a sieve. The Shah had set safeguards. She would have done the same. She was glad her face was concealed behind her veil and she knew that if the Shah penetrated it, she would be warned. But he was respectful, and did not. The veil did not protect her from the thing in her head, however.

Whatever the Shah had learned from the ring, he seemed satisfied.

"You've done your best. There have been—difficult—elements to this case."

You're telling me. "Thank you," Shadow said. There was a pressure behind her tongue, as if the ifrit was willing her to say more. With an effort, she forced it back; she would not be a completely pliant puppet.

"Of course, you'll remain on the payroll," the Shah said now.

"Oh, good."

She felt the Shah's sharp gaze through the veil.

"I shall, also of course, be calling on your services again." He handed over a small leather bag. It was heavy, and gave a metallic *chink* as she took it. Gold. How old-fashioned. But it was how you were supposed to pay an alchemist, in coin. Shadow murmured her thanks and, at a gesture from the Shah, rose to go. She needed to get out of the Has, for all sorts of reasons. She could feel the spirit looking out of the back of her head as she left, an odd sensation and intrusive.

"This will take some getting used to," the ifrit said. Perhaps it felt the same way. She knew, without being told, that there were deep levels in her mind the spirit could not access, not without a proper set of keys. That was not beyond the realms of probability, either. But on the way through the bazaar she took care to focus on the purely quotidian: which spices were for sale, which pieces of machinery.

"How boring your life must be," the spirit said, in wonder.

"I need the downtime," Shadow said, and thought of different kinds of tea for the rest of the journey home.

⚘Interlude⚘

It was easy to succumb to despair. She had lived all her life under a benign hand. When doubts had come, or conflicts, she had been encouraged to express her own opinions, knowing that beneath the tightrope of uncertainty, there had been a safety net. She had loved her life. Her speciality had been in investigating the storyways to do with children-in-the-forest and even today Tope's mind could be soothed by the thought of gingerbread houses, darkened pines, poisoned apples, mad old hags. So many of them, yet not a lifetime's work, one would have thought, but there had been other stories, too. A worthwhile life, ever since she had trembled on the edge of her initiation at seventeen. That had been during the war—one of them—and she had been filled with an ardent blaze, a desire to keep this fortress of civilisation against what was coming at it out of the night.

Now the night was once more coming fast, it seemed to her, and there was nothing to hold it back. She knew she should have had more faith in the Library itself, in its capacity to remain a tower of strength. Because it was an open secret that the Library itself was a living thing, an entity with a myriad minds and a thousand tongues. She just hoped that this would be enough.

⇌Twenty-six⇌

Mercy was worried about the airship. It had come out of nowhere, and it was anomalous to this primitive wintry world through which they now trudged. True, the airship had not come back, but it had been automatically hostile. On top of that, she was concerned about the disir themselves. This was their territory and even though they were supernatural beings—legends that had come from the minds of men—some laws of evolution still applied. She wondered what they were sharing their world with. She had the feeling she was about to find out.

With Benjaya and the *ka*, she had now been following the river for over an hour. The light had not changed and neither had the flow of the river, although the crack and creak of the ice was now more marked. She thought that the temperature had risen a little, as well. A spring, for this winter world? Somehow, that seemed unlikely. She could not help feeling that this was an ice age, and spring very far away.

Mercy's feet were cold. So was her nose. She was hungry (the *ka*'s hunting had not yet produced a result) and tired, but she was not yet exhausted. She and Benjaya had given up conversation, but Mercy could hear the murmuring voice of the Irish sword and it was this that kept her going. Odd, that a weapon should be the link that, she felt, kept her attached to the Library, yet the Library was the thing she had sworn to protect and so it made a kind of sense. And the sword could not tire or falter, although it could be broken. It would not let her down. She gripped its hilt a little tighter and walked on.

The curve of the river took them along the shore of a rocky bluff, and then the ground evened out. Forest spilled down the slopes, encroaching onto the shore. Here was a scattering of pines, filling the air with a fresh astringent scent that wiped out the lingering odour of the disir. Mercy wasn't even sure that she hadn't imagined it. She turned to Benjaya.

"What do you think?"

Benjaya glanced nervously at the forest. "I don't know. I don't like the thought of being in those trees when it's still half dark. You don't know what might be in there."

Mercy agreed, but there had never been any sign that it might get lighter.

"What are you thinking?" Benjaya added.

Instead of answering, Mercy turned to the *ka*. "How about you? Are you up for taking a look?" She did not like asking Perra to do her dirty work for her, but the *ka* was a lot less vulnerable than Benjaya or herself.

"I will try," the *ka* agreed. It padded rapidly among the trees, leaving Benjaya and Mercy standing on the foreshore. Mercy peered into the clouds: there was no sign of the airship.

"I'm worried about getting back again," Benjaya said, suddenly.

Mercy thought about saying something reassuring, but he deserved the truth. "So am I," she said.

"It's as though the city is bleeding people. First the Skein, then the *Barquess*. Now us."

"We will *get* back, Ben. I'll do my best." But she'd told the Elders that she'd take care of it, and what if her best wasn't good enough?

The *ka* appeared at her feet, as silently as it had gone. "There's something in the forest. A road."

"A *road*? What sort of road?" This land was too long-ago for any kind of buildings. Yet there had been the flying boat . . . "All right. Let's take a look."

It was made of stone flags and cut straight between the trees. She could see it vanishing off into shadow. It did not look right. It did not belong. The Irish sword twitched in her hand.

When she took a step onto the road, the sole of her boot rang out as if she was treading onto metal, a cold, metallic sound. Mercy swallowed. She had the sudden disquieting feeling that the road would snatch her away, whisk her into the darkness.

"Ben," she said. "Let's not lose sight of each other, all right?"

He gave her a rather odd look in reply. It should indeed have been obvious.

"I don't know where it goes," the *ka* said.

"Then we'll follow it and find out."

They had been walking for some time when Mercy became aware the world was changing around them. It was subtle, at first: the trees thinning out, a slight lightening of the sky above their heads. Then she realised that the road itself was altering, the stone becoming less rough and more cleanly cut. They crested a low hill and found themselves looking down on a crossroads. A black stone stood at its heart. The sword twitched in Mercy's hand. This wasn't the landscape they had left, the Ice Age tundra. It looked more like part of the Scottish highlands—rolling bald hills with scattered pines, shadowy beneath the ferocious stars. The bisecting road ran in either direction, across moorland, but the crossroads itself stood alongside a grove of trees. Benjaya and Mercy looked at one another. Crossroads meant magic: the threefold meeting-place of the Greeks, where Hekate's offerings had been left, the junction where you meet the devil at midnight, a place of ritual and magic . . . They headed down into the scent of heather. Dark pools formed mirrors on either side of the road; sparse saplings gradually clustered until Mercy could see the crossroads stood in a grove of oak. Beneath her feet, the road changed, blackening. The oaks were heavy with leaf, a midsummer foliage. She stopped. She did not know what was in the grove, but she did not want to go any further. It felt ancient, laden with bloodshed like the site of a forgotten battlefield. She could smell meat on the air.

"If the disir are anywhere . . . " Mercy said, then stopped. A breeze stirred the oaks, as if the word had become a wind. The sword twitched again like a hound straining at the leash. *But if we don't go, we won't know.*

"I will go," Perra said.

Even though Mercy knew how hard it was to harm the spirit, she heard herself say, "No. We'll go together."

As they approached the crossroads, the smell of blood increased. There was no sign of anything amiss: nothing hanging from the branches. Mercy couldn't help thinking of Roman descriptions of the druid groves of Britain, butchered meat dripping blood on the forest floor . . . this was not a productive line of thought. Besides, she couldn't see anything.

Into the grove. The *ka* gave a compulsive shiver, as though wind had rippled over its fur.

"Perra? What is it?"

"Predators."

"There's an altar," Benjaya whispered.

It stood at the centre of the crossroads, a slab of basalt four foot high and six long. It gleamed faintly in the light of the stars. A skull stood at the centre of the altar, shining. Mercy stared. The altar had a fascination, the kind of compulsion that she associated with controlling magic. Before it was the jawbone of a whale, an immense ragged white arch.

"It's very old," a sly voice said from the trees, making Mercy leap.

"Who's there?"

"Come and see."

She did so, hearing the others close behind her. Deep inside the oak grove, behind the bone arch, stood a rock, an outcrop of granite. Something stood before it and it was a moment before Mercy realised the figure was chained to the rock.

It wasn't human. It was bigger than the disir she had seen, and it was male: a long white face, sharp-toothed, beneath matted pale hair. He wore leather rags, the remnants of armour. His nails had scored the rock: she could see the grooves. He smiled at her, head cocked to one side.

"I don't often have visitors."

The voice was sophisticated, resonant. It held promises and malice. It seemed to Mercy that she had heard it somewhere before, but not directly: like an echo through someone else's voice. Warily, she stepped forward.

"Maybe this isn't an easy place to find. Where are we?"

She wasn't expecting an answer, but to her surprise, one came. "It's called 'the place of the crossroads.' I'm afraid your ancestors were rather literal."

"*My* ancestors?"

"This is the far north of the storyways, the far deep, but not as deep as where you've been. I can smell the tundra on you." He raised his blade-like nose and gave a prim sniff. "An archetypal place, somewhere that's found in the hollows of the head. You know how it works."

"So how come there are roads? Someone must have built them."

The thing laughed. "Logical, aren't you? It's my world. I can shift the furniture around if I want to." She saw the glint of his eyes, silver-dark in the long face. His jaw worked. She felt a sudden tug of desire and it made her skin crawl.

"Who are you?"

"I am a god. But currently, I am a god under restraint." He nodded upward and she followed his gaze. High on the rock, something writhed. She saw a long sinuous shape: a serpent. "It's sleeping. But when it wakes, it opens its jaws wide, wide, and the poison that has accumulated while it sleeps drips down onto me." For a moment, he inclined his head and she saw a line of blackened, festering blisters running down the back of his scalp and his spine. She should have felt sorry, but instead there was only revulsion.

"Isn't there anything you can do?"

"No. It comes from an older magic than I, and I am among the oldest things in the world. I was born in the age of ice, very early, with my brothers and sisters." A wolfish smile. "Only the sisters, these days. Well, mostly. And their daughters."

"The disir."

"As you say, the disir. That's men's word for them. They call themselves something else, but you won't be able to pronounce it."

Mercy suspected he was right and she knew who he was, now. *Loki.* After the first moment of realisation, she forced the name out of her mind, in case it provided a way in. "If you'll forgive me for saying so, you don't look very far from human. But the others—"

"The males are closer to men. To humans, that is, and their offspring are closer yet. The females—they have reverted, to an older type. We may be gods, but we still have genes."

"You know about that sort of thing?"

"I know what the world knows. As the world changes, so I change. Besides, there's not a lot to *do* here. I have to keep myself occupied."

"Did you bring us here?"

"Us?" asked the creature, sly once more.

Mercy spun round and saw that she was alone. "Shit! Where are they?"

"Looking for you, I should imagine. I wanted to talk to you on your own, away from your colleague and the spirit."

"Why?"

"I want you to do something for me."

Mercy had the sensation of drowning, of events closing over her head. "What is it?"

"I want you to find a story for me."

For a moment, Mercy glimpsed what he saw. The tree stretched before her: its root deep in the heart of the world, the fires of the world's forge, and its crown in the stars. Its branches arched into air and then air's lack: its fruit were planets. She saw suns spinning among its eternal leaves, moons hung cold from its shoulder—and she was whirled up into the branches, the pathways and permutations reaching in all directions, breaking, splitting, merging with each word spoken and each action done. It echoed in her head: *the tree is time,* and she knew then why that image had spent so long in the heads of men, why its power remained. She saw a man who was not a man, who was something else, not human, walking through the streets of Worldsoul. A man in a dark coat, dark-eyed, who smiled and spoke softly, who knew the words of magic that could change the world. She thought she'd seen him before. She did not know where for a moment, then it came to her with a rush of dismay: the fake doctor, Roke, who had taken her blood. Now she knew him for who he was: Jonathan Deed, the Abbot General of the Court.

"What story?"

"The legend of a Pass between the worlds. The story of an angel with a flaming sword and demons who roam within a garden."

"I've never heard of that story," Mercy said.

"No," the god said, patiently, "that's why I want you to find it."

And in return? Her thoughts must have showed on her face, because the god said, "Magic. I'll give you power. It all comes down to power in the end. Stealing necklaces, stealing horses, stealing spells. I may be chained. Doesn't mean I can't act." He gave a wolfish grin. "Doesn't mean that at *all.*"

"I—"

But the scene in front of her was gone. The rocks, the chained god—everything vanished. Mercy was left staring stupidly at a grove of trees. She turned, to find Benjaya.

"Thank the Skein! You're all right."

Benjaya gave her a look that suggested she'd taken leave of her wits. "What do you mean? You've just seen me."

"Twenty minutes ago, perhaps. I was talking to the god and you disappeared."

"What god? We haven't lost sight of one another."

Mercy felt as though she was going mad. "Perra? You saw?" But the *ka's* golden eyes were blank.

"I saw only the trees, and you."

Great, Mercy thought. For all she knew, she'd imagined the whole thing. But then she looked down. A thin silver chain encircled her wrist, snicking against the ward bracelet: a fetter, a band. A slender key hung from it. She stared at it, stupidly.

"What's that?" Benjaya asked.

"I don't know—"

But they heard again the long, low cry.

"Wolf," said Benjaya.

Mercy shook her head. "That wasn't a wolf. I don't know what that was."

They headed back to the crossroads, swords drawn. The altar and the skull were gone. The road stretched, empty, to the bleak horizon. The cry came again, closer. Mercy and Benjaya began to walk, warily, along the road: at least they could see.

It was Mercy who caught the first glimpse of the thing, travelling fast over the moor. It was four-legged, but bigger than a wolf, perhaps the size of a horse. As soon as she'd seen it, she realised that there were others following it. Three dark shapes bounded behind. She could not tell what they were: they had long, sinewy legs and whiplike tails and they were thin to the point of emaciation. And therefore, probably hungry. Mercy looked back but the trees had vanished: they were standing on open ground. One of the creatures bayed, a low echoing howl. Mercy brought the sword up and she could see the thing closely now—all sinew, with a narrow questing head. It was vaguely doglike, apart from the size, and wan. Its ears were scarlet and it had no eyes. The dreadful head swung from side to side like a pendulum.

Mercy brought the sword up as the thing took a great leap, sailing over the side of the road towards them. The sword sang as it flashed through the air, but it did not connect. A white lightning bolt split the air between Mercy and the hound. The air was filled with bells and there was the sudden smell of blood and shit as the beast, bisected, fell in a heap of rubble by the roadside. A pale face was looking down at Mercy.

"Get in."

The face and its owner were in a sleigh, drawn by deer. Mercy scrambled over the side and fell into the body of the sleigh, followed by Ben. Then, to her own disgust, she screamed. The sleigh was full of heads.

"Take care!" one said. It was the face of an ancient, wizened man, bound with silver. "You trod on me!"

"And on me," said another, a redhead bound with brass.

"Sorry." Mercy said. Familiarity was tweaking at her: she knew this, she had come across this story somewhere—but the sleigh was racing away, along the road and up. She looked back and saw the road fall away beneath them with dizzying speed, the hounds no more than white specks along its length. She struggled to the back of the driving seat, trying not to step on protesting heads.

"Who are you?"

The woman looked down at her from under a crown of pale hair.

"Aha," she said. She reached into the tatters and rags of lace that she wore and took out a small golden phial. Tucking the whip under one arm, and transferring the reins to one hand, she took a stopper out of the phial and held it over Mercy's head. "Sorry. But you'll thank me later." A droplet of liquid gold oozed out of the phial and fell between Mercy's eyes.

The sigil should have protected her, but it did not. She was conscious of a sudden warmth, a cocooning, and then she was falling painlessly down into sleep as the sleigh sped on through the midnight air.

Twenty-seven

Keep her away from me! Shadow woke with a shock, flung awake with all her nerves jangling. It took her a minute to realise that the alarm was the ifrit's, not her own.

"What are you talking about?"

"Keep her away!"

Her next thought was that the disir had come back. Shadow jumped off the bed, reaching automatically for the sun-and-moon blade.

"You won't need that," a voice said. In a shaft of moonlight, Shadow could see someone sitting in the chair by the window. She fumbled for the lamp and flicked it into light. On the table beside the bed, Shadow's sigilometer was ticking off the scale.

"Who are you?" Then she realised, and bowed. "You are a demon."

"I am a duke of Hell," the woman said. She wore crimson armour and a great gold ring that reminded Shadow of the Shah's. Her hair was unconcealed. A demon does not wish to hide her hair from the sight of God; a demon does not need to be concerned about modesty.

"Do I alarm you?" the demon said, with cool amusement.

"The thing in my head does not like you. That's enough to predispose me in your favour," Shadow replied. The demon laughed. It sounded genuine.

"I can see why you might think that."

"Will you tell me your name?" Shadow asked, expecting the demon to say no. But the Duke of Hell answered readily enough.

"My name is Gremory. You may have heard of me."

"Yes. Your name is inscribed in the *True Grimoire*. You find hidden treasure, and draw the love and desire of beautiful women. I'm afraid I'm not up for the latter."

The demon laughed again. "You're used to this, aren't you? One can tell you're an alchemist." She uncoiled herself from the seat and walked across the room. She smelled of fire. "Those things are my main remit, it's true, but I can do a lot of things. Demons like variety. You'll be wondering why I've come to visit you." *Back, back!* the spirit in Shadow's head insisted. She ignored it.

"I've had a number of visits lately. From various . . . entities."

The demon cocked her head on one side. "I gather it's been quite the circus. Well, you need not worry. I have no plans to create havoc. On the contrary. I'm here to help."

"Oh," Shadow said. It sounded unconvincing. "I don't want to seem rude, but . . . "

"I understand." The demon did not seem offended. She stared at Shadow out of cold red eyes. "You are acquiring powerful patrons, powerful enemies."

"You're telling me."

"The Shah, the disir, the Court . . . " Gremory's voice was sly.

As she was supposed to, Shadow bit. "The Court? I know about the first two."

"The Court is at the heart of things. The Court wants you."

Shadow shook her occupied head in bewilderment. The spirit seemed to have gone to ground, for the moment, and that in itself was interesting. "What in the world does the Court want with me? It's got its own personnel. They're powerful magicians and their interests lie in the West, not here." But she was not surprised to hear Gremory mention it. The Court concerned themselves with demons, with grimoires and Goetic magics.

"Yet you have attracted their attention. Or at least, the attention of one of them. A man named Jonathan Deed."

"I've heard of Deed," Shadow said, slowly. "But I can't remember where."

"Deed is disir."

"What?"

"He is of that lineage. He's a male, of course. They're different. The females are more savage." Gremory looked modestly down at her talons. Their scarlet colouring ran down into her long fingers as far as the first joint, as though her fingers were dipped in blood. She blinked and the talons changed to bronze, then back to blood. "Naturally."

Shadow's mind was working fast. "So there's a connection. Did Deed send the disir? Why did it come after me?"

"I think Deed wants you. You ought to know how it works by now. The Court wants what Suleiman wants; he desires what the Court has. Each of them feed off one another—the Court and the Has. Under the Skein, it didn't really matter: balance was kept no matter what. Now the Skein are gone and the city's up for grabs. Guess who's grabbing?"

"Makes sense," Shadow said. "So the thing in my head—the ifrit? What does it want?"

"I don't know," Gremory said. "Shall we take a look?"

Being possessed by two entities was not a comfortable experience. Shadow sat, trying not to squirm, while the demon evaporated into smoke and drifted into her lungs, then into her blood, then into her mind. Shadow felt as though she was standing in a crowded elevator; one that might, at any moment, break a cable and start to plummet. She took a deep breath, willing stillness.

"I know you're in here!" the demon sang, like a child playing hide and seek. "I can fi-i-i-ind you!"

Shadow, eyes shut, tried to look within. The ifrit, which suddenly seemed very small, was running, bolting down neural pathways, disappearing into the labyrinthine causeways of the mind. Shadow, pursuing, felt herself drop, as if she'd fallen down a well. Her eyes snapped open.

The laboratory was gone. The fronds of acacia waved gently above her head, higher than they should have been against a vivid blue sky. One of Shadow's hands was raised, imprisoned in someone else's. She looked up to see her aunt, familiar behind the lace-edged veil that she always wore. Behind the veil, her aunt smiled.

"Would you like an ice?"

"Yes, please!"

They walked along a sandy track, through a pair of ornate iron gates with curling letters above them. Shadow spelled the words with only a little difficulty: *City Zoo*. Her adult awareness had retreated, distantly watching: it was a little like being in a lucid dream, but with the sense of self dulled. Shadow was a child again, excited about the zoo and seeing all the animals.

"Can we see the tiger?"

"Yes, and the marmosets. You like those, don't you? We've got all afternoon. We can see whatever you like."

Shadow, happy, walked with her aunt along the track and they came to the first of the pens. A stout spotted hyena basked in the afternoon sunshine, fast asleep. Shadow did not like hyenas very much—they smelled—so they did not linger.

"Look! Do you see the camels?"

The pens were large and spacious, with plenty of room for the animals to roam. This one was the size of a field, with troughs for the camels to feed. Each had one hump, and their sandy coats made them blend into the earth.

"Aren't they funny?" her aunt said.

Then one of the camels turned and looked directly at Shadow, who stopped in alarm. The camel's coat was black and so were its eyes, with a flicker of scarlet within. Its lips drew back, displaying sharp, pointed teeth.

"Look!" Aunt Behamiah said again. "Isn't he funny?"

It was evident that she could not see what Shadow saw. From a long way away, the adult Shadow realised what was happening: the fleeing spirit was taking refuge in her memories, hiding out at a day at the zoo. She remembered this day, now: it had been a happy one, with no peculiar incidents. The camel was Gremory. The beasts—a figure of strangeness to Europeans—were linked to the moon and to certain demons. Gremory, as camel, winked a black-red eye at Shadow and took a graceful leap over the barrier. Aunt Behamiah did not appear to notice. Shadow watched as the camel raced down the sandy track, and she could see something running now, flickering in and out of the trees. She let go of her aunt's hand and sped after it, glancing over her shoulder to see Behamiah standing in complacent ignorance.

"Hey!" Shadow shouted at the fleeing dark shape. "Leave my memory alone!" She was outraged that the nice day at the zoo was being hijacked by this demon-and-ifrit show. "Not so smug now, are you?"

But as she came around a thicket of flowering oleander, the camel stood alone.

"Lost him," Gremory said. It sounded odd, coming out of a camel's jaws. She worked her mouth and spat sideways into the bushes. "Sod it."

Shadow had a splitting headache. The ifrit had gone to ground, hiding deep within. Occasionally she felt a twitch, like a nervous tic, and it made her jump, but she wasn't sure whether this was the spirit resurfacing or her own nerves.

Gremory perched on the arm of the divan. It looked unbalanced: a human would have toppled it, but the demon appeared to have no weight. Shadow filed that away for future reference.

"Sorry." The demon sounded remarkably sincere. "Nearly had him but he gave me the slip." She raised a long, elegant hand and Shadow saw a wisp of smoke emanating from the tip of her taloned forefinger. There was the smell of sandalwood; Gremory inhaled.

"Do you know what he wants?"

"He's a prince of the air. Do you know what that is?"

"I've done my studies," Shadow answered, irritably. "In fact, it's what the Shah told me to ask the ifrit in the first place—that was the ruse to get it to talk to us. I suppose he did that because if this thing is also a prince, it would be bound to know, and it was probably interested. They're true spirits—ifrits, not demons or angels—neither good enough for Heaven nor bad enough for Hell. So they wander, in groups. They have ships." The *Barquess* came suddenly to mind: not much difference, perhaps.

"This one is either a renegade, or he's lost. I say a 'prince.' He might be lower in the hierarchy than that—in fact, he almost certainly is. He's possibly a duke, or something: someone who's fallen out with the Prince himself and who's had to go on the run. The Shah found him, trapped him, called you in and now he's—"

"—in me."

"Unfortunately, yes." The demon touched her smouldering talon to her lips. "He's going to be difficult to dislodge. Knows a lot of tricks. I do know someone who could help, bu—"

"But?"

"He's out in the Great Desert. The Khaureg."

After a moment, Shadow said, "Oh."

"You've been beyond the city?"

"Yes, once. My knife comes from the desert."

For the first time, the demon looked genuinely intrigued. "Does it? That means you won it."

"Yes. I killed someone for it."

"Who?"

"No one important."

"Everyone's important to someone," the demon said. "I'm wondering if your knife is connected to the spirit that's possessing you now."

"If this is some elaborate plot, then the Shah could just have taken it, couldn't he?"

"I don't think it's a plot. I think it's a fortuitous incident."

"Well," Shadow said. "I won once. And I'll win again."

⊷Interlude⊷

There was a burning tree outside the open window. The Duke leaned on the sill and looked out into its smouldering branches. There was fruit among the blazing leaves, globes of glowing gold. The Duke was almost tempted to reach out and pluck one of them, but she did not think Astaroth would approve. Beyond the tree, the metal walls of the city rose up in concentric rings towards the molten sky.

"She's ready to see you now."

The Duke's boots rang out along the floor as she made her way into the audience chamber. Astaroth was standing by the window, staring down at a document. At least, the Duke thought, her own life was not constrained by paperwork, whatever other problems she might currently be encountering.

"Gremory."

"My prince." The Duke bowed.

"How is it going?"

This required delicate handling. "Well," Gremory began.

"You haven't found it, have you?"

"Not *exactly*. But I have found the thief."

This got Astaroth's full attention.

"Have you, indeed? Where is he?"

"He was captured by Shah Suleiman of Worldsoul, and is now residing in the body of an alchemist, one Shadow."

"How very original!"

The Duke sighed.

"A bit too original."

"So why have you not extracted him?"

"It became—complicated. I chased him, but he has taken refuge in the woman's memories. It's not within my power to retrieve him." Gremory paused. "He's very skilled at evasion."

"He would be," Astaroth said. "He was well trained."

Gremory knew better than to ask leading questions, but the Prince said, "He is a spy."

"I see."

"That which he has stolen is information."

"I had surmised as much. What course of action do you want me to pursue now?"

"Am I to understand that killing the woman would achieve nothing?"

"I had considered it," the Duke said, "but it could simply provide our quarry with another escape route. The woman is devout, and if your spy hitched a ride with her outgoing soul, I would not be able to follow them."

"I see. I seem to recall that during the wars you had some sort of—liaison—with a gentleman from the opposite team."

Gremory had the grace to look abashed, and knew it. "Young love. You know how it is."

"Oh, quite. We've all done it—there's no shame. On the contrary, in fact, it's far worse for them, given that we're such rough trade in their masters' eyes. The reason I mention it is because certain Messengers are good at that sort of thing: their remit is souls, after all."

"I had already thought of it."

"I can rely on you, Gremory, to conduct yourself intelligently. Usually. Is your paramour still on this plane?"

"The last I heard, he'd become a hermit."

Astaroth looked pained. "Oh, how tediously typical. They all want to become closer to their God, whereas most of us would do anything to stay away from ours."

Gremory laughed. "It's how they're made."

"Send him a message. Ask if he'll help. If he's that boringly typical, he'll do anything to enable you to have a chance at redemption. They can never resist a crack at a demon's soul."

The Duke smiled. "He can crack away. I'm happy as I am."

⊷═◉═◉═⊷

Later, she walked down among the burning trees, into the streets around the fortress. It was quiet, at this time of the day. She made her way down a winding passage to an opening in the wall. Here, sat an old demon, with the brick red skin of a previous generation and yellow eyes.

"Duke!" He rose and bowed. Around him were a hundred or more birdcages, filled with fiery doves. Their whispering and chattering consumed the air.

"I need to send a message," Gremory said.

Twenty-eight

Mercy woke, sweating, in her own bed. She was disinclined to put the whole thing down to a dream and when Perra leaped in through the open window, Mercy asked the *ka*.

"It was not a dream," Perra said. The *ka* frowned. "I do not like being put to sleep."

"Who the hell was she? I've heard of something like that before but I can't pin it down. And why did she rescue us?" Although Mercy was glad that she had.

"I can't answer your questions."

Mercy flung back the blankets. "I'd better get in to work."

⊷⇒ ⇐⊶

Having checked up on Benjaya, now safely back at his post, and given her report, Mercy spent the rest of that day in the Library. She was restless and tired, but not displeased to have an afternoon to herself. She roamed the Library with the *ka* at her heels, uncertain as to what she was searching for. Perhaps it wasn't anything in particular, just a sense of dislocation. The appearance of that rift in the air, apparent to Perra but not to anyone else, had disconcerted her. Knowing where it led was even more unsettling. She wanted to know what the hell else was breaching the Library's defences. Once, it had seemed impregnable, now it felt more like a leaky colander.

They took it systematically, top-down. The upper floors held the oldest texts, being perhaps paradoxically, the easiest to defend. The cellars were too easy to breach, to burrow and worm into. Hence the heights, in which Mercy now stood.

On this top-most floor, there were no books. Instead, there was a collection of astronomical and weather-reading equipment: astrolabes at one end, where a dome could be opened to the night skies, wind and rain gauges at the other. The dome had not been an original feature of the library of Alexandria, but added later: maybe it had added itself, which was the way things usually worked in Worldsoul. You could wake in the morning to find a whole new block, the city re-arranging itself around the incomer and then settling back into place as though the addition had always been there. But the observatory dome had been in place long enough for Mercy to take it for granted. They searched anyway, Perra scanning the air like a hound tracing a scent.

"I can't see anything. Only songs." The *ka's* small face was wistful.

"Songs?"

"Songs of stars. Songs of clouds."

Research left its traces, Mercy knew. She felt a brief envy. "Sounds nice."

"Mm," the *ka* said. But there was nothing sinister here. As they headed down the stairs, Mercy glanced out of the long windows towards the Court. Its dark roofs glistened with recent rain; the golden spell-vanes turned in the sea wind. Unfinished business. She wondered if this search of the Library wasn't just putting off a confrontation with Deed.

Deed, who still had a vial of her blood.

Deed, the Abbot General of the entire Court. You couldn't just walk in and start flinging accusations.

Downstairs, the light faded abruptly as they entered the upper stacks. This was where Mercy had first encountered the disir, the place of the oldest texts. The rift that had let them into the world of ice was now closed, according to Perra.

"It would be helpful," the *ka* said, "if you could see this for yourself."

Mercy looked curiously at the *ka*. It was unusual for a spirit, even one as benign as Perra, to offer a secret freely. "You can teach me to do that?"

The *ka* leaped up onto an empty shelf, so that they were at eye height. "I can. Close your eyes."

After a second's hesitation, Mercy did so. She felt a feather-light touch on her forehead, between her brows. The sigil marked there burned cold for a moment, making her gasp. Then the *ka* was through the ward.

Flashback. She was standing in the great chamber at the Heart of the Library, in front of the Skein. The woman who stood in front of her was holding a sash, of black, white, and grey silk.

This binds you to the Library. If you accept it, then you belong to this place, you are tied and indentured for the rest of your life, unless we choose to sever you. Is this your choice?

And Mercy, seventeen years old but feeling very grown-up, had said, "Yes. Yes, I accept."

A touch on her forehead, as Beheverah of the Skein reached out an ivory hand and inscribed the first warding sigil between her brows, the sigil that she would have to re-administer every day of her life from now on.

Unless she retired and left the Order entirely, but then, Librarians tended not to do that.

Mercy blinked. It was as though she had grown an inch, and could see a different world around her. The stacks shimmered with magic—she was used to that, and she could see small cracks and chinks in the field of blue, with tiny lightning strikes and fizzes of electricity, as though insects were being fried around the texts. The spellwards, trying to hold back leaks in a sieve. Perra's impassive golden gaze was fixed on her face.

"I think it's worked," Mercy said. "Whatever it was."

"Let's see what else you can see," the *ka* replied.

Plenty of small cracks, but when she mentioned it to Perra, the *ka* said that these had always been there.

"What if they widen?"

"Then you have a problem. This sort of magic can only be contained with great difficulty. Even the Skein found it hard. And perhaps inadvisable."

"Inadavisable?"

"Magic is like pressure. Damming it up can be problematic."

"Perra, how do you know so much about the Library?"

But the *ka* only blinked.

The upper stacks were relatively clear. Mercy did not, however, hold out much hope. What if there were breaks which the *ka* couldn't see? She was thorough nonetheless, taking each floor in turn until she glanced at her watch and saw that it was close to five o'clock. The Library was huge, that was the trouble, and they'd only done three floors, out of eleven. At six, she decided, she would go out to a café, snatch some food, then come back in and work through the night if necessary.

It was, however, on the fourth floor that they discovered a major break. Like the one upstairs, it was a vertical crack in the air. Here, however, the breeze that filtered through it was hot, and smelled of spices.

"Where's it coming from?" Nerren stood in front of it. She was, she told Mercy, able to feel the breeze, but not see the break.

"I don't know. And thanks for coming upstairs so quickly, by the way. How are you feeling?"

Nerren grimaced. "I get nightmares, I don't mind telling you. But I'm all right."

Mercy recognised this as a Librarian's 'all right.' The sort that would have civilians gibbering under the bed. "Good," was all that she said.

"The smell's familiar, though."

"Is it?"

Nerren nodded. "Reminds me of being a kid. It used to smell like this down at the shore—there was a market, where they offloaded the spice cargos." She closed her eyes. "Cinnamon, nutmeg, sandalwood . . . "

"Sounds lovely."

"See—" Nerren said, and for a moment, Mercy could: the island shore, a rich intensity of colour, the mounds of spices on the market stalls and the clipper unloading against a sunset sky.

"I'd forgotten you're a visualiser."

"Not everyone's receptive."

Mercy smiled. "You miss the Southern Quarter?"

"Yeah, but my life's with the Library." She sighed. "Let's hope it lasts."

"Anyway, it might be a nice one, but we've still got a rift."

⚞Interlude⚟

He was sitting in prayer outside the beehive hut when the message arrived. At first he thought, with wonder, that it was a meteorite, streaking down out of the sunlit sky, but soon it resolved itself into the form of a dove, alight.

"Well, well," the Messenger said, aloud. He waited until the dove had set down on the low wall and reached out to take the parchment, only slightly singed, from around its leg. Once he had done so, the dove crumbled into ash, presumably remanifesting back in Hell.

"Thank you," the Messenger breathed. His heart lurched against his ribs, an unfamiliar sensation.

The note was brief.

I'm bringing someone to see you. A soul in peril. Why am I concerned? She is my charge. I will be grateful for your help.

It was signed: *Gremory, Duke of Hell.*

He stared at the note for a long time before folding it and placing it within his robe. Memories of the war came to the fore, the long struggle. Good and evil. Darkness and light. But is anything ever that simple?

⊷Twenty-nine⊶

Shadow did not like the idea of riding the demon. It seemed wrong, and there was a subtext to it with which she was not comfortable.

"You can walk if you want," Gremory said. She looked at Shadow out of a sidelong black eye, flickering with red. As a camel, her coat was again a shining black, quite unlike any beast that Shadow had actually seen at the zoo: camels tended to be on the ragged side.

Shadow cast a glance at the shifting sands of the Khaureg. "You know that will take twice as long."

"Probably four times. Up you get."

Swallowing, Shadow placed a foot in the stirrup as the demon knelt. A moment later Gremory was rising again, hoisting her into the air.

"You've ridden us before, of course?"

"Yes." It was easy enough, once one got used to the rolling gait.

It was now early morning. The demon had suggested that they set out at dawn, partly so that fewer people would see them, and also to make the most of the coolest part of the day. Shadow was naturally wary. She did not trust the demon. She did not know what Gremory's real agenda was, as it was almost certain that the demon was lying to her. However, Gremory's presence was a lot less irksome than the spirit's: the Prince of the Air had vanished deep inside Shadow's mind and clearly had no plans to come out whilst Gremory was there. *Stay in your damned neural burrow, then.*

It was some years since she had ventured into the deep desert, the Khaureg. She had been on a mission: to find a haunted knife and release the spirit that possessed it, and to kill the man who had imprisoned it there. That had been the sun-and-moon blade, which hung at her hip, but now she herself was the knife, and taken. She did not recognise any of the land through which they now travelled. The dunes shifted so much that the desert had altered completely and it would not be until they reached the low outcrops of rocks known as the Devil's Ears that she could get her bearings. She knew better than to glance over her shoulder. The stories said if you did that, you ran the risk of losing the city altogether; it would shift and vanish into mirage. In this world, such stories had to be taken seriously.

Gremory seemed to know where she was going. She loped in a straight line, following the roll of the dunes. Occasionally her long black neck twisted round to observe Shadow with a mocking, knowing eye, as if checking that the alchemist was still on board. As the heat of the morning sun grew, Shadow fell into a kind of doze, almost a trance. She felt the spirit inside her, occasionally surfacing like a bubble from the depths of the sea. *You stay where you are,* she told it. It was difficult to reconcile this small inner presence with the memory of the huge ifrit in the cage, but Shadow knew that to spirits, size was an illusion. Only to humans did it matter.

Towards mid-morning, a shimmer appeared on the horizon. Shadow blinked behind the veil, trying to see whether it was mirage or real, but then it solidified and she recognised the ridge called the Devil's Ears. Gremory's head twisted round again.

"Nearly there."

"Is that where we're headed?"

"No. The person we will meet now is not the one I am taking you to see. It's where we'll ride out the heat."

Shadow had been expecting her to head into the outcrop. There were caves here, occasionally occupied with mad old hermits who, for a few coins, would provide food and water. But the demon headed up into the heights instead, climbing towards the sun via a series of steps that were so worn they could have been natural. Perhaps they were. But the summit featured a low wall, and then a small collection of beehive-shaped huts came into view.

They were made of blocks of stone, covered with a plaster that must once have been white but which had now faded to a flaking honeycomb. Gremory knelt and Shadow dismounted, feeling uncomfortably stiff. She flexed her knees, stretched her shoulders, and when she turned back the demon was once more in the form of a woman, barefoot and wearing a flowing black robe. Shadow said the first thing that came into her head: "Are you tired?"

The demon laughed. "No, I do not tire. But thank you for asking."

Shadow looked back across the desert. They were now far enough away for the city to be lost over the horizon, with no chance of an accidental glimpse. The desert rolled on in endless shades of light. Above, the sky was a harsh, burning blue and it was very quiet. She followed the demon, who cast no shadow and who left no footsteps in the sandy earth, around the side of one of the beehive huts. The place smelled of sunwarmed earth and mimosa; the trees nodded above the stone, humming with insects.

"Ator?" The word fell into the silent air. Gremory paused before entering the hut. "Are you there?"

It seemed too still for there to be a human presence, but then a voice croaked, "I'm here." It took Shadow's eyes a moment to adjust to the dimness, but when they did, she saw an old man sitting on a pallet on the floor. His hands were twisted and arthritic; his head was bowed beneath a crown of long, yellowing white hair which fell in knots and snarls down his back. Then he looked up and she saw his face was young. A terrible scar ran down from the left side of his forehead to the right side of his jaw. She would guess it was from a scimitar slash.

"Ator," Gremory said again. His face held a weary resignation.

"Demon. It's you."

"I've brought a guest."

His eyes were yellow, too, like a jackal's, and hot. His gaze lingered on her; she could feel it through the veil and did not like it. It held a kind of bitterness, an amusement, something more.

"Not a demon."

"No. I'm human. I'm from the city. I—" She had been about to say *an alchemist, an assassin*, but stopped just in time. She was not prone to spilling her secrets like water out of a cracked pot, so what was it about this unkempt person that had nearly drawn them out of her? He smiled, charmingly, but his teeth were blocky, with sharp incisors.

"My name is Ator."

"I gathered that."

"Tea?"

"Why not?" the demon said. She slid easily down to her heels. The black robe billowed around her like a personal night. After a moment, Shadow, too, sat. Ator poured a thin stream of brown-gold tea from a pot on the hearth, adding mint to the glasses. It was sharp, refreshing. Shadow listened while Gremory and the man talked, discussing people and places whose names she did not know in a kind of staccato, sparring shorthand. It had the tenor of a fencing match; Shadow felt that it would be wiser not to play. Wiser, in fact, not to open her mouth at all, given that Ator had already demonstrated an ability to worm information out of her. When they had finished the tea, Gremory stood.

"We'll stay. For a few hours, then move on."

"As you wish."

Shadow felt the weight of his yellow gaze as they walked to the door: the sunshine should have hit her like a blow, but somehow it felt cooler and sharper.

"Guest quarters are down there." The demon pointed to another hut, set among a grove of trees. Scrawny sheep meandered among the limewashed trunks. As they took the path that led down to it, out of the main compound, Shadow said in the low voice, "Your friend. Ator . . . "

"No friend of mine."

"I don't think it's sensible to go to sleep anywhere near him."

Gremory swatted away a buzzing fly. "Him? He's not allowed to leave the compound."

"But—"

"Trust me. He can't. He's bound to it. That's what annoys him so much."

"Why?"

"If he comes out, he changes back. Forever."

"And that would be to—?"

"What he was before," the demon said, and marched down the path.

Shadow had not been expecting the demon to take a siesta, but there were two pallets in the guest hut, in a reasonable state of cleanliness, and Gremory lay down on the first without ceremony. She crossed her hands over her breasts, and her face stilled into expressionless marble. Shadow watched her for some minutes, but the demon did not blink and after a while, watching her began to feel intrusive, so she took the second pallet. She was not expecting to sleep, but the fatigue produced by recent events overtook her and she dozed off, awaking with a start some while later.

The sun had moved round, casting long shadows across the doorway of the hut. Something had woken her, with a note like a bell, and after a moment it came again: a cuckoo. Its two-note song fell upon the air. Shadow felt suddenly wide awake. She rose from the pallet and went out through the door, leaving the demon motionless within the hut.

The sheep had moved on, up the valley. She could hear the distant clank of a bell as they grazed. The sun was skirting the edge of the Devil's Ears; she judged that it must be close to five o'clock. She looked back at the compound but there was no sign of movement. Then the cuckoo called again and she swung round. Someone was standing motionless on the other side of the valley. It was a woman, dressed modestly in black, with her face concealed.

"Who are you?" Shadow called, but the woman did not reply. Instead, she raised a hand and made a gesture in the air that Shadow could not interpret: it looked as though the woman had written a word. Then the figure was gone, abruptly, as if snuffed out.

Thoughtfully, Shadow went back into the hut to meet the demon.

⇢Thirty⇠

By midnight, Mercy and Perra had found two more rifts, besides the one leading into the Southern Quarter. One led into the east and was visible; when Mercy put her eye to it, she saw a formal garden, with a carefully arranged tableau of stones and pebbles, and a small bridge over a lily-fringed pool. Nothing could have been more serene, but Mercy didn't trust it. She lingered, but could not see anything that posed an immediate threat, so she reported the rift to security. Nerren had gone home, complaining of an entirely justifiable headache.

The third rift was an anomaly: it didn't seem to go anywhere. She could see the crack in the air, a dark line with a bright knife-edge, but she could not see anything through it, nor could she hear. Eventually, with some trepidation, she cast a revealing spell at it to see if that did any good. The crack did not widen, somewhat to her relief, but a fragment of text appeared in the air, glowing briefly before fading out:

. . . tells all things, both past and future, of hidden treasures and the love of women . . .

Well, that was helpful. It looked like a passage from a grimoire to Mercy, but she did not recognise which one. At a certain level they were all much of a muchness.

"Mean anything to you?" she asked the *ka*, but Perra shook its head.

As the text faded, the rift narrowed until it was no more

than a single dark-bright point of light. *We will*, Mercy thought nonetheless, *be keeping an eye on you.*

⊶═◌═⊷

After the events of the last few days, Mercy kept the Irish sword by her side as she left the Library. No more public transport from now on, either; she planned to walk home. It was now after midnight and the stars were gathered thickly over the Citadel, with the constellation known as the Crown high in the heavens. The lamps were soft and hissing in the summer dusk. Mercy, with the *ka* at her heels, headed down the quiet stone streets to her home.

She was weary, but too wired to sleep. She made tea and sat in the window seat, then, after a moment's pause, got up and moved to somewhere less noticeable from outside. The *ka* watched her, with unblinking golden eyes.

Then she realised, with a clammy sense of dismay, that she could feel Loki in the room. The impression was so vivid that she turned to look over her shoulder: there was nothing there. But it was as though she stood in the grove again, with the old god watching.

"Perra!"

"Yes?"

"Do you—feel anything?"

The *ka's* tail twitched. "I do not."

Mercy looked at the *ka,* conscious of a creeping and sudden sense of mistrust. "Are you sure?"

The *ka* blinked. "There is nothing here, beside the usual ghosts. The girl who died; the little dog."

"All right," Mercy said, reluctant. The impression was fading: perhaps she'd simply imagined it. But then she looked at the window—the back panes, which looked out over the garden from the kitchen—and knew that she had not.

"Perra!"

Cautiously, she approached the window. Flowers had caught her attention; flowers of frost, which even now blossomed and grew, white across the surface of the glass. Mercy knew winter, of course: the Western Quarter was not immune, though not nearly as chill as the Northern. Towards the height of the year, the solstice, mists came in from the sea, rainstorms lashed the western coasts and the morning air was pale with frost, stiffening the blades of grass and the leaves, and making patterns on the glass. But this wasn't winter. It was late summer now and the air that night had been sultry and still as she walked down the hill from the Library. No natural change in the weather could have accounted for these flowers of frost. Mercy made sure that the Irish sword was still in reach and when her fingers closed over its hilt, the blade sang a sudden sharp note of warning, as it had not bothered to do that afternoon in the Library.

Then there was a knock at the back door, a single rap, and Mercy froze.

"Who's there?"

No reply. The knock came again. Mercy brought the sword up.

"I'm not answering the door until you tell me who you are!"

The flowers were blooming across the windowpane, spreading upwards and out until the whole of the kitchen window was whited out. Looking down, Mercy saw frost was beginning to spread under the kitchen door, pallid fingers like a skeletal hand reaching out across the boards. The sword twitched again in her fist, but how do you fight frost? Mercy threw her splayed hand outward and spoke one of the house spells, the warding conjurations which were passed down through the family, peculiar to each household. She increased them in strength, racheting the incantations up in power, but the frost continued to spread.

" . . . *emecherala, halacherala* . . . "

But it was starting to rise upwards from the floorboards in a thin spray of mist, sparkling and crackling in the air. Mercy took a step back. The *ka* was watching wide-eyed, like a cat about to pounce. The frost rose up until it was at head height, when it began to take on shape.

Its lips moved. "*My name—*" The face cracked like a chipped glaze, but then it was solidifying once more, congealing into a human shape. A crown of starlight glittered across its brow. It opened cold dark eyes, brushed a languid hand over the fur collar of its cloak. It was the woman from the sleigh.

"Forgive me for not introducing myself on our first meeting. My name is Mareritt. And forgive my intrusion, but I need to speak to you."

"I'm at the Library most days," Mercy said. The frost-woman smiled.

"House call."

"I was 'here' before. You awoke from your journey to the north in your own bed, did you not?"

"After you drugged us."

"It was necessary."

"So now you're here." Mercy was outraged. "I mean, I'm grateful for you rescuing us, but what *are* you?"

"I am a nightmare."

It was a moment before Mercy, bridling, realised that the woman was not issuing a threat, but speaking literally.

"You're from the Northern Quarter?"

"I get around. But originally, yes."

"Scandinavian?" Mercy's professional curiosity was piqued. Mareritt smiled.

"Once upon a time." She raised her head and scented the air like a hunting dog. "I understand you've had a visit from the Ladies. Not here. Where you work."

"The disir? Yes."

"How unpleasant," Mareritt said. She sounded as though some social undesirable had dropped in uninvited for tea. Then she turned to Mercy and the well of her eyes exerted a sudden pull, as though the gravity itself had altered. Mercy felt herself flinch away.

"You're carrying the touch of the god's hand. Did you know?" Mareritt cocked her head on one side. "But how could you not, unless he's wiped it from your mind."

"He hasn't," Mercy told her, dry-voiced. The *ka* looked from one to the other, as if watching a tennis match.

"What did he tell you?"

Mercy was reluctant to say. Is my enemy's enemy my friend? Hard to tell, in this instance. But she felt the words being pushed out of her throat, as if Mareritt had taken up temporary residence inside her.

"He—he wants me to find a story."

"Does he, now?" The black eyes were bright. "How interesting. What story is that?"

"A story about demons and a garden."

"Loki is a lord of intrigue, you know that? You're familiar with the tales of the north?"

Mercy nodded. "My mother, Greya—she's from a northern clan."

"But Greya isn't here." Did she know *everything*?

"No. She's gone on the *Barquess*."

"I'm going to do something for you," Mareritt said. She stepped across the kitchen, taking care to avoid the frond of a fern which, Mercy saw, withered at her approach.

Standing over the kitchen table, she reached into her mouth with a finger and thumb and took out a key. It was similar in size and shape to the key Loki had given Mercy. She placed it on the table.

"That's for you."

"Loki gave me something, too. What does it open?"

"It opens the door to the Library that belongs to the Court."

"*What?* How did you get that?"

"I picked a pocket."

"In the *Court?*"

"I need a book," Mareritt said, "The name of the book is *The Winter Book.*"

"Have you checked our own lending section?"

Mareritt clicked her tongue with a noise like chiming icicles. "I know for a fact that the book is in the Court's library, not yours."

"I'm sorry," Mercy said. "I don't have visiting rights."

"Oh, but you will fetch it for me."

"I don't think so."

Mareritt turned. "This is the name," she said.

"I don't—"

The woman touched a chilly finger to Mercy's brow.

"This is the name of the clan: they are the People of the Birch Forest and the Stone. I ask you to do this in the name of the People, of your mother's clan. I place you under geas to bring the book to me."

Mercy felt the geas go into her mind like a silver hook, snaring her will in a binding net.

"Damn you," she managed to say.

"Oh, come. That's no way to talk to your—" She reached out and touched the phial of golden oil to Mercy's brow and that was the last thing that Mercy remembered that night.

⊷Thirty-one⊶

The Devil's Ears had fallen far behind. Shadow had not seen the watching woman again, and she had kept the sighting from the demon. Periodically, the spirit stirred inside her head, found Gremory's red-black gaze fixed upon it, and retreated hastily. Shadow was enjoying the relative peace and quiet, but she kept thinking of the woman, and of Ator. She could not help feeling they were connected, that Gremory had drawn her into a wider web. Yet there were advantages: the immense weight of heat that lay upon the desert diminished the disir in Shadow's memory, diminished even the Shah. She did not think the creature of the north, of those great ice wastes, would pursue her here. The Shah's influence did not stop at the city wall, however. She would be wise not to discount him entirely. That left the demon herself.

Beneath her, Gremory's camel-feet relentlessly pounded across the desert. It was evening. The sun had gone down in a burst of rosy flame and the sky was now green and water-cool. A single star hung like a lamp over the dunes. The demon had, before changing back into animal form, told Shadow that they would be there by nightfall, but Shadow did not know where "there" might be. Asking Gremory had merely resulted in the shapeshift from woman to dromedary. This was not a slow process; one moment Shadow was talking to a woman, and the next, to a large and insolent camel. She found this disconcerting.

As she rode, she scanned the horizon for signs that they might be approaching a destination: there were hills ahead, a ridge that was higher than the Devil's Ears and still catching the last red light of the sun. Gremory veered towards the hills and Shadow became increasingly sure that this was where they were heading. As they drew closer, a bright sword-tip appeared over the summit—the crescent moon. Shadow greeted it like an old friend.

Gradually, the sand became interspersed with rocks jutting up out of the dunes like a cliff from the waves. Gremory slowed, halted, kneeled, and Shadow climbed down, to stand—wobbling a bit before regaining her balance on the sand. A blink, and the demon was back in female form. This time, Gremory wore black armour, heavily ornamented with silver. Shadow had a brief moment of demon-envy; a pity humans couldn't carry their wardrobes with them.

"So," Gremory said. "Here we are."

"Where is 'here'?"

"Where the person I want you to meet lives."

"Is he like Ator?"

"No, not like Ator. I don't—" the demon hesitated. "Ator is sometimes an ally, but one can't rely on him. Besides, he doesn't have the ability we need."

"So who are we going to meet?"

"Come with me," the demon instructed, and walked between the rocks.

A pathway, very rough, was cut into the face of the stone. As she began to climb, Shadow saw that it was not badly made, but simply very old, worn away by erosion and time. The scouring winds that crossed the desert were not kind to stone, and few structures lasted long. But the sickle moon hung above the steps like a guiding lamp and Shadow climbed on.

Halfway up, she turned and looked back. The desert stretched below, undulating miles of shadow. Far on the horizon she could see the uneven line of the Devil's Ears, but the city, as she had risked to hope, was happily invisible, unbetrayed even by light. The stars were thick and brilliant now, so vivid that they cast their own faint glow, and in its pale light Shadow, for a moment, thought she saw someone standing on the opposite ridge. Then it was gone. She turned to where the demon waited with a terrible patience.

"I thought I saw someone," Shadow said.

"This place is too crowded," Gremory replied.

At the top of the steps, the stone levelled out into a platform and there was a black arch in the rocks beyond, some kind of entrance. As Shadow stared, a flame flickered within and she glimpsed a chamber cut into the rock. The demon strode forward. Shadow heard a murmured incantation, a ritual greeting. She ducked to avoid the low lintel and stepped into the chamber.

She knew at once that the person sitting on the other side of the chamber was not human. Yet there was nothing ostensibly to suggest this. He was tall, white-haired, and although his face was unlined, it seemed filled with a great weariness. His eyes were the no-colour of clear glass. He wore a grey robe. He should, Shadow thought, have faded against the stones of the wall and yet he was vivid, drawing the gaze and snaring it.

"Not a demon," she said, and did not realise she had spoken aloud until it was too late.

"An opposite number," Gremory said, and smiled thinly.

"Fallen?" Shadow asked and was appalled she had said such a thing.

The person said, "You cannot help but speak the truth in front of me. It makes social conversation very trying, I know. No, I am not fallen. I choose to be here. Duke, it's good to see you again."

"His name is Elemiel," the demon said. Shadow noticed Gremory—Duke?—took care not to step too close to Elemiel: around the entity's feet, a faint golden glow spread outwards.

Protective measures. Shadow had no doubt that the entity needed them.

"I got your letter," the angel said.

"We've come because this woman is possessed," Gremory said. "She needs your help."

"I may not be able to give it."

"Yet, you may." They stared at one another for a moment.

"All right," Elemiel said, at last. "Let's see."

The world was filled with light. It was as though her veil had become transparent, and Shadow's eyes had opened wide as a door. Illumination flooded into her; she breathed light. She was a doorway, she realised, and the angel stepped lightly in.

"Now," Elemiel said. "Where is this person?"

It was not like being possessed by the spirit, or invaded by the demon. The angel's step into her soul was thistledown soft, as imperceptible as a moth. But she could not more have resisted it any more than she could have flown: there was an inexorable push behind it, sunlight-strong. She stood quietly back and let the angel in.

And then she watched, passive, but this time not minding, as Elemiel strolled down the walkways of her mind, quietly and methodically opening doors. He walked into rooms that Shadow had long since forced shut; chambers filled with cobwebs and matters of the dark, and the light wind of the angel's passing stirred up the dust and opened windows, letting in the air of the spirit.

Housecleaning, Shadow thought, and the angel laughed. Illuminated by the light that he brought in his wake, she was able to look on things that she had thought long buried—her mother's death, her father's disappearance—all without pain. She could sense the demon watching with detached interest. Gremory did not attempt to intrude. But always the spirit that had possessed her ran, fleeing swiftly down the corridors, and the angel went after it like a silent hunter.

He caught up with it at last in a basement room, somewhere small and walled and tucked away. Shadow recalled it as an early memory: a tense night of arguments, the family shouting around her as she lay, fearful, in her small bed. There were slamming doors and hissed accusations. She had never known what it was about. Yet she remembered now that on the following day, her aunt had taken her to the zoo, and the happy memory had eclipsed the other one, forcing it from her mind until now. She again had that feeling of miserable oppression, filled with lack of understanding and *wish-you'd-just-stop*, until the angel's touch banished the unhappiness and brought healing in its place.

The spirit's back was up against the wall; she sensed Elemiel closing in. The angel did not have wings, but colours swirled around it, shades that she was unable to name, colours of the soul and not of the manifest world. She could see the spirit over Elemiel's shoulder, and it was as bright as a dancing flame.

"Come now," the angel said, commanding, and a blade that was a fire and a leaf and a word appeared in his hand. The flame shrank back and then it dispersed into a mass of fragments, much as the ifrit itself had done. Elemiel gave a wordless cry and the light around him folded, faded, diminished to a small glowing point, coal-hot against the cool dimness of the room.

Thirty-two

The Irish sword was not the only weapon in her arsenal, Mercy reflected, and not all weapons are swords. The mind is the best weapon of all and thus she had taken herself early in the morning to the Library in order to do some emergency research.

Mareritt and the Order of the Court itself were the objects of her enquiries. A superficial search revealed a great deal about the Court, all of it on public display and none of it startling. Mercy could probably have amplified much of it herself, through common knowledge. That mean a deeper investigation, and she decided to leave this until a later hour and track down Mareritt instead. The nature of the woman who had come to visit her seemed to entail a focus on the Northern Quarter; there was something tugging at the edges of her mind, some half-recalled memory that rendered the name familiar.

The name meant "nightmare," and it seemed this was what Mareritt was. But whether she was an avatar of that phenomenon, or an entity with the same name, remained to be seen. Mercy followed the trail down through the forest tracks of a dozen books, along a sequence of winding etymological trails, words which conjured snow and the scent of fir, fragments of legends which brought in the ice and the winter wind, just as the disir had done. She did not think Mareritt was the same, but she did not like the thought of the risk. She tracked her quarry down into story, running her to ground in fairy tale.

And the little boy took the spinning top and spun it as he spoke the magic words, and Mareritt appeared like sugar taffy curdling in the air. At first Jan was very frightened, but she spoke kindly to him and told him not to be afraid. Then she asked him to show her the golden ball that his stepmother had given him. When he put it into her hand, she uttered a word and a knife came out from the middle of the ball, as sharp as an unkind word. "If you had done as she asked you and thrown this to the dove, it would have killed her." Jan did not say anything, but a tear came to his eye because of his love for the dove. "Don't cry," Mareritt said. "Come with me." She took his hand. Her glove was as soft as silk but he could feel the coldness of her flesh inside it and her breath made patterns on the air, like flowers. She led Jan to the window and he could see her sledge hanging on the air: it was made of snowflakes and silver and it shone like the moon. The white swans that drew it stamped their feet upon the air and Mareritt helped Jan into the sledge. "We'll rescue your dove," she said, settling a fur robe around his shoulders, "and leave your stepmother to me." Then the sledge sailed up into the clouds and—

That was all there was of the story. Mercy was sorry. She would have liked to know what happened next, a good sign in any tale. The legend suggested a number of things: Mareritt was honourable, perhaps fond of children, or at least willing to take their side. The wicked stepmother was, of course, a staple of fairy tales, often a witch herself. What had happened to the stepmother in this story, Mercy wondered? Had Mareritt breathed on her with a cold breath, brought winter nightmares to her bed? And what had happened to Jan? What *did* happen to boys in fairy tales who meet a fascinating woman? Did they become an army of acolytes, a loyal band of followers? Or were they damaged forever, like Kay with the Snow Queen's splinter of ice in his heart? Thoughtfully, Mercy tucked the notes she had made into her pocket and placed the original fragment back in its place.

As she walked back down the stairs to the central hall, where the Great Book stood on its plinth, the birds whisked and whirled around her head. Jan's dove: what had that meant? Had Mareritt saved it from the evil stepmother? Mercy stopped mid-step, looking up, and as she did so, the bird-ghosts began to change. From shadows, they became solid: some white, some black as soot and night. They began an aerial ballet, turning and twisting until they formed a column of light and dark. They soared up in a pillar of flight towards the ceiling, until they reached the roof, when the pillar broke apart and fell into a flickering mass of birds, shadows once more.

⊶═◉═⊷

Mercy did not know what the behaviour of the birds meant. She had never heard of such a thing happening before. Was it a sign? Did it mean the Skein were coming back? Frustrated, because she had no time to spend thinking on the matter, Mercy headed out into the day, a plan forming in her head.

Across the square, the Court towered around the Citadel. It was massive, built of black stone and wood: Mercy was reminded of the birds, but usually she thought of the Court as a chess player, moving pieces around the city as if it were a huge chessboard. The official entrance was found between a set of stone columns, a pair of iron doors that were shut at twilight and opened again at dawn.

Mercy gave the Court a long, hard look, and then she walked on down into the narrow cobbled streets which led through the Quarter. At the bottom of the hill, there was a rickshaw with a golem standing placidly in the shafts. Mercy hailed it.

"Heart of the World, please."

The rickshaw rattled across the cobbles, taking her past streets of ancient inns, their heraldic signs blazing, past colleges and galleries and markets, under the monorail line and over one of the many bridges which crossed the canals. Mercy stared at the back of the golem's round head and tried not to think too hard about what she was going to do.

The dreams, of the north.

The disir.

Mareritt.

There was one place where answers lay. She'd found the address in Greya's effects, after both her mothers had disappeared. It had been scribbled on a scrap of paper and it had been the only address that Mercy had not recognised among her mother's things.

It had been the only address from the Northern Quarter.

⇥≡◐⊖⇤

When Mercy got down from the rickshaw, the *ka* reappeared out of the air.

"This *ka* is coming with you," Perra said. Mercy felt a distinct relief. Perra was not a talisman, yet she could not help feeling that nothing too terrible could befall her if the *ka* was present. They walked across the square to where the monorail terminus for the North Road stations was situated; there was a train already in. Mercy paid the fare and they got on.

It took them past the empty palace of the Skein where the light still burned, past the statue of the *Barquess*. The scenery shifted and blurred in a small fold of time, and they were going up through the northern part of the Western Quarter, where the river palaces were distantly visible through the gaps in the parkland woods, up over the Speaking Cliffs and towards the Northern Gate, which was now visible on the horizon, towering over the surrounding buildings. The Northern Wall extended outwards from its nexus, heading right and left into the city.

When the monorail reached the Gate, it slowed to a halt. Guards got on, accompanied by security golems: this was not like crossing from West to East. Mercy had to hand over her sigilometer, which was checked, and her city pass. She was subjected to a scan of the eye, and then, to her great distaste, a drop of her blood was taken. After studying the results of that test, the guard unthawed noticeably and said, "Heading home?"

"Visiting family," Mercy said. It might have been true, after all.

"Have a nice time." After a quarter of an hour, when the other passengers were checked, the train slid through the Gate into winter.

The snow had melted to some degree, leaving patches of black stone along the pavement. Here, the buildings were massive—fortresses of wood, iron, and stone, away from the grace of the Eastern Quarter or the whimsicality of the Western—yet still impressive. Mercy still did not feel she belonged, however.

When they reached the first terminus, she got off the train. The person she was hoping to find was loitering at the entrance, reading a newspaper: a small middle-aged man with a long nose, and the universal badge of a City Reader on his coat.

"Good afternoon," Mercy said. "I'm looking for an address."

"You're in luck," the Reader said, folding his newspaper. "Maps won't help you, but I can, and I can also tell you that there was a significant shift around the Black Canal region last night, resulting in a rearrangement of some blocks."

"I rely on your expertise," Mercy said.

"You're very kind. *Some* people," here his expression became bitter, "begrudge the expense and no doubt they are still wandering lost about the city. On Earth? Fine. Things stay put. Here they don't."

"I value knowledge," Mercy said.

He nodded. "As a Librarian should."

She showed him the address. His long nose twitched in surprise, like a mouse's.

"This is old Mr Salt's place."

"You know him?"

"Everyone knows him. He mends lamps."

He gave Mercy directions and summoned a steamsled for her, happily devoid of severed heads. Well worth the money, she thought as she dropped the coins into the Reader's gloved hand and thanked him for his assistance.

The sled headed up the road and into a maze of back streets: Mercy could see an enormous building towering over the rooftops. She reached out and tapped the driver on the shoulder.

"What's that?" she shouted, over the roar of the sled's engine.

"Bleikrgard," came the driver's reply. "Where the Lords meet."

Mercy nodded. The lampmender's place, tucked away between two taller houses, was more her style, she felt. It was half timbered, in black and red, and bore a small crest above a leaded window. With Perra at her heels, she knocked at the door.

⊷Thirty-three⊷

Shadow woke, blinking at the stars. The veil was thin across her face, its infinitesimal weight a comfort. She lay on her back, on what felt like a pallet of straw, on the courtyard in front of Elemiel's dwelling. As she watched, a star shot overhead, bolting down in a trail of green fire. She groped at her sash and found the sun-and-moon blade hanging safely in its leather sheath.

Once she was assured of her veil and the knife, Shadow was more concerned with what was happening within. She shut her eyes and looked inside her mind: there was nothing there, except a sense of unfamiliar peace. The spirit had gone. Shadow breathed out, a sigh of relief and got unsteadily to her feet. Neither Elemiel nor Gremory were anywhere in sight. The crescent moon was riding high above a handful of cloud, but the desert seemed to shine with its own faint light, casting odd moving shadows across the rocks. Shadow remembered the figure she had seen and shivered.

Across the roof, steps led down to the platform of rock by which they had entered. Shadow went down the steps and looked in through the black arch, but there was no sign of the demon or the angel. The chamber was dark and quiet. She took the slope that led down from the platform, out into the desert.

Its peace mirrored the landscape within. She was reminded that it had been years since she had last been truly alone in the desert, without angel or demon or passenger. The journey she had made to find the knife had been like this, with the great starlit bowl of the sky hanging over the shifting sands and the green glow of twilight and dawn.

But now she was not alone; at least, if Gremory and the angel were still even here. Perhaps, their work done, they had departed for other realms, and she *was* alone. Shadow was not arrogant enough to think this had all been done as a favour to her. There were other agendas, more layers of meaning.

Then she came around an edge of rock and there was the demon. Gremory was in human form, barefoot and wearing a robe of black silk. She was crouching among the stones and as Shadow watched, her hand darted out, re-emerging with something spiny and wriggling. A scorpion. The demon stood, opened her mouth, bit it in half, and then swallowed each half. She turned to Shadow, a bead of venom glittering on her lip. She licked it away with the swipe of a long tongue and smiled.

"You're awake."

Shadow nodded.

"I—it's gone. Where did it go?"

"Ah." The demon had the grace to look a little abashed. "I need to explain something to you."

"What?"

"Come up to the chamber."

"Gremory?"

"Come." The demon strode past her up the slope, beckoning. Shadow followed with a sinking sensation in the pit of her stomach. Gremory did not pause at the angel's chamber, but went past it, up onto the roof.

"There," she said. "Do you see?"

Shadow frowned into the darkness. Something was sitting on the lip of rock opposite, something small and tailed. It raised its head and she caught a glimpse of eyes that were the colour of roses, a curl of horn at its brow.

"It's a demon."

"Only a little one. A small spirit, a genus loci. You shouldn't be able to see it, Shadow."

"Then why can I?"

"Well. Elemiel did his *best*."

"And he got rid of the thing in my head." The demon was looking somewhat shifty. "Gremory? Didn't he?"

"He was largely successful," the demon said. "He got it out of your mind, but it went—elsewhere."

"What? Where?"

"Into your flesh. I don't know whether it even meant to. I think it was so afraid of him that it split into a thousand pieces, and those fragments went into you—into your fingertips, your eyes, your ears . . ."

"So now I'm—what? Infested?"

"Look on the bright side," the demon said. "Try to see it as an *upgrade*."

Thirty-four

"I can't do anything before next Fourth Day," the lampmender said when he opened the door. "If it's urgent, it'll have to wait."

Mercy had been expecting a little old man, like Einstein in an apron, bristling with eccentricity. It just went to show that you shouldn't jump to conclusions. Salt was large and lugubrious, with bloodhound jowls and a figure like a pear. He looked at her without expression.

"I didn't come about a lamp," Mercy told him.

The stare increased in intensity. "You'd better come in."

Once inside, he sat her down in a leather armchair. The shop did, at least, ring true to type. It was crowded and, for a lampmender's, surprisingly dark. Maybe they were like cobbler's children, going unshod.

"My mother had your address in a box," Mercy said.

"I've got a lot of customers."

"I don't think she would have kept it if she'd just been a customer," Mercy said. She did not add that romance was unlikely to have been a consideration; regardless of Greya's sexual inclinations, Salt was not an immediate candidate for a burning lifelong passion. But she did not want to hurt his feelings.

"What was your ma's name?"

"Greya Fane."

This did produce an effect. Salt's chilly eyes, which resembled those of a cod, widened. "Oh!" he said.

"You obviously remember her."

"I'll say. The last time I saw Greya Fane, she was drenched to the skin, shivering fit to bust, and had just killed a man."

"I see," Mercy said, blankly.

"That was—what? Over forty years ago now. I was an apprentice at the time. This was my uncle's shop. I knew Greya from up north; we'd both come down together from Aachven. Didn't know one another well—different backgrounds. My family were woodcutters. Uncle broke out, wanted to make something of himself. Greya wanted to get away from the north and her family; I paid for her train ticket. Didn't hear from her for several months, then one night, she turned up on the doorstep and said someone had attacked her. She'd killed him, apparently, though she never said how."

"Did you call the authorities?"

Salt hesitated. "No. And I'll tell you why. I felt us northerners ought to stick together a bit and I was . . . quite fond of Greya. I dried her clothes on the stove and gave her a day's head start before I spoke to the Watch. But then, no body ever turned up. I did make some enquiries but no one missing, no one hurt . . . so I thought, forget it. And I did, pretty much until now. Funny, you don't look a bit like her, and yet I can feel her in you. Otherwise I wouldn't have told you all that. That, though," he nodded in the direction of the *ka*, "that's not hers."

"No. Greya's family were Wolfheads."

"They were more than that. They were shamans. But for all that, they were good to the people around them."

"If they were so great, why did Greya want to leave?"

"She wanted more. You know what girls are like. Wanted to see the bright lights."

Mercy had the impression that there was something Salt wasn't telling her. There was something else she wanted to know. "Have you ever heard of a woman named Mareritt?"

⊷Thirty-five⊷

Being a partial ifrit was, Shadow was discovering, a step up from being merely possessed. Perhaps the demon had not been so sarcastic after all, in her talk of an upgrade. The voice in her head had gone, and she was conscious of another dimension, opening around her. She could see the lines of shimmering light around things, their essences and souls. She could hear the faint song of the stars, the whispered incantations of the moon. And the desert was busy, filled with flickering, darting spirits and the ghosts of small creatures.

Another star was falling. Shadow stood on the roof and watched it descend: it was slower than the other meteorite, and the flame it trailed behind it was a sunset pink . . . Shadow dived, straight off the roof. She hit the ground in a curl, arms folded over her head, and rolled under a lip of rock. The flower burst soundlessly, the world illuminated with a searing blaze of flame. She saw the rocks through her eyelids, imprinted in silhouette, and then her head rang.

"Well," Gremory said, into her ear. "*That* was exciting."

⊷◉⊷

The angel's beehive hut had gone, obliterated into a thousand shattered fragments of stone. Like the spirit, Shadow thought, cascading outwards into the desert of her flesh. Slowly, she uncurled, thinning the veil as she did so. The demon was standing beside her. Gremory wore a cloak and it billowed out behind her in a wind that Shadow could not feel, snapping like a banner. Her eyes blazed like garnets and her hair was free: it streamed out. She said something in a long string of syllables which should, Shadow felt, have hurt her ears, but did not. She remembered demon speech and it was like fire in the ears—this new possession seemed to mitigate it. She whispered a prayer.

Some distance away, Shadow could see the stamen-core of the flower, burning molten into the sand, which fused around it. Runnels of vitrification spread outwards. Shadow got to her feet and stood beside the demon. She would have taken action herself, but the stamen was cooling, more rapidly than it should have, fading into blue and then growing ashen and black.

"That's all I can do," Gremory said.

"What about Elemiel?"

"What about him? He isn't here."

"His house was."

The demon laughed. "He doesn't need a house. It's just an affectation. What interests me is the target."

"I was in a flower attack a few days ago," Shadow said.

"I heard. In the Medina." The demon smiled her slanted smile. "Looks like you've attracted someone's attention."

Shadow sighed. "That's been happening a lot lately."

She waited out the rest of the night with the veil at maximum thickness. No point in tempting fate—she felt she'd done quite enough of that lately. The demon squatted on her heels nearby, her gaze fixed on the crumbling ash of the stamen. She did not move; as before, she might as well have been carved from stone.

Towards dawn, a faint wind rose up, stirring eddies of loose sand and scattering the ash of the stamen. Shadow watched it crumble, flaking away and skittering across the desert floor. Apart from the glassy sand around it, it might never have existed, a brief, violent dream. With a rustle of robes, the demon stood. Rather to Shadow's relief, she did not appear in search of breakfast.

"So," Gremory said. "The angel has not returned and it looks like someone's trying to kill you. I suggest we return to the city."

Shadow gave a slow nod. She was reluctant to let matters stand, but they seemed to have reached a dead end. "What about the possession?" she asked. Gremory gave her a long, contemplative look.

"I'll see what else can be done. For the moment, make the most of it."

From the sound of it, Gremory was in a terrible mood. There was an eyeblink flicker. The demon sat before her, riding in state on the back of the black camel.

"Hang on," Shadow said. "Which one of those are you?"

The demon looked puzzled. "Both."

The camel knelt, looking at her out of a knowing eye. "Which eyes do you see out of, then? Both sets?"

The camel nodded. Unnerved, Shadow climbed up behind the human half of the demon and the camel wheeled around, heading out of the rising sunlight.

They had been travelling for about an hour, with the sun strengthening at Shadow's back, when the mirage first shimmered up on the western horizon. At first, Shadow thought it was the city itself and frowned, wondering how they'd covered so much ground so quickly. Then, as the image grew clearer, she realised it was an illusion, conjured out of heat and sand and air.

It appeared to be a fortress, rising sheer out of the desert floor. She could see the castellated turrets, the massive battlements. It looked like something the crusaders might have left. A flag, bearing a device like a spiked golden wheel, snapped above the fortifications and she saw the glint of metal—armour? weapons?—on the battlements themselves, catching the sunlight for a moment before flicking out of view. The walls were of sandstone, a warm ruddy gold.

The demon slowed. Her gait became sidling, circuitous, but then she moved on. As they drew closer to the mirage, Shadow began to understand the reason for her hesitation: this image, out of air, looked very solid. Then, as they grew nearer still, she saw that it *was* solid. Her new senses, borrowed from the spirit, caught sight of wisps and curls of mist moving with purpose along the terraces.

"What the hell?"

"We're too visible," Gremory said. "Get down."

Shadow slid off. Next moment, the demon was standing beside her, this time in her human form alone. Gremory took hold of the cloak and cast it outwards. It billowed on the air, a pale, transparent red, covering them both.

"It's like your veil," the demon explained.

Shadow nodded. They walked down the slope towards the fortress. Up close, she could see the immense blocks of stone from which it had been fashioned. It was far larger than it should have been, and she could only presume that it was some relic from a story, inexplicably made manifest here in the middle of the desert. There were still no signs of life, only the faint traces of mist above them. But Shadow could not help but feel they were being watched.

Any question as to how they might get into the fort was rendered immaterial by the fact that the great doors at the base of the rock were wide open.

"Hmmm," the demon said. Shadow laughed.

"I don't know about you, but I'm not the trusting sort."

"This reminds me of something."

"It'll be a tale of some kind. I've been trying to think—it's familiar, but I don't know where it's from."

By now they were immediately under the archway. Soot-black curves of rock stretched above them and there was a sudden cool damp breath, out of the morning heat. Shadow saw a courtyard immediately ahead, sunlit, with a splashing fountain. The sound took her back to the Shah's courtyard and she shivered in the coolness. The demon shot her a sharp red glance.

"What is it?"

"Memory. I don't think we should go further."

"I want to see," Gremory said.

They walked on, cautious. Shadow hesitated, but it seemed that the demon's mind was made up and Shadow did not want to risk heading back to the city without her. She could see diamonds of light about the fountain; they reminded her of the spirit, fracturing. It was not a welcome recollection. The demon's veil cast a rosy light over everything, a distraction. But the courtyard was empty of everything except the fountain and a small striped cat, washing itself.

"Hello," Shadow said.

"Don't talk to it. You don't know what it might be."

A fair point coming from a shapeshifting camel, Shadow thought. The cat glanced up incuriously and rose, sauntering into the dark colonnade which surrounded the courtyard. This was the middle of the building. Above the low colonnade the walls rose straight up for several hundred feet. Looking up was like looking down a well, and gave Shadow a moment of vertigo. They followed the cat under the colonnade. Here, in the shadows, a series of doors and steps led upwards. At the top of the stairs, the demon suddenly hauled Shadow back so hard that she stumbled.

"Sorry," Gremory said, perfunctorily. Ahead, a landing opened out into a high, airy room, with unglazed windows which should have been open to the sky. The entire room was filled with sticky red strands, undulating faintly as if in a draught. They glistened.

"What is it?"

"I don't know. Don't touch them."

Shadow did not need to be told. They moved on, finding the same strange threads filling other rooms, and stretching out above their heads to the ceiling of the passages. There was no discernible smell that Shadow could detect, but the threads looked alarmingly like bloody sinews—fibrous tendons connecting bones to tissue more properly found inside a living creature, not inhabiting a fortress.

═══Thirty-six═══

Deed was speaking to the Librarian's blood. He crouched in front of an alembic, watching as the liquid it contained bubbled and congealed. He had already added the substances that would precipitate the *nigredo* to it—eking out the blood with a fluid condenser—and had carefully scraped the resulting residue from the bottom of the retort. He was now well into the second stage of the process. Around him, the boards of the chamber crackled with spells, keeping any wards contained within the Librarian's blood well within bounds. He doubted that Mercy Fane herself knew they were there, or what the oaths that she had taken had produced. Deed smiled, imagining Mercy as young, ardent, keen, and completely ignorant of what she was actually letting herself in for. The Skein had, Deed was forced to admit, certainly done a pretty effective number on their personnel. If Mercy knew what her initiation had done, and how it had changed her, he wondered whether she would be so zealous in her defence of the Library. Perhaps she would. People, Deed was the first to admit, were weird.

He dropped the preparation of powdered blood into a nearby crucible and took a pipette. With this, a drop of the boiling blood was added, along with a preparation of fuller's earth and copper. Deed, murmuring under his breath, added elements to the mixture until an unwholesome sludge formed in the bottom of the crucible. Not promising. Never mind, thought Deed. There were more ways than one if this didn't work.

Deed recited a long sequence of spells with ease. Disir memory was long, and retentive, especially when combined with human powers of analysis. Then he placed the crucible back over the flame and waited for a moment. The crucible sparked and crackled with momentary electricity and something began to rise and flex in the base. Deed stood back, and watched with satisfaction.

⊷Thirty-seven⊷

Mercy looked at the Court from the vantage point of the Library steps. On returning from the Northern Quarter, they had come straight back to the Library and the late afternoon sun was strong, falling clear as honey over the surfaces of the buildings and the marble of the square, imbuing it with a lucidity that made it almost transparent. It was a relief to be out of the northern part of the city, away from the snow. The Western Quarter felt almost tropical. The sun was going down over the Western Ocean: she could see it in a gap between the buildings, making the sea molten. It was not long till dusk.

She had no intention of telling anyone what she was planning, only Perra, who had seen Mareritt and heard what Salt had to say, but the *ka* kept its own counsel. She could feel the geas at the back of her head: a magical engine, driving her on. Infuriating, but she'd tried everything she could think of to dislodge it and nothing had worked. Followed by the silent Perra, she took the staircase up to the summit of the building and a view of the Court: the black façade, shadowy in the sunlight, and the perpetual glitter of the golden vanes that rode the air above it, testing the direction of the magics that coiled around its eaves.

When she once more stepped out onto the roof of the Library, Mercy had woven a trail of thought, untraceable behind the solid walls of the Library itself, a trail of memory that would enable anyone who knew what they were doing to follow her. If necessary.

She hoped that wouldn't have to happen. What she was doing was risky, but it was the only way in, and daylight—just on the turn—was the safest time. Now, she hoped, with the onset of twilight, the Court would be preoccupied with closing its main entrance and reaffirming its wards, rather than with what might be happening on its roof.

Mercy perched on the roof of the Library, steadying herself on the arm of a stone spirit. The spirit gazed sightlessly out across the city; a sculpture that had been old when the world was young. It had come with the Library from Egypt, a human figure with a bird's head. The beak had long since worn away, impossible to tell now whether it had been hawk or ibis or owl. Mercy had studied it before, and sometimes when it rained, she thought she detected the gleam of life in its sightless eyes, like a flicker of movement at the bottom of a pool.

It was not raining now. The sun was a line of flame above the horizon and as she watched it slipped below the world into night. Behind her, above the Eastern Quarter, the sky was already deepening to aquamarine. On the stone spirit's shoulder crouched the *ka*.

Mercy took her notes from her pocket. She had jotted down a number of things relating to the Court: old tales, ancient stories. No poems, though, although she had found several; they were too unstable for the purpose she had in mind. Glancing down at her notes, she began to speak.

" . . . *and there was a guild of Magicians, who summoned demons from the storms of the air* . . .

Once upon a time, there was a boy . . .

The nature of the Lemegeton is this, that it is the word of Solomon the King . . .

She did not know who the old man might be, but . . .

. . . *and the conjuror took his handkerchief out of his pocket and from it, he brought a dove* . . . "

As she spoke, she looked out across the air. A fragile bridge of words was beginning to link the summit of the Library with the golden-vaned rooftop of the Court. Mercy spoke on, weaving words into the air, drawing in the last of the light to power her tale, rendering it into a storyway: a story of a boy and a magician and a dove. No demons, though: she didn't want to take the risk. The *ka* stirred, restless, on the stone spirit's shoulder. When she was sure that the story had taken form, Mercy stepped out onto the storyway, praying to the stone spirit behind her that it would bear her weight.

The storyway held. Mercy stepped out onto words, snatches of phrase, trailing sentences. She walked a careful tightrope, not looking down, although the sparkling sunlit cradle beneath her, woven out of the lastlight, would conceal her from view from below.

And from the Court? Well, hopefully.

She did not look back, and did not know whether Perra was following. But when she stepped onto the battlement of the House of the Court, still shrouded in story, she looked down to see the *ka* at her feet.

Behind her, the story faded into the dusk. Mercy tensed but there were no sirens, shrieks, betraying cries, even though both her feet were now balancing on the parapet. She glanced back to see the stone spirit directly opposite, several hundred yards away. She thought she must have imagined the look of disapproval on its weathered face.

Not wanting to speak aloud, she motioned to the *ka*. The parapet led onto a sloping roof, mazed with spell-vanes. Golden griffins, dragons, cockerels spun in the twilight breeze. Mercy tasted magic on her tongue; the flavours of fire and nutmeg, of charcoal and iron and wood smoke. She tasted metal, the alchemical drift of currents slipping up between cracks in the floorboards below, between the tiles. She smelled roses and ash, myrrh and pine resin, and weaving between the spell-vanes she saw a drift of colours against the twilight air: azure and gold, jade and swallow's-wing indigo.

The trick was to avoid these tides of magic. She did not want to run the risk of sending something back, disturbing a trace and advertising her presence on the roof. She stepped cautiously, taking care that her sleeve should not brush the spines of the spell-vanes. Mercy knew they could not see her, although their golden eyes seemed to follow her, knowingly. She breathed spells of invisibility, drawing disguise from the air, but she knew that these would not last for long. The *ka* padded ahead, wings carefully furled.

At the far side of the roof stood a turret. It had no door, being open to the four winds. Symbols of coloured glass hung in each quarter: blue, green, yellow, red, turning lazily in the wind and catching the light from a lamp that hung beneath the eaves of the turret. Cautiously, Mercy ducked under the arch. The turret was wider than it appeared and a set of stone steps led downwards in a spiral. Mercy looked at Perra, mouthed, *Ready?*

Side by side, they began to descend the stairs.

Halfway down, Mercy and Perra heard footsteps, coming up. There was nowhere to hide. Mercy cursed, and brought the sword up. The footsteps turned away, into a lower room. Mercy exhaled. Quickly, they padded down the stairs and onto a narrow landing.

The Court was a maze, labyrinthine passages and very little sense of symmetry. It was impossible to tell where they were in the building: they went up steps, down steps, through doorways and around sudden sharp corners. Once Mercy heard voices and retreated, retracing her steps, but the rooms here looked completely different and she began to despair of ever finding her way out again, let alone of locating a lock that Mareritt's key fit. She whispered her concerns to Perra.

"Ask it," the *ka* advised.

Feeling foolish, Mercy did so.

"Straight on," sang out a small, metallic voice, obligingly. Raising an eyebrow, Mercy followed its instructions, which began to come more and more quickly. The key led them down further flights of stairs, through empty chambers, skirting the sound of voices, footsteps, the sudden whir of machinery. Mercy was used to the convoluted corridors of the Library, but the Library possessed a harmony, a unifying conception of architecture that made it feel as though you ought to know where you were, even if you didn't. The Court, in comparison, was cramped or overtly spacious, too dark or lit by searing lamplight. Its proportions were wrong and nothing seemed even. Mercy wondered whether this was to confuse visitors, or its occupants. The atmosphere was filled with competing magics: sigils which hissed and spat at one another like warring cats from opposing doorways, bristling wards which raked the skin with icy needles or which scored with scorches of flame. The House of the Court seemed made of dark oak, worn stone, ancient glass, and to Mercy's trained Librarian's eye it breathed out stories. She could detect the scraps and tatters of legend embedded in the framework of the building, imprisoned and jammed together in an enforced attempt at control.

"Left!" sang the key, and Mercy obeyed.

⊷═◉ ◉═⊶

Deed stood back, pleased with his endeavours. The thing was taking shape, curdling and writhing in the crucible. As he watched, the eyes opened in the rudimentary head, a dull toad-gold.

Deed squatted down on his heels to bring himself level with the crucible.

"Can you hear me?"

A pause. Then the thing gave a slow nod.

"And clearly you can understand," Deed said. "Good. I want you to listen carefully. There's something I want you to do . . . "

"Where now?" Mercy asked the key. They were standing in front of an old oak door, black with age or fire. The door, which was closed, lay at the end of a passage, which smelled of damp stone.

"This is my door," the key sang.

"Oh!" Mercy said. She looked down at the *ka*. "Did you hear that?" Exhilarated by the discovery, but knowing it would be a mistake to be too gung-ho, she asked the key, "What's behind the door?"

"The library."

Good.

"Is there anyone likely to be in there?" she asked the key. Presumably not, if the door was locked, but you never knew. They could have locked it from the inside and it was doubtful that this was the only key.

"I do not know."

The geas twitched inside her mind. Bending, Mercy slipped the key into the lock. It fitted and the lock turned. Mercy stepped through into the library of the Court.

Deed leaped back as the glass of the crucible shattered. Like birth, he supposed, with an element of the violent and bloody about it. The homunculus, toad-eyes blinking, spat a sliver of glass from its mouth and sprang to the floor.

"Go, then," Deed hissed. He brought down the black-handled knife and the wards around the apparatus fell noiselessly away.

The homunculus raced towards the open window and shot out into the night.

"Homing instinct," Deed murmured. He reached out an arm and swept the glass shards to the floor.

If she'd stepped into the room with her eyes closed, Mercy would have recognised it as a library. It had something to do with the weight of the air, with the quality of soundlessness inside the room. But she had no intention of closing her eyes and the purpose of the room was evident from the rows of stacked books. Most were leather-spined and cracked with age, their gilt peeling, although she noticed a row of scrolls, piled edge on.

Mercy took a deep breath. This wasn't just a private library. These were the books The Great Library of Worldsoul had failed to procure, the books which fell through cracks in realities, the books which were the most dangerous of all. This room contained grimoires: she could tell that by their iron-blood-charcoal smell and the wincing sensation of her skin, as though spiders walked across her flesh. These were the books of magic and sacrifice, of punishment and control. Some of these books, like the text from which the disir had sprung, would be bound with human skin flayed from a living victim. Mercy had met several books of which she was actively afraid, and a number which merely made her nervous. She did not, yet, know which category the books in this library would fall into.

Mareritt had said: *You'll know when you see it.* Not very helpful, thought Mercy, but she was here now and she had to try, so she stepped further into the library and began to work her way as quickly and methodically as possible along the stacks. Even the shelves here were enchanted, made of bog oak and bound with silver and iron bands on which rows of runes had been inscribed.

She recognised these as aggressive wards, a level of protection which the Library for which she worked rarely deployed: she could think of only a couple of cases. Something, or someone, had died to make sure that the contents of these books remained contained within those shelves. When she had come through the door, all manner of complex magics had reworked themselves around her, responding to the crucial presence of the key; if she had not been wielding that, she doubted whether she would now be still alive.

She concentrated at first on the scrolls, but they felt dead, or very inactive. That was probably a good thing, and she moved on to study the spines of a dark-bound set of books standing on a neighbouring shelf. All grimoires, but at the far end of the shelf beyond, the geas gave a violent start, like a startled horse, and in front of her she found a book with a bind-rune stamped on its skin cover and a title: *The Winter Book*. Bulls-eye! She took the book cautiously down from the shelf and opened it.

The book was written in what looked like Danish. From the scrolled gilt on its leather cover, she thought it was probably Victorian.

Perra said, "Someone is coming."

"Shit!" Mercy had, with the assistance of the key, locked the door behind her, but Perra was right, she could hear shuffling sounds outside. She tucked *The Winter Book* under her jacket, darted to the end of the library and took refuge behind a stack. The library was relatively dimly lit, though Mercy could not see why, and hopefully large enough to avoid the person.

The door opened. Footsteps came along one of the rows, then stopped. Mercy held her breath. She didn't think it was the same row from which she had taken the book and she hoped *The Winter Book* would keep its pages shut: books had been known to shout out before now. It must be nice, she thought bitterly, to live in a place like Earth, where inanimate objects didn't have their own opinions. A jumbled montage of stories—millstones and necklaces and spinning wheels that shouted, "Help! Help!" when stolen—rapidly crossed Mercy's mind's eye. It was all Earth's fault, anyway, for being a place where folk had imaginations. She clutched the book a little more tightly, but it did not speak.

The person was coming along the stacks. Mercy didn't have any great impression of stealth, but if the person suspected she was there, why didn't they simply accost her? Although it wasn't like the Court to do things in an obvious manner.

The footsteps—a quick clicking tapping sound—abruptly stopped. Mercy looked down and saw that Perra was as still as a hunting cat. Only the tip of the *ka's* leonine tail was twitching. She could hear a second, smaller ticking sound, but she did not know what that was. She was reminded of beetles, of bombs. She took a breath and peered, very cautiously, around the edge of the stack.

A woman stood further down the row, tapping a fountain pen against her teeth. It was this that had produced the clicking sound. The woman was young, with ice-blond hair bound up in a chignon. Her face was wide at the forehead, tapering to a pointed chin. As if she was aware of Mercy watching, she turned for a moment and looked down the row. Mercy caught her breath but the woman's expression was absent, as if thinking. Her eyes, wide set, were a cold blue. She wore a black suit: a hobble skirt and a ruffled black jacket with a high collar. A cameo brooch clasped it at the neck; Mercy wondered what the cameo showed.

And high heels. With a sudden jolt, Mercy saw that the woman was not wearing shoes. Her bare ankles, visible beneath the long skirt, were pale skinned and extended to long spurs of spined bone. Her toes were talons. Appalled, Mercy looked at the girl's hands; they, too, had long iron-coloured nails.

She heard the library door open and close. Someone said, "Darya?"

A male voice that slid across the skin. Mercy remembered the voice, a soothing doctor's tone that reassured and held promises. Promises that were then violated.

"Abbot General?" Darya sounded nervous. Mercy was not entirely surprised.

"What are you looking for?" Deceptively casual.

"Why, I—just an idea."

"What sort of idea?"

Darya was silent. Mercy saw her take a teetering step backwards on those bony spines of heels.

"What sort of idea, Darya?"

"About the Library. I remember—I heard something once . . . "

Mercy instantly felt herself on the attack. It wasn't a rational thing, but a magical one: an instinct which stemmed directly from the vows that she'd made at her initiation. Any attack on the Library was an attack on a Librarian, and Darya's comments could not bode well. It didn't quite work the other way, but it was close. She forced herself to remain still but her fingers itched to move towards the sword. Beside her, Perra gave her a warning glance.

"Enterprising, Darya," Deed said. "Did I sanction this search?"

Mercy saw the girl become very still. "I thought—"

"Thinking's good," Deed said softly, and he reached out and drew a sigil in the air above Darya's brow. The girl wavered, as if a line of light had passed through her and her expression grew blank. Mercy saw Deed reach out and pluck something from the centre of Darya's forehead, before the glowing green sigil faded. Then he turned and slipped out of the library without a backward glance.

Darya swayed and her face shuddered, showing sharp bones beneath the skin. Mercy thought: *disir*. And as if she had spoken the word aloud, the girl's head came up and her lips bared back in a hound's grimace. Long teeth slid out of her upper jaw and the bones of her face began to shift and slip, the skin moulding itself to the new structure beneath.

Mercy rammed the book more securely into her jacket and drew the Irish sword.

⊸Thirty-eight⊸

By now, Gremory and Shadow had climbed to the top of the fortress. They avoided the red threads filling every room and snaking along the passageways, and kept to the stairs, which were bare of the red material and made of stone. Narrow slit windows, the kind from which arrows could be fired, pierced the staircase at intervals and Shadow glanced out of these as they climbed. She realised, from these glimpses, that the landscape around them was changing.

"Look at that," she said to the demon. Gremory came down a step or two and stood beside her.

"What do you see?"

"The desert's not the same." She did not think it was the sight that the spirit's presence had lent her.

Gremory smiled as if a theory had been confirmed. "You're right. It isn't."

They had come across pale golden sand, from the ridges of Elemiel's shattered beehive hut. Looking back, however, the desert was now made of black and red grit, with high undulating ridges of dark shale. Shadow could see some kind of equipment in the distance from which they had come, like a mining rig. It was not moving, but it had certainly not been there when they'd crossed the desert the day before, or that morning. Further away, a huge metal wheel stood, also unmoving, below one of the ridges.

The demon, to Shadow's alarm, appeared nonplussed. "This is new to me. Although I'll confess it's why I came up here.

There are stories . . . a fortress, from which you can see different times. I've never seen this kind of country before."

"Not even where you come from?"

The Duke of Hell gave a snort. "My country is nothing like this. It is magnificent—the oceans of fire, the iron cities, the massed legions with their banners. Nothing like this little landscape."

"I do not think I would last long in Hell," Shadow said.

"You are not a demon or a devil, an ifrit or a spirit, it's true. But do not be too sure. Your new passenger might give you some immunity." Gremory's red gaze slid to Shadow's face. "Perhaps I will take you there."

"We've got to get out of here first," Shadow said, concealing alarm.

They climbed higher, checking on the changing land through the windows. Two storeys up, it had altered again, becoming darker, the ground changing to a plain of slate. The machinery had gone but a second fort stood in the distance, as grey as a great ship and with the spires of radio masts at its summit. Shadow had never seen anything like it before, either, and said so. The demon was silent.

Eventually, they reached the top of the fortress. Here, it was blisteringly hot, but the wind occasionally lashing the summit in eddies was cold as ice. Shadow shivered. This was no place for humans and she wondered anew who had built the fortress, or whether it was the outer carapace of something living. The red threads reminded Shadow of seaweed, drifting in the world's tide.

The top of the fortress was a flat paved surface, surrounded by battlements. Shadow and the demon walked across to the edge and looked down. Gremory did not seem to suffer from vertigo, but Shadow was obliged to hold on to the edges of the stone, warm under her hands, and reassuring. From here, the view was once more very different.

She was looking out over a garden. The desert had retreated and was only visible at the edges, where a line of ochre stone showed above the foliage. Beneath, at the foot of the fort, radiating lines of trees reached outwards like a wheel, and it was only this symmetry that told Shadow she was not looking out over a forest. But the trees were not saplings; they were fully mature, their canopies arching up towards the sky in full leaf. From this height, however, they looked as tiny as toys. Shadow could see something moving methodically between them: a small dark figure.

Beyond these trees stretched others, but they did not seem to have been planted with planned regularity. She could see groves and clusters, with lines of pale grass in between. These trees, too, were in full growth, with high arched branches and scatters of green, gold, and flame-coloured leaves. The air, drifting up from the garden, smelled warm and fragrant, heavy with pollen. Shadow thought she could almost hear the distant humming of bees. She did not know if it was the spirit's senses that made the colours so vivid, the scents so strong. It was as if every colour contained a thousand shades within it, too rich for a human to comprehend. Shadow took a breath and felt dizzy. She stepped back.

"Where is it?"

"I—" the demon stopped.

"Gremory. Do you know?"

"I think so. But I'm not sure."

"Where, then?"—but the Duke shook her head.

"I won't name it. If I say its name, it might secure it—like an anchor."

"It looks pretty secure already to me," Shadow said. "And there's someone down there. But if we go down, will it change?"

"I don't know."

A thought struck Shadow.

"Tell me what you see."

"I see a garden. It's full of decay; everything is rotting. The trees are dying and I can see bones in the grass. It's quite magnificent, actually. An excellent place to spend a quiet Sunday afternoon. Why? What do you see?"

"Not the same thing."

"No," the Duke said. "I didn't think so."

On the far side of the fortress, they found a flight of steps, leading down. There must have been a thousand or more.

"After you," Gremory said.

Rather sourly, Shadow lowered herself over the little break in the battlements and began her descent. She half expected the landscape below to alter, reversing itself back into desert, but to her surprise the garden stayed put. She was now worried that they'd become stuck: there had been no sign of the city from the other side of the fortress and given its height, there should have been. Nor had she been able to see the Devil's Ears, or Ator's hut, beyond the limits of the garden.

But as they descended, the garden became more vivid, its features more pronounced. She could still see the figure moving between the trees but it showed no signs of having seen either her or the demon. Just as well. The scent rising from the garden was still overpowering: Shadow detected roses and lilies, the heady musks of jasmine and frangipani. She wondered, from the demon's description, whether it was somehow designed to be appealing to whoever beheld it: perhaps Gremory was assailed by the odours of blood and forges and smoke. She asked.

"You would not wish to know," the Duke said, her eyes glittering.

"I was just curious."

Soon, they reached the final flight of steps and Shadow could feel the muscles of her calves vibrating as though they were the strings of a harp. She was in good physical condition, but even so, it had been a long way up to the top of the fortress and it was a long way down again, too. She felt she would be lucky to be able to stand once she reached the ground and, indeed, her first step was a stagger. Gremory caught her arm in a grip like a steel band.

"Take care. This is not a good point to show weakness."

Grimly, Shadow nodded. She could see a shape moving beyond the trees: that distant figure. It would have been nice to think that it was just a gardener, but in Shadow's experience, things rarely worked out under the category of "nice."

There was no sign of desert sand beneath her feet. Instead, thick grass covered the ground, a dense vivid green and somehow unnatural. Shadow was not sure whether this could be attributed to her new senses or to something about the place itself. She could see cushions of moss and small starry flowers in the grass: there seemed to be a richness of species, as if different ecological layers had folded themselves into one particular space. Then her vision, quite suddenly, narrowed down so that she could see a tiny ant labouring up one of the blades of grass. Definitely the spirit's sight, she thought, with its spatial differentials. With Gremory, she skirted the trees, trying to keep out of sight of the gardener.

She thought it had worked, until they were quite far into the orchard. Shadow did not recognise the fruit that grew on the trees: the leaves were like an apple's, but the fruit was oval, small, the colour of sunsets, and they emitted a strong pungent fragrance.

"Do you know what they are?" she asked Gremory in an undertone.

"Don't eat the fruit," the demon replied.

"But you can see them, yes?"

"Yes. They grow on bones."

Clearly Gremory was still apprehending the garden in a somewhat different way.

Shadow was tempted to pick one of the fruits, but reason told her this would be insane. She moved in and out of the trees, zigzagging, then movement caught her eye. She turned. To her dismay, the gardener was watching her.

It was a hunched, dark shape. The shoulders were massive in proportion to the rest of its body, tapering to a narrow waist and strong legs. She could see the small dark eyes, whiteless in its broad face. It looked more like an ape than a man, something primitive and ancient. It was watching her with a stillness that suggested intelligence, however, and when it saw that she had observed it, it began to bound forwards with long, loping strides.

Shadow drew her blade. She was conscious of the demon turning beside her, but Gremory's hands remained at her sides. The gardener leaped. Shadow threw herself to the side, rolling out and down. Teeth snapped along her arm, grazing her sleeve and she thickened her veil to maximum across her shoulders and head. An arm like a club shot out and struck, knocking a numbing blow over her left shoulder. Her left arm grew limp; ignoring it Shadow feinted, then lashed out with the sun-and-moon blade. It hit home, just beneath the gardener's collarbone, but there was no blood, just a small powdery shower. The thing's lips, rubbery black like a dog's, pulled back from its teeth and it gave a soundless growl, a vibration which Shadow felt rather than heard. Behind it, the demon took a dancing, mincing step backwards. Shadow took a chance and threw the blade. It struck the creature in the centre of its throat and should have severed the windpipe. The creature gave a breathy cough and spat something out into the grass: it looked like a small leaden cube. Shadow reached down and snatched it up with a corner of the veil, not wanting it to make contact with her skin. Then the creature fell apart. Its head burst like a melon dropped from a turret; its chest exploded, fragmenting outwards until only the legs were left, twin crumbling trunks which tottered and fell. Soon, the only thing left was clots of soil, dark in the greenness of the grass.

"Thanks for your help," Shadow said sarcastically to the demon. Gremory shrugged.

"I didn't want to steal your kill. You looked like you had it under control."

"Well," Shadow said, wiping the earthy blade on the grass. "Maybe I did."

Thirty-nine

Darya's transformation was over almost as soon as it had begun. The teeth drew back, the bone structure returned to human-normal. Mercy's hand, clasping the hilt of the sword, relaxed by degrees. Darya bent and swiftly took a book from the lowest shelf, near the back. She gave the impression that she knew what she had come for. She placed it inside her ruffled jacket and went quickly from the library. After a moment's consideration, Mercy followed.

She knew relatively little about the lives of the members of the Court. Unlike Librarians, and other functionaries, they were a closed order, living mainly within the Court itself and its satellite houses. Their initiation practices were a closely guarded secret and said to be grim, but everyone said that about their own initiations, with a kind of magical machismo, so it was hard to know what to believe. As with any closemouthed system, rumours about it were rife.

Still, during the years of the Skein, the Court had contributed substantially to the upkeep of the city, working in many instances alongside the Library itself and reining in the more elaborate or obtrusive stories. Several rogue bits of legend had been tracked down by Court magicians and stuffed back into their ontological places, in more than one case saving the city itself from disaster. There was known to have been some exchange of manuscripts.

With the disappearance of the Skein, matters had gone downhill to some degree. Mercy supposed that this was only to be expected: two powerful organisations, plus a power vacuum at the top, do potential chaos bring. But because she had not been involved with the Court directly, and because the Elders of the Library would naturally not be inclined to confide issues of higher policy to their underlings, she wasn't entirely sure how far things had gone.

She pursued Darya at a distance through another maze of passages. She had quickly lost any ability to discern direction and the lack of windows did not help. Darya was, however, heading upwards and this was helpful, if only because it reassured Mercy that she was heading back towards the roof.

A few minutes later, Darya dived through a doorway and vanished. Mercy, hovering at the entrance of the door, was surprised to hear the sound of weeping, although it took her a moment to work out what this was. It sounded like a gull or a mewing cat rather than anything human.

She peered through the door. Darya sat on a low couch, her face buried in her hands. When at last she looked up, staring sightlessly at the wall, Mercy saw that her face was sliding back towards disir: she no longer looked human. Miserable Darya might be, but Mercy had no intention of having her throat torn out in a misguided attempt at consolation. She shrank back against the wall. The sobbing died away to a hoarse rasp like the sound of a saw, then silence.

Mercy once more looked around the corner of the door. Darya was lying on the couch as though she had been thrown there. The tight skirt had ridden up over her long, spiny legs and her hair was a tangle. She looked like a broken doll and if Mercy had found another woman like that, she would have suspected rape at the very least. But she was sure that there had been no one else in the room.

"Perra," she mouthed. "Watch for me."

The *ka* gave a single nod. Mercy slipped into the room, holding her breath. The book which Darya had taken from the library lay on the floor by the couch; it had fallen from her jacket. Her heart hammering, Mercy whisked it up and fled from the room.

At the end of the corridor she slowed, expecting to hear the disir girl coming after her, but the passage was silent. Perra murmured, "We are close to the roof. Do you see?" A narrow window above the landing showed a sliver of moon and a curve of stone: one of the eaves of the House of the Court.

Mercy exhaled. "Good. Let's get out of here."

She reached up and grasped the windowsill, then pulled herself up. After a moment's grappling, she managed to force the window open. A gushing wind immediately rushed through. Mercy swore.

"Come *on*, Perra!"

The *ka* flowed through the open window and Mercy squeezed after it, turning so that her legs were dangling back into the stairwell. She eased herself out backwards, arching her back so that she was, for a moment, aware of a dizzying glimpse of the inverted city. There was the bulk of the Library, the domes of the Western Quarter and far away, the silver line of the sea. As she started to draw her legs up, there was a sudden blazing pain in her ankle.

"Shit!" Mercy kicked out. The pain decreased and, clinging to the frame, she went backwards out of the window. Her legs were now free, but razor sharp teeth sank into her hand. Mercy bit back a scream, mindful of an entire building full of Court magicians below and herself a trespasser. The thing that had bitten her also squealed, though a mouthful of flesh. She could see the thing: a hideous wizened face that was yet, somehow, in miniature her own. It had her wide brow and a flow of black hair. She didn't have room to draw the sword. Instead, she wrenched her hand free in a spray of blood and whipped one of the sharpened pins out of her knot of hair. Her first stab at the thing missed as it dodged, but her second connected. She stabbed the thing through one eye and a terrible pain assailed her own.

"Damnit!"

Someone—probably Deed—had made a homunculus of her. When it hurt, so would she, and vice versa. But the alternative was to give into the pain, let the thing bite her fingers off and fall from the roof to the stone flags a thousand feet below. Not much contest *there*. Mercy drew a breath, gripped the windowsill as tightly as she could, whipped both books out of her jacket and stashed them on the windowsill. Then she rammed the pin through the homunculus' brain.

The pain was too much. She heard it shriek as it shrivelled around the pin. The burn inside her head was overwhelming: it numbed her fingers and she let go of the sill. As she dropped past the upper windows of the House of the Court, mercifully, she blacked out.

⇌Forty⇌

Shadow had become paranoid about the earth on which they walked. It was all very well preparing oneself from attack by unknown spirits, but what about the ground itself? She expected at any moment that it would rise up and assault her.

Gremory seemed prone to no such fears. She appeared amused, occasionally smiling satirically at things that Shadow was unable to see, as though she walked through a private world. Shadow found this annoying, but she did not want to anger her only ally, so she said nothing.

Once past the orchard, the garden was indeed beautiful, but it was overpowering. The flowers were too large and highly scented; the trees were immense. Shadow would not have described it as a garden of giants, but things were bigger than they should have been and this made her nervous. Looking back, the fortress itself had again altered: it stood in a series of high steps, like a ziggurat.

Eden. Babylon. Both? Shadow did not know; the legend of which this was a part was possibly too old to know much of, dating back to the very dawn of Earth's Fertile Crescent. There were signs of some kind of occupation, apart from the golem-gardener and the orchard rows. There were stone spires, like totems, but decorated with winged birds that might have been vultures, and they looked very old. They pricked something in Shadow's memory, something primal. She was inclined to avoid them, and did so.

And she felt they were being watched. When she asked Gremory, the demon simply shrugged again, as if this was a matter of no consequence. "I haven't seen anyone living. There are plenty of the dead."

"What do they look like?"

"Ancient. Their skulls are strange; their heads are too narrow. I think they are an earlier form of man."

"There were other peoples before the Flood, so it's said." She had once heard that, on Earth, a volcano in the region of Sumatra had wiped out three-quarters of the variants of the human species, leaving behind only their boring old ancestors.

Did these unknown plants and trees date from then, the dawning of the human world? Shadow wondered as she walked.

Some distance from the fortress, the trees began to thin out and eventually Shadow and the demon stepped into a glade that fanned outwards to become a valley. The sides were wooded, but faded into golden cliffs and finally, Shadow recognised an echo of the Great Desert through which they had travelled. The valley floor, perhaps a quarter of a mile wide, was grassland, with trees only at the edges, so that it resembled a natural park. Along the valley, a black rock jutted up from the grass, a boulder so dark that it resembled a fragment of night.

Gremory hissed when she saw it.

"What's the matter?"

"It's from the heavens. A meteorite."

"It's not the Ka'aba."

"No, another. Older. Still worshipped."

"We don't—" Shadow stopped. "Well, never mind. I don't see any signs of people."

They approached the black stone. It had fused with the surrounding earth, reminding Shadow of the flower strike that had destroyed Elemiel's hut. Something flickered along its length as Shadow thought this, and then the demon cried out.

"Shadow!"

She felt the scorch of it through the veil, but the veil itself saved her hair from catching fire. The thing shot over her head, rolling against the base of the rock. Shadow scrambled up; to her dismay, this was not another earth-creature. It was made of fire, a flicker of bright flame in a shift of rainbow colours. It smelled of hot metal. It turned to come at her again and Shadow ran.

Her first thought was to find water. Paper, scissors, stone . . . Metal trumps earth and water trumps fire. She needed a stream and she found one, but it was only a rivulet of water, a trickle, running between narrow crumbling banks in the grass. It was perhaps two feet wide and shallow, not enough to cover her. The thing hissed as it sprang and at its brightness, Shadow shut her eyes and stepped backwards over the stream. Then there was a sound like a crack of lightning and flame erupted behind Shadow's eyelids. She opened her eyes, half-blinded, to see only a thin wisp of smoke. Elemiel stood before her, with a flaming sword in his hand.

"Hello again," the Messenger said.

⊹═◉═⊱

"So this is—what? Your home?"

They sat by the stream. Shadow's feet were in cool water. Elemiel sat cross-legged in the grass. Some distance away, Gremory paced like a prowling cat, intent on her own thoughts.

"No. But I can come here."

"When we met you—"

"Still the same place. It's changed over time. Thirty thousand years or more."

Shadow eyed the Messenger with respect. "You're a long-lived species."

His smile was sad. "Too long."

"Your house has been destroyed, I'm afraid," Shadow told him, but she wondered whether this would really mean anything. After all, a garden had died; a desert had taken its place and that desert itself had shifted and changed so much as to be almost unrecognisable. He did not seem surprised.

"I know. Are you all right?"

"I think so. Were they aiming for me, or for you?"

"Both."

"So who's the enemy?"

"I said I'd show you. And so I will."

"The spirit—" Shadow began.

"Yes. I'm sorry. I did not succeed in what I set out to do; I've made matters worse for you."

She did not want to say: *it's all right*. It wasn't.

"I don't know what to do now," she said.

"Nor do I," the Messenger admitted. "But I think it's brought you here. That's a good thing and a bad thing."

"I don't like 'bad thing.'"

"Who does?"

Forty-one

Mercy woke to a room thronging with shadows. They hummed and whispered about her head, like a host of moths. Her skin crawled with them and there was a buzzing in her ears. But she knew what it meant. Unless she was greatly mistaken, it meant she was alive.

"*Ka*? Are you there?" she hissed. She did not want to speak Perra's name, not knowing who might be listening; a name could be used against its bearer. She waited, but there was only the sibilance of the shadows. Light was coming from somewhere, but it was diffuse. It was enough to see the flitting, flickering shades.

And the place stank. After a moment, Mercy decided she was not detecting this with her nose: it was more like a spiritual stench. She sat up. She did not seem to be restrained in any way, and this in itself was ominous, suggesting as it did that her captors did not need to place her in bonds as they were confident of her inability to escape.

Captors. Her hand hurt like hell. She remembered falling from the turret but not anything after that, although her back and the backs of her legs felt bruised. What had happened to the homunculus? Evidently not with her in the room, otherwise she doubted she'd be alive. If she had died, then so would it, but they were programmed to finish the job. It evidently didn't work the other way around, as she was fairly sure that she'd killed it, but then she was the original and it was just a copy.

Stiffly, she got off the low pallet on which she'd been lying and looked around the room. Enough light to see that it was an even square, windowless. She could see the faint rusty traces of sigils on the walls: a containment cell, then. But perhaps not usually for human beings. Then she turned and saw with a shock that ran electric through her that the light was coming from something's eyes.

They shone out, huge and a pallid yellow, from the other side of the room. As she stared, the head tilted. She could see it faintly: a long hairless skull, ridged with cartilage. Its body was white, with long arms hunched around its knees. When it was sure it had got its full attention, it uttered a shriek, leaped to its feet and threw a handful of something at her.

Mercy ducked and the stuff whistled over her head and splattered against the opposite wall. There was the sudden, overpowering smell of shit. The thing capered, ran up the opposite wall and clung, upside down, from the ceiling, where it gave voice to another gibbering shriek. It was at least the size of a man, but its arms were longer.

A shit-flinging monkey demon. Great.

Frantically, Mercy ran through a mental magical arsenal. The Irish sword had been removed and so had her hairpins. The charm was no longer in her ear and her ward bracelets had also been taken away. That left the tattooed sigils, which she had reaffirmed with a paste made of powdered myrrh and dragon's blood resin that morning. She clapped a hand to her brow, transferred the sigil to her palm and threw it. Her injured hand burned with its passage.

The sigil spiralled outwards like a throwing star. It stuck the monkey-demon full on and knocked it from the ceiling. Howling, it rushed forwards, its arms flailing. Mercy threw herself to the side and dodged under its arm, hurling herself to the other side of the room. She knew she could not keep this up indefinitely, but what was the alternative?

The monkey-demon turned with frightening speed. Mercy kicked it in the stomach, grabbed its wrist and threw. The demon sprawled to the floor but her move, which would have broken a human's arm, had merely twisted the demon's. Mercy saw its muscles rippling back into place as she watched. The thing grinned at her, displaying long yellow teeth. It wasn't quite a monkey, and not quite a man either.

"Nice try," it said, and buffeted her on the side of the head. Mercy went down, feigning more dizziness than she felt and kicked its feet from under it. It fell, sprawling, then reached out and grabbed her by the wrist. It was certainly as strong as a gibbon. It hauled her first to her feet and then off them. Its other hand came up, clasped her round the throat and banged her head against the wall. The room exploded into a firework of lights.

"That's enough," a voice said. Mercy was abruptly released.

"No! More!"

"Do as you're told." The man spoke perfunctorily, almost absent-minded. Still seeing stars, Mercy heard him cross the room. He bent down. "Nothing broken."

"No thanks to you."

"I wanted to see what you'd do," the man—Roke, Deed—said. "Now I've found out. Anyway, I rescued you in the first place, so be grateful. I'm Jonathan Deed, by the way, although you know me as Roke. If it wasn't for me, you'd be making a mess all over our nice courtyard."

"How did you do it?"

"Magical net." He squatted on his heels by her side. She could see him more clearly now, and he held a lantern.

"The Library took a major risk sending you here."

"I was acting on my own initiative."

An eyebrow was raised. "I don't think I believe you, though it's very public spirited to claim sole responsibility."

"You can put me through a truth process." Mercy had no idea what was involved in such a process, but she could guess that was beyond unpleasant. "I'm not lying."

"All right," Deed said. "I might do that. On the other hand, that rather begs the question that I actually care."

"Ah," Mercy said.

"Because it's a great excuse to pick a fight with the Library, you see, something I've been needing to do for some time."

"Thought so," Mercy croaked. "Now that the Skein have gone . . . "

"Be reasonable," Deed said, pained. "You can't have Librarians running a city. You'd spend all your time shushing people and cataloguing things. Forgive me, but you're not known in your profession for wide-ranging vision and overall perspective; you're more the fine detail sort."

Mercy said nothing to this, partly out of annoyance, and partly because she was secretly afraid he might be right.

"So what are you going to do?" she asked at last. "Keep me here?"

"No. This was just an experiment; we're not barbarians. As I said, I wanted to see what you'd so. That's what we do—we experiment. We're scientists, after all. Come with me."

He pulled her to her feet, not ungently, and ushered her ahead of him through the door. Mercy began planning strategy: a backwards kick, elbow to the face . . . But he was staying too far behind her, even when she deliberately slowed, and when she glanced over her shoulder she could see from his amused expression that he had read her mind.

She was expecting to be led to another cell. To her surprise, however, he took her into a parlour. Panelled walls, brocade seats, and a pianola. Very nice.

"Sit down. Would you like a scotch?"

"I—actually, yes."

Deed grinned. "Good girl. You've no chance of getting out of here, but if you cooperate, we'll see what we can do. Please don't take any of this personally."

"Likewise."

"You're angry about the theft of your blood. I can tell. Well, fair enough. I'd be cross, too."

"I can't blame you for taking an advantage. We're not on the same side."

"But you think we should be."

Mercy paused. As long as he thought she was working for the Library, and not for Mareritt . . . if he wanted an excuse to go up against the Library, he'd got one anyway, no matter what the truth was, and if she kept quiet about Mareritt it might give Mercy an advantage. She accepted the heavy crystal tumbler of whisky that he offered her, and took a sip. Peat-flavoured fire spread through her.

"Good whisky."

"It's a magician's drink," he said. "Like red wine. Claret."

She couldn't tell whether he was making a veiled threat or simply expounding a personal theory; oddly, she got the impression that it was the latter. He took a seat opposite her and sat comfortably, long legs stretched out in front of him. The ruff made it look, disconcertingly, as though his head had been cut off. An angular face, a thin mouth, not without humour. An oddly compelling face. She did not want to even think about going down that road.

"So," he said. "What were you looking for?"

"A book."

Again, the eyebrow was raised. "Because you don't have enough of your own?"

"That actually was part of the problem."

Deed laughed. "So what was this book about? Medieval drainage systems? Growing better cauliflowers? Marxist dialectic?"

Since she did not know what *The Winter Book* contained, Mercy decided to shake the tree of speculation and see what fell out.

"The disir."

His face did not change.

"I see."

"Do you? We had one in the Library."

"Did you? I don't imagine it's the sort of thing you'd want in a Library. I should think that the monkey-demon might even be a little higher on the desirability list."

"The disir didn't throw shit," Mercy said. "Though she did try to kill me."

"Perhaps not, then. So, a disir came to kill you and you decided that the best way to deal with this was to do some reading up. Why didn't you just call me and ask to borrow something?"

"Would you have lent it to me?"

"I might have, actually. Let this be a lesson to you, Miss Fane. Always ask your neighbours *before* burgling their premises."

"My apologies."

Deed waved a hand. "Doesn't matter. As I said, it's useful to me. So what did you find out about the disir?"

"They're old. They come from the Ice Age. They're not human but they were probably conjured up by some shaman or other, part of a story that we no longer possess."

"Fairy tales," Deed said. "That's the engine that runs this city, after all, isn't it? That's what drives us on. Was that all you discovered?"

"Yes."

"Well, I'll have to do some research," Deed said pleasantly. "And see what else I can find out for you."

⊰Forty-two⊱

The orchard fruit was not, Elemiel told her, safe to eat. But there were seeds and a number of bracket fungi that were edible. Shadow did not feel like eating them, despite Elemiel's assurances. There were no animals to hunt and at this, the demon pulled an expression that, after a minute, Shadow interpreted as eye rolling.

Night would soon fall, but that didn't matter, so the Messenger said, because there was a moon.

The moon, whenever they were, was a lot closer to the Earth than it subsequently became, at least in myth, as became apparent when it rolled up over the summit of the hill. This was a young moon, its face a little less starred with craters. Shadow felt a comfort in its light, and it made it easier to see where they were going.

Elemiel led them deeper into the valley, past the black stone. Shadow had interrogated him about the elementals: the earth spirit, the fire, thinking he must know them well. But the Messenger told her that the fire spirits were new.

"Only the gardeners are original. The golems. Ancient technology, rediscovered anew closer to your day."

"They have them in some quarters," Shadow said. "They're not always very reliable."

"They were designed to be close to the earth," the Messenger said, "and sung into submission, but in your time, most of those songs have been lost." He walked up over a lip of land and pointed. "This is where we start to climb."

There was a path leading up through the groves, into the hills. Shadow and Gremory followed, breathing in the scent of fir, still warm with the sun. Shadow could hear a nightingale, singing far below in the valley, and they came out into starlight.

"It's only safe to come here now," the Messenger said. "And even now, not very."

"Why?" Shadow asked.

"They're growing nightblooms. But most of the plants flower during the day."

"What sort of flowers?" Shadow asked, with a sudden prickle of suspicion.

"The sort you're afraid of." He guided her to the edge of the rocks. "Be careful."

She was looking down into a ravine. It was full of flowers, a garden in itself. The huge blooms were all folded, tightly as parasols. She was reminded of hibiscus, but each flower was the height of a man. The tip of the stamens protruded at the end of each curled flower, like an obscene tongue. She recognised them: she'd last seen one bury itself in the floor of the desert and destroy Elemiel's hut.

"This is where they come from? Are they natural? You said 'they' grow them. Who are *they*?"

"I'll show you. But keep close behind me—there are guards."

As they walked, Shadow was conscious of things moving around them through the darkness. She heard no voices, but once someone ran past them, disappearing swiftly down the valley. She nudged Elemiel, not wanting to speak, although it seemed impossible to her that whoever was out there could be unaware of their presence.

"They aren't interested in us," the Messenger said, in what seemed to Shadow to be an unnecessarily loud voice. "They don't know we're here."

"We're pretty obvious, Elemiel," Shadow said.

"They're not in the same story-stream. Look above you."

Shadow did so and saw that the stars overhead had changed their configuration again. The couple of constellations that she had recognised, low on the western horizon, had disappeared, but not enough time had elapsed for them to have sunk down below the rim of the world. These stars were new.

"That makes no sense, astronomically," she said aloud.

"This garden is where stories overlap," Elemiel replied. "You're not seeing the world as it ever was: you're in storytime now. Or more than story. Mythtime. In your city, there are many legends, but time doesn't shift so much. Here, it does. The people around us can't see us because I've taken the path that leads past the storystream. We're not in the same space. Look—"

For a moment Shadow saw a fleeting sequence of impressions: the garden itself, a desert city made of low domes and huge walls, buried in a terrible storm of sand. Then other settlements rising in its place, abandoned when tribes swept down from the north. She saw a battle, between people who looked scarcely human. Then djinn and demons, stalking the battlefield and devouring the spirits of the slain. She did not see Gremory among them, and was grateful.

After that, the desert bloomed again, as if the blood of the fallen had watered it, only to sink down into the sand once more. A ghost city arose, but was dispelled by a magician who could have been the grandfather of Suleiman the Shah. And then the familiar outlines of the Khaureg, the Great Desert that had lain beyond Worldsoul since the city's rise. Which was, Shadow was reminded now, relatively recent in the great scheme of things. She tried to pay no more attention to the beings that surrounded her in the darkness.

"The only thing you need to worry about is the guards," the Messenger said.

"How will I know when those appear?"

The Messenger laughed. "Don't worry. You'll know."

⟨Forty-three⟩

Mercy Fane had been confined to a secure room in the heart of the House of the Court: windowless and warded. Deed could have put her back in the dungeons with the devil-monkey, but it amused him to keep Mercy off balance. He suspected that she knew exactly what he was doing, but for now, it would do. He didn't want to have her killed, not just yet. She was too useful as a bargaining chip. The initial homunculus had disappeared, probably going to ground, rat-like, when Mercy had been captured but he had fresh blood with which to make another if the need arose.

He spent a peaceful night and rose at dawn to prepare a letter. This was on official Court parchment, with the identification sigils prominently displayed around its crest. It gave a brief account of recent events, more in sorrow than anger, and invited two of the Elders of the Library to visit their recalcitrant employee. Once that was done, Deed wrote in his letter, they could begin to discuss terms. Phrases like: . . . *long association between our two institutions . . . a pity if anything were to damage our hitherto excellent relationship . . . city as a whole taking a dim view of internecine rivalries at a time of crisis* . . . all rolled fluently from the tip of Deed's quill.

When he had finished the letter, he rolled it up, sealed it with the Court's usual method of bloodwax, and dispatched it by golem across the square. Then he sat back to wait.

He did not have to wait long. Mid-morning, a golem trundled back again. It thrust a sealed letter at Deed and waited, staring at him from incurious eyes.

"You may go," Deed told it and perused the reply. The tone of the reply pleased Deed. It read as if it had been written by someone unnerved, and Deed liked *unnerved*, particularly in an adversary. The Elders would, he read, meet with him as soon as they had received his reply confirming a time.

Deed cast a small astrological divination and discovered that, given the planetary alignments, two o'clock would do very well. He duly inscribed the appointed time in a second letter, summoned the golem, gave it the missive, tucked an instruction slip between its ridged jaws, and sent it on its way.

He then went down to visit his captive. "I hope you spent a comfortable night?"

"Yes," the Librarian said blandly. "Thank you for providing me with a book."

She was sitting in an armchair, with the book in question spread open on her lap. It was the official history of the Court.

"What's your professional opinion?"

"Of the book? Bit of a hagiography, isn't it? I didn't find any mention of that regrettable episode in the nineties when a small castle got flattened by accident."

Deed laughed. "It's an edited version."

"Heavily edited, I'd say."

"You can't expect us to betray trade secrets."

It was, apparently, Mercy's turn to laugh. "I didn't think there were any left. What with disgruntled magicians heading off in a sulk to tell everyone else what your methods are, and the fact that most of your magic is grimoire-based anyway and therefore accessible to anyone who can read . . . "

She had a point, but Deed kept smiling.

"Most of our magic. Not all."

"No," Mercy said, giving him a considering look. "Not all."

"Did they bring you breakfast?"

"Yes, thank you. I don't think Persephone and I have much in common, and I was hungry, so I ate it. They've taken away the tray." She held up a cup. "I still have tea."

Deed studied her. The sigil marks which were a part of her craft had not been renewed, and they had taken her weapons from her. Interrogating the sword had not proved successful; the thing had clammed up and refused to speak even under geas. Up close, Deed could see those betraying traces of ancestry in Fane's face: the wax-pale skin and the elegant bones that seemed to be a trait of the wolf clans when they bred out into human. But the black hair and blacker eyes were more reminiscent of southern Europe. He would not be surprised to learn that there were traces of Spanish in her ancestry.

"Ever been far north?" he asked.

"Once." Her eyes were wary. "Visiting relatives."

"Wolves?"

"Perhaps."

"The old clanholds and fortresses still stand, I believe. An interesting heritage."

"And your own?"

Deed smiled at her. "Me? Oh, I come from a long line of accountants."

⊷═◯═⊶

Once he had made sure that the door to Mercy's chamber was securely locked, he went back down to the laboratory. The homunculi were coming on nicely: three of them, which was all that the blood could produce, growing like mandrakes in jars of black earth and fluid. Even with fresh blood, the process was not limitless; the most anyone had ever been able to make was seven and the last had been too sickly to really count. Deed's other alchemical preparations were proceeding well enough. In the furthest crucible, red lion was devouring white eagle, the symbolic representations of the magical chemicals writhing above the apparatus. Deed watched the process for a while, then checked on the spying eye that looked into Mercy's chamber. She was sitting in the chair, looking at the history of the Court. Satisfied, Deed went down to the atrium to await the arrival of the Elders.

He had taken care to select the two most conservative members of the Library: Elder Vande, and Elder Egrim. Both, Deed knew from his enquiries, were old, querulous, and wanting a quiet life, which they were unlikely to achieve any time soon. They looked at him with palpable anxiety.

"Naturally, we are eager to avoid any unpleasantness," Vande quavered. "This is most embarrassing."

"Young people will be young people," Deed said, sententiously. "I'm sure she thought she was doing the right thing. However . . . "

"Can't imagine why she didn't go through official channels," Egrim lamented, clutching her reticule.

"Doubtless she had her reasons. I suggest you confirm her presence here—I called you in because these things can be falsified, as I'm sure you're aware—and then," Deed paused. "Then we can begin to discuss terms."

It was possible, of course, that the Library might simply decide to hang Mercy out to dry. But in that case, Deed would declare open war, and he was counting on the Elders' timidity and caution. The disappearance of the city's masters had hit them hard, much harder than the Court, which had, after all, sensibly put a number of contingency measures in place after a prophecy, which, though at the time unlikely, one would have to have been a fool to ignore.

On Earth, a prophecy was a prediction, and quite often false. In the Liminality, with its different ontological basis and the shifty temporal underpinnings of the nevergone, a prophecy could be something quite different, not a prediction at all but a fact which had slipped backwards down a storyway and lodged in the past, or a possibility from an alternate timestream which had flaked free of its rightful place and drifted through the overlight.

"You'll want to install your own disciplinary measures," Deed said, sorrowfully. "She hasn't been ill treated, although regrettably she did have an unfortunate encounter with an entity . . . " He watched the two elderly faces grow pale, and inwardly smiled. "She'll tell you herself that we've put her in comfortable quarters."

"Thank you for your restraint," Egrim said.

"We have to work together," Deed replied, with a degree of piousness. He led them down the winding passages of the Court, making sure that a maze-spell was in place just in case his two guests were a bit more clued-in than they appeared, and were able to trace where they'd been. When they reached the door of the incarceration chamber, Deed said, "Here she is," and opened the door with a flourish.

The room, however, was empty.

Forty-four

It felt like the edge of the world. Shadow stood beside Elemiel and the demon on a great lip of rock. Behind them stretched the narrow valley, filled with dangerous blooms. Below, was a howling pit of air. Shadow looked down onto a boiling storm; clouds scudded beneath her feet and a sudden bolt of lightning illuminated a landscape far below that looked like the surface of the moon. She stepped quickly back as something huge and black-winged soared close to the edge, veered, and was gone.

"What was that? What *is* this?"

"This is the Pass of Ages," Gremory said, surprising her. Shadow looked at the demon. Gremory's impassive face didn't do "startled," but Shadow thought there was a trace of disconcertment in the demon's eyes. "Even I thought this was a myth."

"It isn't a myth. It was closed in the apparent world aeons ago, after the first fall of the Garden. But it opened again when the Skein vanished."

"Do you know where the Skein have gone?" Shadow demanded.

"If I knew that, I would have gone after them."

Angels cannot lie, she had once read. She nodded.

"But they kept this—this gap closed?"

"Or they professed to do so."

"What do you mean?"

"The Skein deal in the highest of high magic. They were the lords of the world: their cities spanned the shores of Earth before the Flood, and those were drowned when a meteor hit the planet. Those of the Skein that were left vowed it would never happen again: they created the Liminality, wove it out of the legends of the ancestors of man, and then took refuge in it. Their magic is a blend of demonic and angelic: the forces which powered creation, two halves of the same whole. But the Skein didn't know everything and they did not realise that their sanctuary was built on a crack: the Pass of Ages. Or perhaps they did realise, and thought they could control it. Stories enter the Liminality through the Pass, it's part of the overlight. When it was closed, they seeped around its edges, and when it opens, they rush through. It is not fully open yet, and it is guarded. And there is a spell to close it."

"Was that one of the guards just now?" Shadow looked down into the roil of indigo, silver, black. "That thing I saw?"

"No," the Messenger said. "That was one of the servants of the Storm Lords. *That* is a guard."

It was coming towards them, stepping on the clouds like someone walking across a thundering sea. It was a bright outline of a man, a silhouette shot with light, and its hair flared in a nimbus of golden blue around its head. It carried, upright, a flaming sword. Shadow drew the blade.

"Leave it," the demon said, sharply. "Not even star iron will cut it."

The Messenger held up a hand. The guard strode out of the storm, onto the rock and it sizzled and fused beneath its feet. Shadow could see its eyes now and they were so bright that she had to look away. Elemiel spoke a name and the thing faltered, but only for a moment. It swung the sword. Shadow felt the Messenger summon his power, drawing it into himself and sending it out but she could also feel this was not enough.

"It shouldn't be able to see us!" the Messenger said.

His hand shot out and a curling whip of light knocked the sword aside but the guard swung again and the whip split apart.

"I can see," Shadow heard Gremory say, "that I'm going to have to help you out."

Black fire joined the whip of light. The ground shuddered beneath Shadow's feet and she stumbled. As she went down on one knee she saw the sun-dark lash of light strike out and tear the sword from the guard's hand. It fell backwards into the abyss without a sound and Shadow was falling too, into a hole of night.

⇒Forty-five⇐

"**I** know the sword can look after itself," Mercy hissed, "but I don't want to leave it here unless we have to." It wasn't as though it was her own sword: it belonged to the Library, but the thing was at least partly alive and the thought of it in the hands of the Court stuck in her throat.

"It will be under lock and key," Perra warned.

"But do you know *where?*"

Despite the loss of the sword Mercy was, however, in reasonable spirits. The thought of the look on Deed's face when he opened the door and found her missing was a notion she would treasure for some time, whatever other advantages he might have taken during her time with the Court. That, Mercy thought with a trace of smugness, was what came of underestimating other people's reading habits.

She had not slept, although to anyone watching—and surely such a chamber would be under observation—it would have looked as though she had lain down on the couch, covered herself with the blanket and passed into slumber. She had certainly closed her eyes. But no power of the Court could keep someone who knew what they were doing from investigating matters on the astral level and she had spent the night examining the wards of the room. Each of the four walls was locked with a quarter-sigil: unfamiliar in particular to Mercy, but familiar when it came to type. A sigil is a group of words and symbols, bound together like weaving or knitting. Find the end, even if it has been woven into the pattern, and you can unravel the sigil.

Deed's own strengths lay in the north, and in the Western Quarter where the Court resided. Mercy wasn't too familiar with the South, but she did know the designs of the East; her other mother, Sho, had taught her well. Magic that tasted of aniseed and ginger. Not the snow-and-sea-salt of the north, or the greengrowing spells of the Southern Quarter, but something with which Deed was not, Mercy thought, all that familiar.

She found the sigil's end in a name: a demon of the East. She did not speak the name aloud, but she whispered a syllable, over and over again, beneath her breath and without moving her lips, until the name began to fray like a pulled thread. Mercy uttered another syllable, pulling gently. In her mind's eye, on the astral, she crouched by the sigil, which was inscribed in red and gold upon the wall, tugging at its corner. And quite suddenly the sigil began to unravel, looping out into Mercy's hands until deactivated.

She did not act at once. She yawned, mumbled, stirred, and sat up, hoping that the sigil's demise wouldn't trigger some kind of alarm. If so, she would soon find out. Mercy got up from the couch and stretched, then wandered around the room. When she reached the western wall, she glanced up. A transparent oval had appeared in the middle of the wall, with the golden-eyed form of Perra peering through it.

Mercy let her gaze glide over the *ka*. She saw Perra mouth, "Wait." Then the *ka* breathed out. A mist began to fill the room, feeding from shadows and the play of the flickering lamp that stood by the bed. Mercy stepped forwards to the hole in the wall and suddenly it was like facing a mirror. She stood there, looking into her own dark eyes.

"What the hell?" Mercy breathed.

"When you fell off the turret, this *ka* took the homunculus and extended it. This is just an illusion; the core remains. It will replace you for a time, then it will decay into dust. But you can't leave now. Deed's on his way. Once he's gone, we will do the switch."

"All right," Mercy said. If Deed had placed anything else in the cell, anything that would betray she was no longer present, the homunculus would hopefully be enough to fool it. She backed into the room and the mist dispelled. When she once more looked at the wall, it was solid.

⊷═◉ ◉═⊷

Later, when Deed had gone, Perra once more opened the hole in the wall. Mercy had been on tenterhooks throughout Deed's visit; she had been sure he would notice the damaged sigil. But he had given no sign of having done so and now, for him, it would be too late. Mercy left her mute, unresponsive double sitting in her place with the book and fled through the wall.

This led them to the point of rescuing the sword. Mercy knew they had to act fast: it was only a matter of time before Deed or someone else discovered her escape and sounded the alarm.

"The library? Do you think he'd have put it in there?"

"I can find my way back," Perra said, "if we need."

But first, the roof. The two books were still where Mercy had left them, on the ledge by the window. Then they raced around the passages, down steps and up stairs. The library door was opening. As Mercy flattened herself behind a wall hanging, the door banged and the disir girl came out, heels clicking. Today she wore a gown of grey velvet and her face was once more remote and cold. She was writing something on a pad as she walked.

As soon as she had gone, Mercy slipped into the room. The same rows of grimoires; the same air of fermenting occult strangeness. The Irish sword lay on a slab of slate, bound in silver.

Mercy reached out and wrenched it free. Moments later, an alarm sounded, shrieking at astral level throughout the building. She did not know, and cared less, whether it was as a response to the theft of the sword or in answer to her own escape. With Perra at her heels, she ran out of the lab. A door at the far end led onto an outside balcony, which opened onto the same courtyard that had come close to being decorated by Mercy's plummeting body the day before. It was perhaps ten feet to the ground. Mercy ran along the balcony and at the end a door opened and the white gibbon-thing from the dungeons was loosed. It screamed, bounding towards her. As it leaped, Mercy skewered it with the sword, gutting it mid-flight. The monkey-devil howled and like the homunculus, wizened around the blade, diminishing until only a few bloody white ribbons fluttered about the hilt. The sword cried out in triumph; Mercy was not inclined to tell it to shut up. She ran to the end of the balcony and looked through the door. The Court was now chaotic with shouting and running footsteps. Mercy sprang over the rail and dropped down to the courtyard, trying to orient herself. The outer perimeter wall of the Citadel had been visible through the windows of the laboratory: that meant that the main square lay directly ahead and they were at ground level. Mercy ran through a door, down a passage, and came out into the atrium.

"Shut the doors!" she heard someone shout, but it was too late. Mercy threw herself through the iron doors of the Court and rolled down the outside steps into the square. She dodged into the maze of passages that ran between the Court and its neighbours, and was swallowed by the city.

⊷Forty-six⊷

Shadow stood alone in the middle of the Khaureg. From the position of the sun, it was late afternoon. The sky was a hot burn of blue above her, and the distant dunes were ringing and singing as they shifted. There was no sign of the garden of flowers, of the storm-swarming abyss, of the angel or the demon. Why had Elemiel taken a risk that had nearly killed her? But he had said the guard should not have been able to see them: presumably because they were with Elemiel himself, and he was allowed to walk there. Then she wondered how vulnerable she had really been. She wasn't quite human any more, after all.

On the western horizon she could see the walls of Worldsoul, with the golden crescent moons of the Eastern Quarter rising above. Facing the city, there was no chance of losing it. Tears came to her eyes and she clenched her fingers around the hilt of the sun-and-moon blade. She had wondered if she would ever see it again, and now—

It was dusk when she walked through the Desert Gate. The evening bustle of the Medina lay ahead. Shadow felt as if she had been gone for years, and she did not trust the Messenger's view of time. When she checked the great water clock that stood at the entrance to the Medina, however, she found that she had been gone for three days, as she had thought. She let go of a breath that she did not know she had been holding and walked into the Medina.

"Shadow!" She turned at her name. Sephardi came out of a dark doorway, smiling. "I haven't seen you for days. There was talk . . . "

Shadow returned the smile. "There's always talk."

He looked at her. "You smell of the Khaureg."

"I've been—outside the walls." She probably simply smelled, Shadow thought with distaste.

"Mariam Shenudah has been asking about you."

"I was going to see her," Shadow said.

Three days, but it was not just that it felt longer. She felt no hunger and only a little thirst. There had been a shift, a reorganisation of her guiding principles. She'd gone to get rid of a spirit and she'd found a war. Even the Shah could be regarded from a different perspective: a potential ally, or part of the problem? The sight of the café destroyed in the flower attack, charred and with its walls still reeking of smoke, only hardened her resolve. She needed advice and if Shenudah was unable to give it, she would at least know where it was to be found.

Mariam worked throughout the night, but it was early enough for her to be out and about, catching up with Medina cronies. Shadow found her on her own doorstep, unlocking the door.

"Shadow!"

"I need to talk to you," Shadow said. Sephardi had melted away into the Medina, pleading urgent business, and she had been relieved: it was not precisely that she did not trust him, but he conveyed rumours. It was his job and she did not begrudge him that, but she thought the news of what she had been shown in the desert needed more careful handling than being scattered around the Medina like blown leaves. And not much stayed in the Medina, either: fermenting in its crucible, information became alchemically transformed, eliding and changing, until, released, it sprang forth into the city. Had Sephardi gone straight to the Shah? Quite possibly so.

Mariam, however, knew how to keep her mouth shut. When they were behind her locked door, and Shadow had, with some gratitude, accepted the ritual of tea, she told Shenudah what had happened. She had some concern that Mariam might not believe her, but the other woman listened without expression.

"I've heard of the Pass of Ages once. It's in a very old text that was brought with the Library when it came from Alexandria. It's said that Eden fell into it after Adam was thrown out."

"Eden apparently did."

"The story of Eden has many variations. Some of the oldest say it was born from the desert. Historians are starting to think it was a real place, a forest that formed a wild garden for the early peoples of the Fertile Crescent. There would have been areas they'd seed and tend: the Fall came when they gained knowledge and tried to control it. They destroyed the balance and the Garden died."

"That doesn't account for the Pass."

"But if what the angel told you is true, it's part of the overlight."

"Who are the Storm Lords?"

"In legend they are the children of Lilith, who is herself many entities—the Lilitu. They're bird demons, storm devils. They came into being when Lilith, who was Adam's first wife, left Eden on her own because Adam tried to control her. Who can blame her? She danced with demons in the desert and bred with them to produce the storm children."

"So Lilith left Eden of her own free will, and when Eden fell, her children came back to make use of it?"

"Perhaps. Someone's attacking this city, after all, and the Storm Lords are ancient enemies of mankind."

"How do we stop them?" Shadow asked.

"I think you need to pay a visit to the Library," Mariam Shenudah said.

⊷⊜⊜⊶

That night, Shadow had a dream. She was back in her own rooms, with mingled reluctance and relief. Mariam had offered her a bed for the night, but given that so many things were trying to kill her, Shadow was unwilling to place the older woman in further danger. Shenudah was the closest thing remaining to family, and she'd lost too much already. So she had come home, to spend a weary hour re-warding the laboratory, followed by a bath—essential after three days in the desert, it had been amazing that Mariam had let her in through the door—and finally going to bed.

In the dream, she was once again out in the desert, and she knew despair at the realisation that the return to Worldsoul had been the illusion, and *this* the reality. She had not escaped, but was once again in that unknown place, where the tides of time shifted like the dunes. Elemiel's beehive hut, undamaged, stood before her. It was night, with the stars thick overhead.

The man came up the path towards her. She had a curious rush of feelings: hope, resentment, desire, shame. The young man was tall and wore black robes. His face was beautiful: symmetrical, with high cheekbones and liquid dark eyes. His skin was the colour of gold and it shone. He wore no headgear and his hair fell to his shoulders. He wore a short black beard.

"Who are you?" Shadow said. He touched his brow and she saw a fillet of gold around it. She was sure that this had not been there before.

"I am a prince," the young man said. His face was grave. He reached out and Shadow stepped back.

"Do not touch me," she said.

"I know you are a virtuous woman. I mean no disrespect. But I am within you."

"You're the spirit who is in my blood?"

"Yes." He bowed. "I did not intend to possess you. But I have to hide."

"In me?"

"A human is the best hiding place. They're surprisingly difficult to see into."

"What are you hiding from?"

"Everyone."

"Why?"

The spirit drew his right hand up and in it was a scimitar. It shone in the moonlight, fire-bright.

"I am the scabbard and the blade," he said, and before Shadow could stop him, or say anything, he raised his arm above his head, reversed the hilt in his hand and plunged the scimitar into his own skull. It vanished and at that moment Shadow understood that both scimitar and man were part of the same thing, just as Gremory was both girl and beast and both, and all demon.

"How do I get rid of you?" she said to the spirit, and he—the Prince of the Air—began to spin, whirling around in a dervish-wheel of dust and air. Then he was gone, winking out. A single drop of blood fell glistening to the desert earth. And Shadow woke up.

⊷Forty-seven⊶

The disciplinary committee hearing was remarkably tedious, and a waste of valuable time. Eventually, since Mercy herself could not, Nerren took issue with the Elders.

"You don't have any proof that she was even there. Deed was lying. He said they kept her in a chamber, but there's no record of it. She's here now, isn't she?"

Mercy, sitting in the interrogation chair, forced herself to stop staring out of the window and look helpful.

"Then why undertake such a rigmarole?"

"Because the Court is trying to make trouble. That's what it does. They're magicians. They're tricksters."

"With the Skein gone"—*and you lot dithering*—"they've seen that there's a power vacuum and they're trying to take advantage," Mercy said.

"But why do they think you were trying to burgle their premises?"

Round and round it went, but in the absence of proof, and with Nerren backing her up, they eventually placed Mercy on a three-day suspension.

Good. Now I can do what I want.

Back in Nerren's office, the other woman looked at Mercy. "What did you think you were *doing*?"

"I can't tell you." That much was true. She could feel the geas binding her tongue. Presumably it would only be over when she delivered the book. "But it's to do with that business with Section C."

Nerren rolled her eyes. "I might have known."

"And I'd like to say that I know what I'm doing, but I don't. I wish I did."

"That's very reassuring, Mercy."

"I'm off for three days. That means you won't have to worry about me."

A snort. "As if. What are you planning to do?"

"Some light reading," Mercy said.

⋆⇒◎⇐⋆

Darya's purloined book was about the disir. It was old, though not nearly as old as the text from which the thing had come, and it was both in English and surprisingly informative. Mercy read it over tea in her office at the Library, paying close attention. She could tell that a lot of it was conjecture, and yet more of it, legend. But the kernels of the story were there, the seeds of truth from which the myths had grown.

The old god, chained.

Poison dripping from a serpent's mouth.

The Ladies, who came from before the ice.

And a name: *Mareritt.* The Ladies' enemy.

All of these things were connected to the disir. What had become of the one who had leaped through a story-gap into the Library, and run out into the city? The one whose hand Shadow had cut off?

Mercy had tried to contact Shadow since then, but without success. The alchemist seemed to have gone to ground. She'd tried again. But Shadow was not there, or was not answering.

Perra, leaf-light, jumped onto the desk.

"Do we go home, tonight?" the *ka* asked.

"No. It's not safe. I've angered Deed; we're safer here."

Safer, if not wholly safe. She did not have total confidence in the Library's defences, but it would be a lot easier to hide here than in her house. She could sleep on the couch in her office; she'd done it often enough. Nerren had agreed to tell the Elders that she'd gone to a friend's for the days of her suspension, though she was not banned from the Library's premises. There were stories of people who lived in the Library, after all: hiding out among the stacks, venturing out at night when all was silent. Living off crumbs and flakes of tales, so faint that they were almost ghosts . . .

As she had told Nerren, Mercy planned to do a little late reading.

⋯▻═◉═◅⋯

When everything was quiet, and the Library had been locked for the night, Mercy ventured out of her office. The slam of the huge main doors was still echoing throughout the building and she caught sight of one of the night staff whisking down a corridor. Mercy waited until the man had gone, then climbed the stairs. The ghostly spirit birds were beginning to flutter down to their invisible roost; she could see the last golden fire of the sun reflected on the tall windows.

She headed for Section C. The sword was at her side, and she had re-applied the sigils on her brow. Pity about the ward bracelets that she'd lost to Deed; she was cross about those. She had another pair, old and in silver, an apprenticeship gift from Sho. She did not like to wear them for everyday use; they were too fine, but on the other hand, these were exceptional circumstances and Mercy felt these bracelets had more power. Fortunately, she kept them in a locked drawer of her desk rather than at home. She had taken them from the black velvet interior of their box as though armouring for battle.

Which in fact, she was. *Deed: Game on.*

She was looking for one of the translators on the Ninth Floor. She did not think that Mareritt was anyone's friend but her own, but she'd be interested to see what there was to be found in *The Winter Book*. When she got to the locked stacks, therefore, she sat down at the translator, put the book under its thick glass panel, and began to turn its brass handle.

Paper spewed out of the other side and Mercy looked at it with interest. It was a book of fairy tales, like *The Red Fairy Book* and *The Green Fairy Book*. She found again the story of Jan and the dove. She remembered that in the tale, Mareritt's sleigh was drawn by swans, not deer; she wondered if it was significant. And another tale, too, of a ship made of ice that sails the northern seas, crewed with the ghosts of drowned sailors. The original had delicate watercolour illustrations behind a thin film of tissue paper. Here was the ship and—yes!—a picture of Mareritt in her sledge, running over the ice. Clouds of mist steamed out of the mouths of her deer and Mareritt's face was beautiful and cold. The ship was plunging among the floes.

Mercy read the story. It was not clear if Mareritt was heroine or villain: she saved the ship, but for her own reasons. This ambivalence did not seem to bother the author, concerned mainly with the protagonist of his story, the ghost of a young cabin boy. But at the end of the tale, Mareritt told the boy something useful: *If you need me again, call my name three times in moonlight and I will come.*

All right, thought Mercy. *We'll see if that works.* Anyway, Mareritt would want to see her, wouldn't she? Mercy had been successful: she had obtained *The Winter Book*. It was too early as yet: the sun had only just gone down. But she would be able to see the moon's rise from the top of the building easily enough. The geas gave a twinge.

She put the book back in its place and locked up. Walking down the next row of stacks, she heard a sound.

Night watchman? Probably. But the sound did not come again, as if someone was keeping still. Mercy drew the sword. She tiptoed along the row of books, paused, waited. Nothing.

Then a floorboard creaked. Mercy turned and was struck blind. Something billowed over her head, shutting off sight and hearing. The sword was entangled and she could not strike.

Then it was whisked away.

"Sorry!" Shadow said. "I didn't realise it was you."

"We're going to have to tell the Elders," Mercy said, some minutes later. They were sitting back in her office. Shadow, unveiled, looked haunted. She wore a long-sleeved blue shirt, with an indigo tunic over it, and loose blue trousers. Her feet were booted. She looked weary: unsurprising, if what she had told Mercy was the truth.

"Mariam Shenudah is taking it to the imams and the magi of the University," Shadow said. "She has contacts: they'll listen to her."

"It ought to go to the city council," Mercy remarked. "Oh wait, we haven't got one. The Citadel doesn't count—all they do is pointless inspections which have to be written up in triplicate."

Shadow sighed. "Maybe this is heresy of a kind, but I'm beginning to realise what a stranglehold the Skein have had on this city."

"No, you're right. We're not geared up for anything. It's been a year. Everyone's put their heads in the sand and pretended that we can just bumble along as normal. We deserve to be attacked, frankly." She paused. "A tale for a tale. This is what's been happening here."

When she had finished her story, Shadow stared at her. "The members of the Court have always wanted more power than they've been entitled to. But they'll have to work with others now. If they don't pitch in, the city could crumble. And I think we'll need their magic to fight the Storm Lords."

Mercy thought she was probably right, but she was not so sure that the Court would not want Worldsoul to fall. "We need to look at possibilities. The disir wouldn't have been able to come through if the Skein were here. The flower attacks began after the Skein vanished. If the Skein were keeping a lid on rifts between the Liminality and parts of the nevergone, then we don't have two problems: we've only got one, but it's a big one."

"Elemiel said there's a spell which will seal the gap," Shadow said. "But he doesn't know where it is. We need to find it."

"And if we do find it, it could shut out the *Barquess*, and probably the Skein as well."

"Your mother is on that ship, isn't she?"

"Yes." Mercy did not trust herself to say more.

"I'm sorry about your mother," Shadow said. "But for the rest—for the Skein, I mean—I think it's time we stood on our own two feet."

⊷═◌═⊶

The emergency session of the Elders could have been embarrassing, but the matter was serious enough to override Mercy's professional transgressions. Shadow addressed the dismayed Elders, speaking with clarity and force, and backed by a deputation from the Eastern Quarter that included Mariam Shenudah.

"The University has texts about the Storm Lords. They're ancient. They're story-eaters—that's the aim. Devour and destroy the tales of men, so the nevergone will belong to them. But we have a choice," Shenudah said. "We can squabble and fragment, or we can stand together."

"What proof do you have?" Elder Tope asked. "This is a fantastic tale and we are used to fantastic tales. But what proof is there?" Moonlight flooded in through the tall windows of the council chamber, vying with the illumination from the lamps. So much light, Mercy thought, and yet none of us can see clearly.

"I know this woman," Shenudah said. "She would not lie."

Shenudah spoke quietly, however, and Shadow said, "But *they* don't know me. I have no proof, only my word, and why should they believe me?"

"It is not that we think you are lying," Tope said. "But people can get things wrong. Stories can be deceptive."

"And this is as you said, a fantastic tale."

Mercy began to have the terrible suspicion that all this would be in vain. After the hearing, things would simply remain as before. But what could they do except be reasonable? She thought Shadow's story was indeed extraordinary, but she had spent her lifetime among extraordinary stories.

"The flower attacks didn't come from nowhere," she said.

Tope sighed. "We can't just accept this without some kind of evidence."

"No, I understand that."

"Maybe I can help," an unfamiliar voice said.

In the hours that followed, desperate though they were, Mercy found a few moments in which to treasure the sight of the faces of a Library committee confronted with the sudden manifestation of a talking camel.

"Oh, sorry," the demon said, without a trace of apology. "Wrong one." It now took the appearance of a woman, armoured for war. The armour was crimson and made of supple leather; the demon's hair was braided and she wore a band across her brow with the symbol of a crescent moon. Mercy heard Shadow sigh.

"I wondered where you'd got to."

"I was annoyed. Elemiel put us both at considerable risk— typical of someone indestructible to underestimate danger. I ended up at the ends of the Earth—it's taken me all this time to get back."

"You are a demon," Librarian McLaren said. He looked amused rather than alarmed.

"Yes. My name is Gremory. I am a duke of Hell."

"How did you get past the wards?"

"I don't think I'll tell you that," Gremory said. "For reasons that should be obvious." She strode forward and put taloned hands on the council table. "But this woman is telling the truth. I realise that a demon's word is subject to some doubt, sadly, and thus as a gesture of good faith, I propose to lend you this for safekeeping."

She tugged at her hand and placed a ring on the table: a thick band of gold bearing a carnelian inscribed with a sigil. The Elders' eyes bulged: the demon had handed over her own domination.

"Why?" Mercy heard Shadow breathe.

The Duke of Hell looked at her. "I'm not really the altruistic sort. It's because of the Court. I am a Goetic entity; they work with us, as you know. I come from the book known as the *Grimoire Verum*. This you can easily verify. The Abbot General, Jonathan Deed, has broken a pact made between the Court and my masters. He has sought power from elsewhere and that power, when it comes, will undermine ours."

"From the disir?" Mercy asked.

"His god Loki has a disir army amassing in the nevergone. Plans to bring them into Worldsoul, take over the city. Meanwhile we've got the Storm Lords planning much the same thing, except they want to strip everything back to basics: obliterate humanity's tales, replace them with their own. As one of those stories," the demon said, looking modestly at a talon, "I am naturally a little concerned."

Mercy could feel relief emanating from Shadow. "I'm glad you have an agenda. The lack of it was worrying me."

The Duke of Hell laughed. "Help from demons. Always a worry."

Tope was still staring at the carnelian ring as if mesmerised.

"We have to do something," Mercy said.

"But what?" All the Elders were looking hopefully at her and Shadow; she should never have made that earlier promise. Mercy opened her mouth to speak, and the tall windows that flanked the council chamber burst inwards in a shower of glass. Mercy was flung against the wall and threw her arm across her face to shut out the glare of an explosion, but it did not come. She could not smell the firework odour of a flower, but the light beyond the windows was becoming steadily brighter.

"What's that?" she heard an Elder say, shakily. Mercy pulled herself to her feet; beside her, Shadow was scrambling up. The demon stood, apparently unmoved, in the centre of a blizzard of glass shards. Tope was face down across the table.

"I've seen it before," Shadow said, gripping Mariam Shenudah's arm. "It's the Pass."

═Forty-eight═

For purely dramatic reasons, Deed found that he profoundly resented being pipped to the post. After the debacle involving Fane and the Library, Deed had stepped up his preparations, making frequent checks down the long lens that connected Worldsoul with the nevergone, a periscope between dimensions. The periscope was not entirely reliable, showing as it did contingencies that had not in fact occurred, or at least, not yet. But what it did continue to show him was reassuring.

The bleak line of the horizon. The scroll of the oxbow river across the barren land. The disir army massing along its shores.

The lid had been removed from Loki's memory jar during the night; he'd woken to find the sour smell of the old god filling the room and new knowledge in his head. He knew, now, what he had to do.

So Deed had continued to send out the necessary summonings, dropping knowledge into the heads of the shamans as they lay in that disir state of not-quite-sleep. Disir brains didn't work in the same way as humans; it was fair to say that they were not completely conscious. As with ancient humans, the two halves of the brain were not entirely connected, so messages from one half would be interpreted as voices from elsewhere. Deed, his eye glued to the periscope, whispered instructions, coaxed, cajoled and threatened, until the shamans—moved by that murmur out of the darkness—drew the tribes into position.

Deed had few illusions about his ability to control the disir. They were savages, and feral. They would run amok in the city, following their own whims, but with Loki's blessing at the tip of his tongue, he could destroy them if he had to. That was the plan: bring them in, and when the city was thoroughly cowed, remove the nuisance and bring the Court into centre stage as heroes. It was a simple, brutal plan, Deed felt, and it lacked elegance and subtlety, but it was at least historically tested.

He had already set the spellwork in place to open the rift in the Library. That the disir would make their grand entrance there, probably destroying hundreds of rare texts in the process, appealed to Deed. It would give the literary advantage to the Court in years to come, and he was prepared to sacrifice the odd grimoire to greater ambitions. With the Library crippled and the Court predominant, plus the existing support from Bleikrgard—that left only the Eastern and Southern Quarters to subdue and Deed was confident that with the disir plunging through the city, he would be able to persuade the relevant authorities in those areas that the Court would be an appropriate guiding force.

He was, therefore, both alarmed and annoyed when Darya ran into the room where he was undertaking his preparations.

"Abbot General! Something's happening?"

She looked dishevelled. Strands of hair had come loose from her chignon and tendrilled across her face, and her jacket had been misbuttoned. Deed regarded her coldly.

"Would you mind knocking in future?"

"Look out the window!" Darya pointed a quivering finger. Deed did so and to his shock saw a vast chasm opening in the sky above the Western Sea. It was as if the sky was splitting in half. The windows of the Court bulged briefly inwards, but held. Deed took a hasty step back. Within the gap surged a tidal race of cloud in all the colours of fire. Rose, gold, scarlet and a livid white turned the night sky into a terrible false day.

"What the *hell* is that?" Deed breathed. Darya was wide-eyed, her appearance slipping further into disir.

The ground shuddered under their feet. In the laboratory next door, alembics and retorts rattled and the rattling did not stop. Deed looked at the window and saw the frame was shaking. He cast out a spell for stability, but it was like spitting into a hurricane. Battening down panic, Deed said, "The roof."

They ran up shaking flights of stairs. Magicians were pouring out of the rooms of the Court and Deed heard the rising note of hysteria in their voices. The building gave a huge, convulsive shudder, then stopped. Followed by Darya, Deed burst out onto the roof. The sky was alight. The spell-vanes, gilded surfaces catching the rosy fire, spun wildly in all directions and the air tasted of wild magic, pungent as petrol.

Deed was running for the turret, Darya at his heels, when the Court shook again and a great section of roof broke off and plunged into the street. Deed didn't look back. Good thing he had a penchant for emergency plans.

⊷⧟⊶

Tope was unconscious, but not dead. Librarians were running from the room in a panic. Shadow was bundling Mariam Shenudah through the door. Mercy hesitated over Tope's still form.

"Go on!" Benjaya Vrone shouted. "I'll take care of her."

With the other Librarians, Mercy and Shadow fled down the stairs. A brief glance upwards told Mercy that the ghostly birds had gone to roost, just as living ones do during an eclipse. As they were halfway down, the stairs rippled like the skin of a stroked cat, flinging them against the banisters. Mercy lost her footing and sat down hard. She was thus in a position to watch in horror as the entire front façade of the Library split in two. Tiles fell from the roof and she saw the bird-faced spirit follow it, twirling down through the air to crack in two on the marble floor below. The crack widened so she could see all the way out into the square, which was filled with frightened groups of people running to and fro and a golem in the midst of it all, trudging stolidly about its business. She glimpsed McLaren, with Benjaya at his side, directing people to safety.

Shadow pulled her to her feet.

"Look!" But she was pointing up the stairs.

On the Ninth Floor, the rift that had begun as no more than a slit in the air along Section C, was now spreading. Icy air gusted through with a swirl of snow and Mercy caught her breath. She saw rather than felt the *ka* pluck her sleeve.

"Up or down?"

"I don't think we're going to have a choice," Mercy said. By now, along with the Duke, poised elegantly upon a tilted step, they were the only ones left on the upper staircase. Everyone else was pouring out through the crack in the front of the building; Mercy hoped they would at least have a chance at survival. She couldn't work out whether it was an actual earthquake or not. The city wasn't prone to them as geological phenomena, which suggested to Mercy that this was some massive ruction along the storyways themselves, some heave in the fabric of the nevergone.

But the rift from Section C was coming on fast. Shadow reached out and gripped Mercy's arm as the curve of arctic air and twilight swept down the staircase to engulf them.

⋅⊷⫯○⫯⊶⋅

Deed could hear the engines powering up as he neared the turret. The building had stabilised for now, but Deed wasn't taking any chances. As he drew close, the doors of the base of the turret burst open. The nose of an airship slid out, a dark, iridescent green, whirring with spell-vanes of its own. He could see the pilot in the cockpit, insectoid behind his goggles and flying mask.

Deed scrambled up over the running blades and through the open hatch. He didn't bother to find out whether Darya had made it as the airship began to glide down the roof, but a thud and a curse behind him indicated that she had. Deed sighed. He stumbled into the cockpit and tapped the pilot on the shoulder.

"Keep away from that!" He pointed to the rift in the sky.

"Do you think I'm an idiot?" the pilot demanded, belatedly adding, "Sir."

Deed flung himself into a seat before acceleration did it for him, and strapped himself in. A moment later, Darya joined him. At least there were no accusing glances about his unchivalrous behaviour; disir expected everyone to act on their own behalf.

Good thing he'd had the airship tested recently. Its maiden voyage through the overlight had been a success.

The airship reached the edge of the roof and lurched into the air. It rose surprisingly quickly for such a bulbous craft, although Deed could hear the increasing whine of the engines as levitation spells took hold. Around him, the mechanisms of the airship whirred: a large brass sigilometer in the centre column of the cockpit spat out data. Deed had a brief, dizzying glimpse of the scene below him in the square as the craft turned: crowds streaming down the alleyways and out of the Library. What was happening to the Library? Deed thumped the pilot on the shoulder.

"Take us around again!"

Muttering, the pilot obeyed and Deed saw that the front of the Library had broken like an egg. *Let this be a lesson to you, Jonathan,* he thought, *next time you plot to bring down your enemies, make sure that the universe isn't planning to do it for you.*

"All right," Deed said. "Get us out of here."

But it was too late for that.

—=◎=—

Mercy smacked down into snow. The impact knocked the breath from her lungs. She inhaled again and the cold seared her throat.

"Shadow?"

"I'm here." Shadow sat up. "Wherever *here* is." Mercy did not recognise the precise place, but she thought they must be in the world from which the disir had come, the world of the bridge and the lands inside the mountain. The landscape was the same: plateaus of snowfield against black shards of mountain, descending through the pines. She got to her feet, to see the Duke of Hell and Perra sitting side by side in the branches of a tree like two exotic birds.

"Where are we?" Shadow asked.

"It's part of the nevergone. You went back to somewhere that emerged out of the legends of the Fertile Crescent; this is further north. The Ice Age. I've been here before."

Shadow nodded, taking it in. "And the way out?"

"Well, this wasn't where we first came in. We went down a particular storyway—there was a bridge and a waterfall of mist. This is further in from that land, deeper. This might not even relate to human memory."

"The Pass comes from demon's stories," Gremory said. She walked lightly across the snow, dusting something from her taloned hands. Mercy thought it was ash. "I've never been here before. Do you know the way out?"

Mercy shook her head. "Not really. We'll just have to keep walking and see if we can find our way back to the bridge."

She thought, but did not say, *And what happens then?* The

world of the bridge had led back into the Library, but that had been when there still *was* a Library. She was by no means sure this was still the case, given the state of it when they had left. Although "left" was rather too active a verb.

They began walking down through the pines. Here, the snow was sparse, kept away by the dense canopy above them. This, surely, was the sort of forest you found in fairy tales: thick, impenetrable and dark. And filled with monsters? Almost certainly. She thought about stumbling over the old god's lair again and swallowed hard. Well, she'd found his story, hadn't she? He ought to be pleased.

Above the pines, the sky was quite dark, swarming with stars. Mercy was only able to see by the light cast by Perra's eyes: golden beams on the snow and the black trunks of the trees. But gradually, Mercy found she was able to see. The sky was lightening to a bright indigo blue and shadows appeared. Dawn? But then, with dismay, they came out onto a high plateau and Mercy realised that the reason she could see was because of the Pass itself.

⊷═◑ ◒═⊶

The airship rocked as if it had been buffeted. Deed had a birds'-eye view of the second rift as it spread outwards from the Library, obscuring the ruined façade from view. He could see through the ragged edges of the rift to a familiar landscape: the world of the disir.

"Take us through!" Deed commanded the pilot.

"Not much sodding choice! Sir."

The little airship was being pulled into the gap, nose forwards. Deed heard the whine of the engine as stabilising spells tried and failed to secure the craft's trajectory. Then the temperature plummeted and they were sliding through the gap into the nevergone. Deed was looking down onto the churn of cold grey ocean and behind them, he saw the rift in the air snap shut.

⋯⟞◉⟝⋯

"What's *that*?" Mercy was looking down onto the plain, at a dark mass of moving forms. From this distance, it looked like an ants' nest, strung out along the looping shores of the river. She could see the glint of the rosy, heaving light of the Pass striking sparks from the metal of weapons.

"Looks like we've found Loki's army," the Duke said beside her.

"There are thousands of them."

"Yes. I must say, it will be interesting to see what happens when these two cultures clash—both ancient, both unhuman. Circumstances have always kept them apart, but now they're going to meet at last." The demon fished in a pocket of her armour and extracted a pair of small brass opera glasses. "Would you like a closer look?"

The army stretched across the plain, far beyond the river. Looking through the opera-glasses, Mercy could see the disir clearly: tall, attenuated figures, wrongly jointed. Their skin was mottled black, white, grey. They wore leather armour, some in tatters. Many of them wore headdresses of wolf skulls, evidence of earlier kills. All were female, as far as Mercy could see. Some had bracelets and headbands of silver, and a pale fire flickered about their heads: those would presumably be the shamans.

Mercy set her feet more firmly on the ridge.

"How many are there?" Shadow asked.

"Several thousand." She could see poles bearing skulls and the tatters of clan banners, carried among them. Some rode beasts: huge horned creatures with shaggy black coats and cloven hooves. "I think those things are aurochs." She took a deep breath.

As they watched the army approach, a black speck appeared above it. It spiralled up like a blown leaf, then, as if snatched by the wind, it shot forwards. Mercy braced herself. It was a raven, the feathers black and shining, but the bird itself was a skeleton. Its eyes were sparks in its skull.

"My mistress wants to speak with you." It wasn't a bird's voice. Mercy thought that something was speaking through the puppet of its skull. The bone-white beaked head cocked on one side.

"Me? Why?" Mercy asked. The raven's skull went up as if its head had been jerked back. It shot upwards, whirling into the sky.

"You have the god's touch on you. It's how she smelled you out."

The raven's mistress, a shaman, was riding one of the aurochs. She spurred it forwards and it gave a bellowing cry, perhaps of protest, perhaps rage. It lumbered at startling speed across the frozen ground until it was close enough for Mercy to smell its pungent cattle-scent, warm in the cold air. The shaman herself wore a necklace of bones, delicately polished and interspersed with river garnet. Her armour was of white hide, linked by iron rings. She carried a flint blade at her hip and her long hair was matted with lime. Her eyes were snowfire pale and her face was bone, not skin. She slid down from the auroch's back with a thud and said pugnaciously to Mercy, "I challenge you for the god's favour. Begin."

"Look," Mercy said. "If you're talking about Loki, I don't want him. You can have him."

"Begin!"

Mercy drew the sword.

"Not that. I meant magic."

"I'm not—" Oh, what the hell. She thought of her dreams and sighed.

It would have to be wolf-magic; nothing else was old enough. She remembered her dream of the homunculus, wriggling in the snare under the ice. She thought of the curse. She remembered the shift, herself changing not into wolf, but wolf-woman.

This was the nevergone. It was *between*—that was important, it was not the final product. No such thing as a finished story. She took a breath and changed.

The world about her shifted. Maybe that was it: you yourself don't alter, but you step into a different narrative, rewriting yourself. Mercy stood on the plateau she had seen in her dream, with the standing stone above the long valley. It was winter, twilight, a thin moon high overhead, but the air still smelled of the pines. And blood: something had been freshly killed.

The disir shaman stepped out of the stone. At first, she, too, was different. She was no more than a girl, her hair white fire against the darkness of the rock. Her eyes were huge and luminous, and she was smiling. There was a touch of Mareritt, but her face was more elemental. Then it changed and the disir was back. She opened her jaws to display long teeth and gave a grating shriek of challenge.

Mercy was hit with a blast of power. Not a conjuration or a spell, but the knowledge of what the disir was. Overwhelming cold, the long Ice Age winter, thousands of years long, when a thin rind of northerly humanity had clung to the chill planet and survived. The disir were their nightmares; they were the sharp-toothed dark and the killing cold. They were the stories and tales of the hunters, and when the ice had gone and the world grew warm, they too survived their long winter in the deep minds of men. And they were female, which men so often fear.

Mercy could see, in that moment of understanding, why Mareritt was their enemy. Later she became a rival. She came from a part of history in which city-dwellers feared the forest, overlain onto something much older. But she wasn't wild. She was an urban idea of the wilderness, and she was far closer to human than the disir would ever be. She wanted the disir gone so she could take their place.

"This is my reply," Mercy said. She thought of the wolf-clan, the hearth. She thought of people in the long night, the arctic cold, banding together against the rigours of the world. Animal and human, finding connection, reaching out. The long winter hadn't killed them: they'd won. Greya and the lampmender Salt, who had helped one another. She raised the Irish sword and it began to sing in her mind a song of its own, a thread of telling about battles fought and won, the green summer hillside and the sparkling sea. It sang of honour and glory, but also of loss and the knowledge that it had been the agent of that loss. It was human-born, human-made and Mercy hung onto its song and pulled herself to her feet. She cut through the wintersong of the disir, the stories of iron ground and iron cold, of the delight in bloodshed, and she ran the shaman through so hard that the blade rang out against the standing stone.

The stone and the valley were gone. Mercy was herself again, with the sword hilt reassuringly solid in her hand. Her arm was still numb with the shock of the blow, ringing up the bones of her arm. The body of the shaman lay at her feet, convulsed in death. The disir army cried out with rage and dismay.

But Shadow, off to her left, was looking behind Mercy, not towards the vociferous disir.

"This is not good," Shadow said. Mercy turned. The clouds of the Pass were opening up. The sky was splitting in a ragged vertical to let more stormlight through. She saw bolts of azure flame rip the clouds, a blaze of golden light, with thousands of black specks whirling against it. Storm demons, coming through. They coiled in a spiral above the black line of the horizon, like bats or birds, but Mercy knew that from the distance, they must be vast.

The horned beasts ridden by the disir were beginning to panic and stampede. Their riders wheeled them back, shrieking: an earsplitting sound which made Mercy clap her hands to her head. But she could still hear the riders' cries and feel the thud of the hooves travelling up through the ground, a dull drumbeat. Something tugged her sleeve and she leaped, her heart pounding and the sword jumping in turn in her hand. The demon's eyes were gleaming.

"Can I make a suggestion?" Gremory said. She gestured with a long-taloned hand towards the oncoming storm. "If that lot sees you, they'll tear you apart."

"I'd worked that out." Mercy nodded towards the forest. "Only way out's through there."

"Best get a move on, then."

With Shadow, they ran for the line of trees. Perra ran ahead, bounding between the tussocks of grass. If the disir noticed, it meant little: their attention was now fully occupied by the oncoming storm. The trees would not protect them—but the rocks might. Mercy was remembering the bridge, and that crack in the mountain behind the mistfall.

The only problem was that once off the open tundra, the trees slowed them down. The pines, their branches weighted with snow, grew closely together and the slope between them was slippery, with ice filming the glassy rocks beneath the thin covering of earth. Mercy could see Shadow was shivering, despite her heavy coat. She held out a hand and pulled her friend up the slope.

"I'll be all right," Shadow said. The demon seemed to have no such difficulties: her boots made no footprints in the snow and Mercy was reminded of a raven, black above the red of a kill. They could hear the onrushing storm through the trees now, a battering wall of sound. Shrieks from the disir army suggested that the meeting was imminent.

Mercy struggled across a short plateau of rock and found herself above the tree line. She looked back. Over the pines, the stormclouds boiled and writhed: she could see the tornado funnel of the winged demons, a black whiplash cracking against the sky. They had a clear few hundred yards of snowfield, before the rocks began.

"Ready?" Mercy said to Shadow, and they ran.

Forty-nine

Deed stood in the cockpit of the Court's airship, binoculars clamped to his eyes. Disir sight was not always so keen and he had enhanced his own over the years with a variety of judicious preparations: sight stolen from the youths of the Western Quarter, vision sipped from the eyes of cats and nightbirds. But the tundra was too wide, and he needed the binoculars to check the magic levels. The readings slid in a sequence of silver sigils down the sights of the binoculars, ticking away the fluctuating degrees of different magics.

As the airship slipped over the estuary, the first great curves of the World's River came into sight. This river had been, in the true past, the first to reappear across Siberia once the ice had begun to retreat. Tales of the disir had first come from its banks, and so here it was in the nevergone. Loki's land. Deed's binoculars registered ancient sigils as they passed overhead, runes which were given by the land, not by man. He could taste them in blood and fire on his tongue; they spoke to him of the blast of the winter wind, of ice and the little flick of flame raised by a human hand, of the hunt and the long chase. Deed smiled, and then he saw the army of the disir.

Thousands of his kindred stretched out across the plain, milling far below the airship. Ahead, he could see the mountain wall: features so ancient their true names had been lost. The pines spilled down the mountainside like ink, black against the snow. In that forest, Loki was waiting for his freedom. Deed's mouth was suddenly dry.

He touched the pilot on the shoulder.

"How long?"

"Before we can take them through the gap? Another few minutes."

Deed nodded. "Good enough." He lowered the binoculars. Around him, the cabin's instruments were showing readings of their own, currently displaying height, pressure, speed—none of these things mattered to Deed. He was interested in the levels of power. He crouched by the brass-clad sigilometer and studied it.

Nehatz.

Rutine.

Gemart.

Each sigil appeared briefly, outlined in fire, and then fading. He knew where this was coming from—the runic invocations uttered by the disir shamans below, keeping the fighting mettle of their sisters up, appealing to their own spirits, preparing a battering ram to hammer down any tales they might encounter on the way in.

But there were other sigils, too, and at these, Deed frowned. A trace like a curling leaf: what the hell was that? It was blurred, as though whoever it belonged to had smeared their signature to prevent detection. And another—a name of God, unless he was much mistaken. Not the kind of magic he expected to find here, and Deed, ever the conscientious magician, did not take kindly to anomalies. He scowled as a hieroglyph chased fleetingly across the screen. The sigilometer whirred, spitting out a small roll of paper, its intermittent record of proceedings.

But these were tiny indications that all was not as predicted below. Deed was far more considerably taken aback some moments later when the sigilometer clicked, made a grinding sound, and revealed a cascading torrent of sigils, slipping too quickly across its screen for individual symbols to be detected.

"What—" Deed started to ask.

At that point the airship gave a dramatic lurch to the left. Deed was thrown against the bulkhead, his shoulder slamming into the iron scrollwork of the spell-protection system. He heard someone cry out, thought for a moment that it was himself, then realised it was Darya, sprawling against the sigilometer. Next minute, the ship righted itself, but the pilot's face was pallid and drenched with sweat.

"What was that?" Deed demanded. "What was it?"

Darya was staring with horror at the sigilometer.

"Look!" The machine was beginning to smoulder, the sigils flashing at white heat over the little screen until the screen itself resembled a rapidly blinking white eye.

Then the steersman brought the ship around and they saw the stormcloud gap in the sky.

"Take us out!" Deed told the pilot. He did not know what this wrench in the heavens was, but he had no intention of sticking around to find out, whatever was happening to the army below. It seemed to extend right through the nevergone. The disir were not, essentially, a cooperative people. "Take us out now!"

"I'm not sure I can!"

The pilot hauled on the wheel. The ship swung, and something large and black like a blown umbrella smashed into the prow windows. It left a smear of green ichor on the glass as its grip was torn away from the ship by the sudden acceleration and its body was hurled up into the raging clouds.

"What was it?" Darya echoed.

"I don't know." An event of massive proportions, the cataclysm foreseen by the Crown divinators was clearly in the process of unfolding; Deed swore. That should have been *his* cataclysm.

"They're all over the sky!" the steersman cried. The ship rocked as if struck by a hammer. Deed flung himself into the neighbouring seat.

"Strap yourself in," he told Darya. He brought the prow cannon around so that it was pointing directly into the storm, now below and off to the left. Then he began to hit the sigil keys, one after another, two or three in combination, invoking spells of destruction and sending it down the prow cannon in a blast of white fire. The recoil reverberated throughout the ship. Deed saw the spell strike down into the heart of the storm; black shapes were flung outward, shrieking. This was not, Deed thought, a moment for subtlety. He reloaded the cannon, bypassing any demonic invocations. From the look of the things in the stormcloud—teeth, spines, spikes, claws—that was likely only to add to the problem. He kept to the runic, therefore: ancient magic, weather magic, conjuring up the deep cold of winter, the spirits of blizzard and gale, the spirits of the deep and bitter air.

And for a few minutes, he almost thought it was working.

But Deed recognised that he did not know what he was dealing with. He didn't know where these entities had come from and that ignorance, combined with the fear that the army would be overwhelmed—for there were far more demons than there were disir and any army that has the advantage of flight will have the edge over one that does not—caused a bitter constriction to rise in Deed's throat and start to choke him. He flung spell after spell, and for some moments watched with satisfaction as the demons that soared in front of the ship froze and cracked, blasted apart in the wake of cold magic, falling like showers of fiery snow to the curving world below. Some, but not all. There was a thunderous crack to the rear of the ship. The little vessel once more rocked before stabilising.

"Darya," Deed said pleasantly, turning to her. "Go and see what that was."

She shot him a look of mingled fear, resentment, and loathing, but she did as he asked. That was good, Deed thought, that she still found him the most frightening thing around. But for how much longer?

He fired another spell. Born of wind, it snatched the demons ahead and scattered them like leaves, but shrieking they rode the spirals of conjured air with glee before they regrouped, and one did not disperse at all, but hung with a hawk's confidence upon the battering storm. There was a crash from the back of the ship.

Deed unclasped the leather seat strap and, clinging to the bulkhead, went to the cabin door. The moment he opened it, he was smacked by a gust of wind, roaring in through a hole in the hull. A white snarling face turned on him: Darya. She had let go of the human in her as someone might release a soap bubble into a hurricane. Her skin was stretched taut over jutting bones and her face was a howl of teeth. The thing that had caught her resembled a lamprey: an oval taper of greying flesh with vaned white wings, beating with a steady rhythm above the storm. It had no eyes. Its mouth, a round series of needles, was wrapped around Darya's leg. She was tearing at the thick grey skin with the talons of one hand, whilst the other clung to a stanchion.

"Jonathan!" she cried, but the name was barely recognisable, coming from that teeth-filled mouth. Deed was quick to react. He kicked out, crushing her hand against the stanchion and causing her fingers to release it. With a soundless cry Darya was pulled through the gap and into the whirling air. Deed saw the final whisk of a pale wing and then she was gone. He spoke a command to the hull and the ragged metal began to seep back together, until only a tiny whistling hole remained.

It was surprising what a relief it was to have got rid of Darya. No more competition? Fleetingly, Deed recognised that his ego would not allow him to entertain that thought and he pushed it away. No more Darya, at any rate.

And what was happening to the army? Furious, and facing the wreckage of his hopes, Deed fought his way along the plunging airship to the cabin.

⭑Fifty⭑

All the way across the snowfield, Mercy expected to feel the plunge of talons into her back. She struggled through the thick drifts, occasionally hauling Shadow along, occasionally being hauled in turn. The demon and Perra ran lightly across; Gremory with impatience, Perra with a *ka's* usual impassivity. The Duke made no attempt to help. Mercy suspected that it simply did not occur to her.

When they reached the rocks, Mercy pushed Shadow ahead of her and dived into the stony clefts. Something shrieked overhead. She looked up to see a shadow moving fast above them. It was enormous, perhaps forty feet long. A hammer-head snaked down to a serpent's tail and as they cowered between the rocks, a stinging lash shot down, raking through the cleft. Mercy felt it whistle past her hair. The thing shrieked in frustration and turned. The sky above the rocks grew dark as it veered and shot back, its small ball-bearing eyes glittering with malice. Mercy ducked. A black-and-scarlet shadow leaped onto the rocky ledge ahead of her. There was a thin hissing sound as a lash whipped overhead, was flung upwards to tangle itself around the storm demon's throat. The Duke, knocked off balance, fell into the rocks in a tangle of metal; the whip blazed up, a bright necklace around its throat, and its head fell severed to the snowy ground. A moment later, Gremory was back, red eyes alight.

"I can't take all of them."

"Aren't they your kin?" Mercy asked. The demon bared her teeth.

"No kin of mine."

They fled up into the mountain wall. Once, Mercy glanced back and saw the storm demons falling on the disir. The shamans were plucked from their mounts and carried kicking into the sky. Mercy saw a demon drop one of them onto the rocks, splitting armour and carapace as a thrush beats a snail against a stone. Then another demon whisked down out of the heavens. They cowered down between the rocks, Shadow's veil billowing out across their heads. Mercy felt rather than saw it rip; it felt as though something had scratched her own soul. She heard Shadow cry out in pain and understood at last what the veil was: part of Shadow herself, a visible part of her spirit. Mercy whispered an incantation, flung it upwards at the writhing white form. Grooves of bloody fire appeared on the thing's flank, but although the demon shrieked it did not fall. But then, as if something had summoned it back, it wheeled away and flew towards the river.

They hurried on through the rocks, emerging onto another plateau of snow. This was much wider, with the black rock wall rearing jagged at its further side. To Mercy, the monochrome landscape was a nightmare fairy tale. What had Nerren said, the day the monorail blew up? *White as snow, black as night. Red as blood.* There was no blood there now, at least, not yet.

She looked back. The disir army was a struggling mass at the river's edge, with the storm a locust cloud above it. When the demons had finished with the disir, they would come after straggling prey. The only reason, Mercy knew, that they had not yet been devoured had been accident, and that only a couple of demons could be bothered. That situation would not last. She shouted to Shadow, "We've got to get across the snowline now. In a minute it will be too late."

But in this she was wrong.

⚬Fifty-one⚬

Deed had just returned to the cabin when the windscreen shattered. There was a heavy thump on top of the airship, and a moment later the glass imploded as a stinging whip-like tail burst through it. The pilot, impaled, did not have time to cry out as he died. Deed ducked as the demon withdrew its tail, then sent it back inward for another lashing thrust. He was unable to reach the controls: the tail filled the cockpit. The airship's engine began to emit a high mosquito scream. Its nose veered sharply downwards. Deed would have slithered uncontrollably towards the shattered windscreen had he not grabbed onto one of the wall stanchions. Didn't matter, though, did it? Deed thought. He was going to die anyway, because the airship was going to crash. He hurled an incantation at the demon, blasting it away from the stricken ship, but by now the engine was making a noise like a tortured tomcat and the ship was corkscrewing down towards the river. He could see the ice-flecked water spinning up in a series of loops and coils as the ship plummeted down.

He was not conscious, for once, of changing. It happened fast: bones jutting out from his skin, his vision altering, teeth extending. The hand that gripped the stanchion now had long iron-coloured talons and the bones stood out like knives. Deed snarled as the ship skimmed over the surface of the river, the breath of ice blasting cold through the shattered glass, and ploughed into the bank.

⊷Fifty-two⊷

Mercy ran, slogging through the deep snowfield. It had an icy crust like a loaf of bread, but her feet were plunging into the depths beneath and the Duke finally had to help both Mercy and Shadow, seizing their hands and dragging them along. From above, Mercy thought, they must look like three children, little dark figures toiling over the snow. It was with a terrible sense of despair, but no surprise, when the demon swooped down out of the sky, a hawk hunting. Gremory's hard hand was torn from Mercy's grasp and she was whisked up into the storm as easily as a captured dove.

"Gremory!" Shadow cried, in a voice of startling loss. Mercy, futilely, brandished the sword, but the Duke was gone. A *dove*, Mercy thought. Aloud she cried, "Mareritt! Mareritt! Mareritt!"

A silver bolt flew out of the shadows of the mountain wall. It shot over her head and buried itself in the storm demon's throat. Blood pattered down, burning Mercy's skin; Shadow threw the torn veil over them both. The storm demon dropped Gremory. She fell, twisting elegantly through the air, and landed in the snow. Mercy heard a hissing sound that was unknown and yet oddly familiar: she turned to see Mareritt's sleigh gliding swiftly over the snowfield.

"Well, get in."

Mercy did not need asking twice. Shadow pushed her over the side of the sleigh, into the mass of heads, then followed. Gremory crouched on the sleigh's side, knees drawn up; she appeared unharmed. The heads gaped, astonished.

"What is happening?" the Brass-bound head asked in a voice like a bell.

"Hush," Silver-Bound said. "You ask such foolish questions."

"It is the time," Golden-Bound remarked. The others looked at him, their eyes rolling in their sockets.

"You never make any sense," Brass-Bound complained.

The Bronze-bound head appeared to be sleeping, but Iron-Bound, the one who must have been a warrior, laughed, silently showing its bloodstained teeth. Its eyes, black and small, met Mercy's for a moment: they exchanged a glance of complicit enjoyment.

Over her shoulder, Mareritt said, "Well done."

"I found your book," Mercy said.

"Excellent."

"I'm just not sure that there's still a city to read it in."

"We'll have to see, won't we?" Mareritt said. She cracked the whip in a shower of silver bells and the sledge sped on towards the mountain wall.

Mercy did not wish to backseat drive, but she did want to know what the plan was. And even if there was one. She crawled to the front of the sleigh, behind the driving seat.

"Careful," Bronze-Bound said, without opening its eyes.

"Sorry." Cautiously, for the sleigh was travelling fast, she stood and found herself looking past Mareritt's white-clad arm, all lace and frost, and over the silvery rumps of the running deer. "Where are we heading? For the gap?"

"Oh, no, dear." Mareritt turned her head and grinned a feral grin. "I can't take this through something that narrow—a person, perhaps, but not this sleigh. We came the long way round when I heard your call, along the Dead Road. I'm not going back that way. I don't think you'd survive it."

Mercy was aware of a cold lump of dread, lodged beneath her breastbone. "Then which way *are* we going?"

Mareritt pointed with the whip, to the lick of fiery cloud that was the newly opened Pass. "We'll be going through there."

⭑⭑⭑

Deed lay, face down, in snow. It was cold enough to have killed a human by now. He raised himself up on taloned hands. The airship rested several yards away. It was burning. A hard blue flame flickered throughout its exposed bowels and occasionally something shorted out with a hiss. He saw a small spirit, released from the mechanism, darting out across the snow, beak gaping, before it faded and vanished.

Deed was reluctant to stand, in case he got snatched by one of the storm worms. He looked across the river. The battle was over: he could smell blood on the faint wind and it was disir blood. He knew that scent very well. The demons themselves were amassing high up in the clouds; he could see the tornado funnel gathering. Deed forced himself to think logically—for that, human heritage was useful. The disir were not big on rational planning: aggression, rage, and death, yes, but not reasoned consideration. If the army had been destroyed, that meant that Deed's own intentions would now have to undergo a serious revision. He did not have the requisite knowledge to repair the airship, even if it could be mended. That meant that, assuming he wasn't killed in the next few minutes, he was stranded here for the time being, on the other side of the World's River. He would have to cross the river, then make his way through Loki's forest to the nearest gap back into the city.

Being disir, Deed was inclined to regard this as an opportunity rather than a challenge. To have the army destroyed was galling, true, but it also meant a lessening of competition. Now, if his understanding was correct, he and the female still loose in Worldsoul were the only disir left.

A breeding pair; how romantic. Deed did not consider himself to be ideal parent material.

He was still aiming at control of the city. He looked on the bright side. The Skein still had not come back. That left all sorts of opportunities to grab at power, assuming he could get back into the city without running into one of Loki's wolves. And that was a rather big "if."

⊷═◐═⊷

"You must be mad," Mercy said. Mareritt looked at her, apparently genuinely surprised.

"Whatever makes you say that?"

"A look up ahead?" Shadow said, coming to stand by Mercy's side. The sleigh was now skirting the mountain wall, running along the air just above the surface of the snowfield, like a skimming stone. The stormcloud was gathering over the bony wreckage of the disir army, whipping upwards in a mass of teeth and stinging tails. Beyond, the Pass was clearly visible, a wound in the air.

"All you have to do," Mareritt said, "is keep your heads down."

"Oh, that'll be all right, then," Mercy said.

"Your friend has a veil."

"It got torn," Mercy told her. She could still feel Shadow's pain: an invisible rent, seeping invisible blood.

Shadow gripped her hand. "It's all right. I'll be all right. And we *have* to do this. I've realised why now."

"I don't want—" Mercy began, but by this time the sleigh was sweeping up, up towards the tear in the sky.

⊷═◐═⊷

Deed leaped. The ice rolled beneath his feet, nearly sending him down into the swift dark water. He jumped to the next floe, which was more stable, a shelf of ice carried on the current. Deed clung to it as it took him around one of the ox-bow curves in the river: using the ice to carry him as far as possible from the scene of the battlefield, away from the attention of the gathering aerial force.

But he could not let it take him too far. Ahead lay the estuary of the World's River and then the sea: eternal, ice-locked, ancient, and cold. He'd seen its slow oily heave from the airship's maiden voyage, the tidal sway of a sea that is on the perpetual point of freezing, and he had no wish to be carried out into the waves. That meant judging his movements across the ice. Deed crouched, sprang, and landed once again.

⊷═◉═⊶

Shadow's veil may not have been able to protect them from demonic attack, but it did save them to some extent from the noise. Up here, the shrieking of the horde that had come through the Pass was close to unbearable: a starling flock magnified a thousand fold. As the sleigh approached the edges of the tight formation that was the swarm, Mercy saw a dozen lamprey heads turning in their direction. She clung on as the sleigh veered, taking the turn around the edge of the funnel. But several of the worms had already broken away and were sailing down, their wings gilded by the light of the Pass into eerie transparency. There was a snap above Mercy's veil-shrouded head as Mareritt cracked the whip, urging the deer on. What struck Mercy, even with the demons soaring down to meet them and the Pass coming up fast ahead, was how hot it had become. The upper air above this ancient land should have been freezing. Instead, a bead of sweat was trickling down her nose and the point between her shoulder blades had become unpleasantly damp. The air smelled of musty spice, the odour of stale musk that was, she realised with nausea, generated by thousands of demonic bodies. Across the sled, Gremory was managing to look superior. The *ka* sneezed.

"Kindly get out of the way!" That was Golden-Bound.

"Yes, how can we act when your soul is all over the place?" Brass-Bound chimed in. Mercy saw Shadow's eyes widen, and she whisked the veil down so that it covered Mercy and herself closely, like a pair of snoods. Brass-Bound made a prim face, as if about to utter some distasteful truth, then spat. A gobbet of liquid fire shot out and struck an oncoming demon in the middle of its lamprey jaws. Mercy saw the flame travel all the way down its long throat, illuminating the demon from within, and then it exploded. Brass-Bound allowed a faint smugness to show across its face. The Duke gave a brief, *I-am-reluctantly-impressed* nod.

Silver-Bound followed suit with a plume of blue-white flame. A demon fell like a singed eel out of the sky, bursting into a brief flare as it sank towards the tundra. As a demon screamed with rage, all of the heads swivelled in the direction of the swarm and spat in unison. A rainbow arc of flame coreolised in the sled's wake as Mareritt whipped the deer on.

⋯⊜ ⊖⋯

The movement of the swarm had sung up the wind. Ice-laden branches of fir lashed against Deed's face. But the disir thought things were looking up. He was far from the swarm now, and into the treeline. He was at home in these forests—for a moment, it occurred to Deed that it might be an option to remain here, run wild through the forests of the night rather than returning to Worldsoul and its tedious politics. A little vacation . . . He rejected this as coming from the disir-self, the feral-self. This back-to-nature business was all very well, but he still had the old god's wolves to contend with and besides, there was too much of intrinsic interest in the city. Deed took a gasping breath of arctic air and trudged on.

⊷═◉═⊶

The demon was on fire, but this did not seem to deter it. It came over the backs of the racing deer and struck Mareritt on the breast, ramming her backwards over the lip of the sleigh and into the well of heads, where it exploded. The heads cried out in a unison of disgust. Mercy and Shadow both scrambled for the reins; Mercy, due to position, was a fraction quicker. She clambered up into the driver's seat and steered the deer towards the Pass.

She had driven a horse buggy, once or twice, in the parks of Worldsoul on holidays. This was different. Taking the reins was like taking hold of something living; they twitched quicksilver in her hands and she felt electricity dance up the bones of her arms into her spine. For a second, it was as though she looked through the ice-dark eyes of the deer, seeing a web of connections spreading out between demons and air, a way of seeing which she could not understand and which momentarily disoriented her. The reins fell slack in her hands, but she grasped them more tightly, bringing them up. The deer turned.

"Is she all right?" A spit of fire shot past her ear, singing her hair. "Careful!"

Shadow was leaning over Mareritt. "I think so. She's trying to speak."

Mercy risked a glance over her shoulder and saw the gaping hole in Mareritt's chest was beginning to knit together: blood, tissue, lace and bone all forming a seamless whole. Mareritt's mouth was open so wide, she looked barely human. *Well, she wasn't, was she?* Mercy reminded herself. She concentrated on the Pass ahead.

Deed was expecting the wolf when it came. He had heard it coming through the trees; soft footed, it had nonetheless betrayed itself by the single rustle of a twig. He pretended to be lost, glancing nervously around him, adjusting his appearance to partway human. It would not fool the wolf entirely—they knew disir when they smelled one—but it might confuse it. Thus he was, deliberately, facing away from the wolf when it sprang. Then he turned, falling backwards, reaching up with taloned fingers to rake the wolf's throat. Its own momentum ripped out its jugular. Deed, exulting, was covered in a bath's worth of blood. He drank it in, an indulgence, for it was the wolf's spirit that he was lapping up, stealing its strength, its wildness, its ferocity. At the very bottom of its animal soul lay something that might be compared to a bright jewel: a shining pearl which Deed recognised as its imprimatur from the old god. A berry of mistletoe. This he did not touch, and it fell snowflake silent to the ground and dimmed away. There was a chance that Loki would be conscious of it, a little candle going out, but hell, animals died all the time. He hadn't been aware of any tugs on the wyrd-web, but he'd taken good care to shut himself off from it, severing any connections that might have curled out, vine tendrils from his spirit. Old Loki was subtle, though. Deed still wasn't planning on taking risks.

It was now obvious that Mareritt would not be mended by the time they reached the Pass. Mercy estimated this to be another thirty seconds or so. The Pass filled the sky: it was like flying into the sunset. As a child, and sometimes now, Mercy had hung out of the back windows of her house, looking into the shining crimson sky above the Western Sea and its the golden clouds of islands, wondering if she would ever visit them. A whimsical notion, but now here she was. These clouds were moving too fast to be islands, however. They were like boiling clouds of golden steam, laced with lightning fire. Mercy couldn't help feeling if she took the sleigh into the middle of that, they'd all be fried.

Then the clouds parted and she gasped. There were gates in the Pass. They reared up in the form of columns of black cloud, soft as ink or soot, then hardening to the resemblance of stone. On a ledge on the left hand gate, someone was standing, holding a sword of flame.

"You'll have to—have to—" That was Mareritt, from the back of the sleigh. Her voice was a reedy gasp, almost inaudible.

"What's she saying?" Mercy called.

"You'll have to stop the sleigh!"

"But what about the demons?" Mercy looked back. They were still being pursued, but the bulk of the swarm was still amassing, readying to pour through the Pass. The heads continued to spit fire. Shadow leaned over the lip of the sleigh. Her gaze was intent.

"Mercy, you'll have to take us down to that ledge. We've got to go past the guardian."

"Do you know who it is?"

"No, but I've got some suspicions."

The sleigh soared downwards. Close up, Mercy could see that the columns were akin to basalt: if this was an illusion, it was a remarkably realistic one. Both the ledge, and the figure, were far larger than they should have been, but as the sleigh grew rapidly nearer they, too, adjusted in size.

Shadow said, "Guardian."

⊹⊨◉⊨⊹

He thought he'd been careful. He'd thought, too, that he knew these woods, and so he had, but that had been when the god had been kind, if you could call it that, still held him in grace. The world was a reflection of the mind of God, after all, and what kind of world can that be, when a god is cruel? Outcast from Loki's dubious benignity, Deed found that he was lost.

Night had fallen some time before. He could still see the rift in the air, a sunset slash, far away to the west, but he was relying on his nocturnal vision in order to make his way through the trees. He was heading up into the mountain pass, the one that led, ultimately, to the mistfall bridge, and he had been on track until, suddenly, he wasn't.

The forest had closed in. Even Deed was finding it difficult to make his way through the trees and it was first with relief, then a chilly dismay, that he stumbled out into a clearing.

But not just any clearing. He knew exactly where he was. The tall spires of trees, motionless despite the wind which had been whipping the branches of the pines into a shower of snow, the basalt rocks. The two wolves came out from the trees, closing in from different directions. Deed knew as soon as he saw them that they were not wolves at all, nor were they from the wolfhead clans, who paid allegiance to Odin. These were men, transformed into the semblance of beasts, and the process had not been painless. He could see the anguish and rage in their trapped eyes; knew, too, that they would not be able to do anything except the god's bidding. They moved as stiffly as automata over the snow. One wolf's mouth moved.

"Hello, Deed," a voice said.

⋇═◉═⋇

For a few minutes, Mercy was afraid that the sleigh might actually melt. The rock on which she stood was hot; she could feel it through the soles of her boots. She cast a nervous glance towards the sleigh, but although its runners had hissed and steamed as they landed, to her relief the sleigh remained intact.

She noticed that Mareritt, now apparently healed, took care to remain seated on the sleigh, or perhaps it was just that she did not want to relinquish her hold on the reins and the deer, whose silver-black eyes rolled in panic. Gremory, however, had joined Shadow and Mercy on the ledge, and the demon looked as though she was enjoying the change in temperature.

But it was the figure ahead of them who was worrying Mercy. He was tall, with pale fiery hair that streamed down his back, and teeth as long and sharp as a disir's. His beautiful face was remote and sometimes it flickered, changing into fire. He wore robes as white as snow, but the sword he carried was a burning gash in the air. Mercy had never met an angel before, but she had a sudden apprehension of all that filled-with-awe business. Or make that fear. She swallowed hard and sheathed the Irish sword, which had become very quiet and still in her hand.

"You would pass through the gate?" the angel asked.

Shadow was staring not at the angel, but at Mercy. Meeting the other woman's eyes, Mercy read the message in them: *Don't trust it.*

"Will you let us?" Mercy said. Mareritt was staring at her, too, but Mercy could not read her expression. Perhaps she realised that an appeal from her would do no good. The demon appeared to think the same. She, on the other hand, was watching the angel, her eyes narrow red slits.

"Of course."

Gravely, the angel inclined his head. "If you pay the fee."

Mercy sighed. There always was one of those. "And what would that be?"

The angel looked her directly in the face. It was hard to

withstand his gaze; Mercy felt her face grow hot, as though she stared into the sun. "A life."

"What?" She was shocked into rudeness. "You're an angel. You're not supposed to ask for that sort of thing."

"To do him justice," Gremory said, as if commenting on some abstruse theological point, "it's not really his decision. He's just the enforcer. The gates run on older rules. Mind you," the demon added, "I can't say that there's any love lost."

"Do you know who he is?"

"I don't know his name. I do know one or two of them."

The angel's gaze did not waver. "You have to choose."

"May I have a word with my friend?" Shadow said to him.

The angel nodded.

She stepped over to Mercy and threw the ripped veil over them both. "I don't think this will stop him hearing us—but anyway. The thing is, I've worked it out. The swarm's hard behind. When they're ready, when they've formed their fighting formation, they'll come through here. It won't matter to them if they have to sacrifice one of their number."

"No, but it matters to us. Perra can't die: the *ka's* a spirit. Gremory won't and anyway, she's a demon. Mareritt's a story."

"So that leaves you and me. If someone dies, maybe they can ask that the gap be closed. We could have it both ways. We've got rid of the disir. Now we have a chance to close the Pass behind us."

Mercy took a deep breath. Then she nodded. "I'm vowed to the Library. I swore I'd give anything to protect it, including my life. This counts as that. I'll do it."

At first, she thought that Shadow was going to protest, but then a change came over the woman's face, rendering it unreadable. She said, "If that's your choice."

"I'm sure," Mercy said, thinking, *Fuck.* All the things that she couldn't now be able to do . . . but if they let the swarm through, she probably would have died anyway. "Let's get it over with. See if it works, for a start."

She ducked out from under the veil and began to walk across the ledge. The hot stone baked up beneath the soles of her feet and the air scorched her lungs. She opened her mouth to say, *Take me . . .*

. . . and the world disappeared beneath an enveloping blue. For a second, she thought that this was death: an azure drowning, sky fall. Then she realised that Shadow had thrown the veil over her head.

"No!" Mercy cried. She fought the veil, pushing back the cascading folds, but it tripped her and she fell, bruising her palms against the hot rock. The fall tore the veil from her face and she saw Shadow walk forward towards the fiery sword.

"If I die," Shadow said, "will you let my friends through and close the Pass?"

The angel looked at her, his head on one side.

"If I do *that*, it's not just your life," he said. "It's your soul. You'll have to stay here, until someone else comes along. You'll have to become the gap."

"Shadow," Mercy whispered. A favourite debate among Librarians involved the nature of the ultimate story. Is it the person who triumphs over insurmountable odds? Is it the child who seeks and finds their own destiny? Watching Shadow now, Mercy thought she knew the answer: the greatest story involves willing sacrifice, the person who gives up their life for others. Christ. Ishtar. Aslan.

Shadow began walking forwards and did not stop. Mercy saw the fiery sword come down and bathe her in light. She was a silhouette, and then she was gone. Around Mercy's kneeling form, the blue veil shimmered and disappeared.

"Get in the sleigh!" Mareritt cried. The demon hauled Mercy up and bundled her over the lip of the vehicle. She tumbled down among the heads, blinking as the brightness of the light that had encompassed Shadow started to fade.

The angel stepped aside. Mercy looked up as they sped past his standing form and he was now a statue, changed to silent stone like the bird-faced spirit that had once stood vigil above the Library. Mareritt cracked the whip. The sleigh shot over the edge of the column into the Pass. Mercy struggled to her feet and looked back over the rear of the sleigh. Behind them, the two basalt columns were grinding together. The Pass was closing.

⊹⟞⟝⟞ ⟝⟞⟝⟞⊹

"Come closer, Deed," the wolf sang out and Deed found he had little choice. His dragging feet took him unwillingly forwards, a zombie shuffle through the snow. "Not too successful, were we?"

"No," Deed croaked.

"I tell you what," the wolf said, in Loki's voice. The long lupine muzzle twisted around the human words. "I'll give you a sporting chance. After all, there were a few unforeseen spanners in the works, weren't there? So this is what I'll do. If you unchain me, we'll see if you can outrun me. After all, I've been chained up for a very long time. Haven't had the exercise I should. Bit stiff."

"Very well," Deed managed to say. If he declined, the god would simply order the wolves to kill him where he stood.

"I'll even take the wolves away. How about that?"

Next moment, both the animals were whisked up into the air. Deed blinked. The wolves were hanging on the whalebone arch, sheaves of bloody meat and fur.

"Didn't like them anyway. Now. Unchain me."

The god pointed to a nearby boulder. Set into it, in a runnel in the rock, was a rusty iron key.

"It didn't look like that originally, of course. Changed with time."

Deed tugged at the key. Even disir talons couldn't make much impact on the imprisoning stone.

"A little joke on the part of my captors, putting the key so nearby. But no one's been able to get it out. You see, you need magic for that."

Gritting his teeth, Deed infused the rock with power. It was hard, harder than any natural stone but at last, when he was almost drained, the rock burst apart and the key fell to the ground.

"Oh, well done, Abbot General."

Deed took the key across to where the old god stood. He moved cautiously; there were eyes in the shadows, yellow and shining. If he just made a run for it, there were more wolves waiting.

He fitted the key into the lock that secured Loki's chain.

"I'll count to ten." The old god closed malevolent eyes. "One . . ."

But Deed was running, disir speed, leaping through the grove. He brushed aside ancient rotting corpses, thrust away skeins of necklaced bones. And then he was on the road itself, the stone hard beneath his pounding feet.

He made it as far as the crossroads before the god pounced. His last thought was that this was at least appropriate: crossroads had always been a place of sacrifice. Loki's long talons closed around his throat and ripped it out, releasing a gush of blood and magic, steaming into the winter air. Deed's spirit, sinking down into the earth, listened to the god's laughter and saw no more.

⋯⋙Fifty-three⋘⋯

The Shah crouched on slippered heels, looking inside the cage. This one was not made of meteorite iron, but of steel: a substance unknown to its occupant.

"Well, well," the Shah said. "So this is who's been causing all the havoc. I'm rather glad we've finally tracked you down."

The disir hissed at him. She clasped the bars with the talons of her remaining hand and spat.

"Now that really won't do," the Shah said, admonishingly as if to a naughty toddler. "You won't be getting out of here any time soon, so you may as well behave." He turned to the milk-eyed girl who stood behind him. "What do you see, Soraya?"

The milky eyes began to fill with light. It overspilled the sockets and ran down her face in dribbles of illumination. She opened her mouth and breathed it out in a glowing stream.

"I see a cold place. Death. Much death. I see the woman I followed into the Khaureg and she is triumphant."

"Is she?" the Shah said, mildly displeased. "Oh, dear. That probably means she's lost my ifrit." He wondered whether Shadow would be coming back to the Eastern Quarter. He hoped so. An enterprising young woman. He had plans for her.

⚒Fifty-four⚒

The sleigh was racing over a calm sea, into twilight green. Mercy could see the prickle of stars above the horizon and they were familiar: the constellation known as the Wain. When she looked back into the sleigh, the heads had drawn to the sides and Shadow's body lay there, bareheaded and barefaced. Her arms were crossed over her breast. She would not have liked the heads to see her naked face and Mercy stripped off her coat and stepped forwards to cover her. She was just about to lay the coat over Shadow's face when the corpse's eyes snapped open.

"Shadow?"

"Oh!" Shadow said. "There's no one here."

"Shadow, you're alive! I'm here, and Gremory and Mareritt and Perra."

"No." Shadow sat up and the veil was back, billowing about her, untorn. She tugged it into place. "The spirit that was in me. He's gone."

"Where has he gone?" Gremory asked, sharply.

"Into the gap. I didn't die. He did. He volunteered. Just before I threw the veil over your head he said that it was the only way he could escape."

"Well, damn me," the Duke of Hell said, nonplussed. "I've known people take desperate measures to avoid capture before now, but—"

"Is that what it was about?" Shadow asked. "You were trying to capture him?"

"He stole something from my mistress," Gremory said. "Astaroth wasn't pleased. Very presumptuous, for an air spirit. She sent me to get him back, but the Shah already had him. By the time I tracked him down, he was in you."

"What was it he stole?"

"I don't know. She didn't tell me."

"Do you think he's still got it?"

"Who can say?" Gremory said. An expression of distinct unease crossed the Duke's features. "Astaroth won't be very happy about this. Frankly, I'm not looking forward to going back and telling her."

"Look on the bright side," Mercy said. "You've helped to save the world."

"Mmm."

"You did tell the Elders that the storm demons would be a bad thing for your people, too. So surely—"

"You've not met Astaroth, have you?" The Duke looked gloomy. Then she frowned. "My ring's still in your Library. I hope it's still standing. I don't fancy spending a week with a sieve."

"We'll soon find out," Mercy said.

The storyway gleamed faintly in the light of the moon. There were lights down below, scattering the ocean. Fishing boats, then islands. Mercy could not identify them but then they came over the rim of the world, the hills of Golden Island rose up below, and the city lay ahead, strung out along the shores of the Liminality. Smoke rose from the Western Quarter. In the east, the sun was rising.

They came in just as dawn touched the city. It had been a turbulent night. Most of the Court's roof lay in the middle of Citadel Square, spell-vanes still creaking and turning in response to the flow of magic. The Library still stood, more or less. Nerren and others were carrying out piles of charred paper.

"If anyone's pilfered any books—" Mercy began. It looked as though the façade would be reparable, but only just. She turned to Mareritt. "When I saw you lying in the sleigh, you know what? You looked a lot like my mother Greya."

"Did I, dear? How odd."

"I spoke to a man named Aelrich Salt some days ago. He knew my mum. And he told me a couple of rather strange family stories about our ancestors."

"Did he, dear? How interesting. Now, I'd like my book back." She raised a hand and beckoned. A small leather bound volume flew out through the gap in the Library wall, its pages flapping like wings. It soared down to Mareritt's waiting hand.

"Oh!" the heads said, in unison. "Now we can find out what happens at the end!"

"I wouldn't count on it," Mercy told them. The geas pinged apart in her head.

Mareritt snapped the whip. "Someone's calling me. I'm sure I'll see you again, dear."

The sleigh spiralled up into the growing morning light.

"What happens to the Court, now?" Shadow said.

"I don't know. Hopefully it will be too preoccupied with setting its own house to rights to worry about the rest of the city. Although I might have to say the same for the Library. What will you do now, Shadow?" Mercy bent to pick up a stray page, caught by a breeze.

"I ought to find Mariam, and—" Shadow broke off.

"Shadow?"

The sun was coming up, but the sky above the square was darkening. Something was coming over the rooftops: part behemoth, part dreadnought, part airship. Its metal sides were pitted as though it had been scored with meteor strikes and one of the great flanking vanes had been broken and hung loose, strapped to the side of the vessel by what looked like grappling hooks. It hissed through the air, heading east-west across the Quarter, and even a passing golem raised its round head and stared incuriously upwards.

The *Barquess* had come back.

The End . . . for Now

About the Author

Liz Williams is a science fiction and fantasy writer living in Glastonbury, England, where she is co-director of a witchcraft supply business. Her books have been published by Bantam Spectra, Night Shade Books, Prime Books, and Tor Macmillan, with short fiction appearing in *Realms of Fantasy, Asimov's,* and other magazines. She is the secretary of the Milford SF Writers' Workshop, and teaches creative writing and the history of science fiction.